Happily Ever Chapter

Samantha Wren

Mood Readers Inc.

Edited by Amy Spaulding, Kelly Siskind, and Sarah Waterman
Cover Illustration by Lauren Gnapi
Interior Design and Formatting by Mayonaka Designs

First Edition 2026

To the bookish community. Thank you for letting me be me.

And my hot husband, that doesn't read, but so supportive he'll spend hours in bookstores anyways.

Chapter 1

Hot Girl Walk

He kissed his way down her neck, over her hard peaks, slow and reverent, claiming every inch he touched as though it were written into the fabric of time, as though loving her was something he had been destined to do long before this moment, and trailing molten, forever-promised kisses down her stomach. It left her shaking beneath the weight of him. She leaned into his touch like a woman undone, felt every ragged breath he stole against her skin, every heartbeat echoing between them. And when his thick fingers dragged up her inner thigh—

"Mazey!" Nova calls from down the hall. "You about ready?"

I love my roommate and best friend, but her timing is the absolute worst.

Although, I should be outlining my plan for the latest project—assigned to me on far too short notice—not indulging in a romance novel. Throwing myself into someone else's love story seems far more interesting, even if I am skimming the storyline for the spicy parts.

It's not the story that's lacking. It's me. This novel has everything my heart desires in a book. An epic—if slightly unrealistic—storyline, witty conversation, and of course, five chili peppers of intimate sex-ua-tions between a strong heroine and a swoony hero. Reading is my all-time favorite thing in the entire world, tied with Wilfred, my Shih Tzu, Nova, and gummy bears.

Nova barges into my room and jumps on my bed. "Ohh, I see what's taking you so long. Are they banging yet?"

"Is it bad that I have no desire to finish my work this weekend?" I ignore her question and close the novel, throwing my legs to the side of my bed. Guilt over the procrastination bubbles inside me. I know what I need to do—sit down in my office, open up my laptop, and do the damn thing. After years of being a project manager, the system I created to map out an implementation for Pixel Perfection, the software company that writes my paycheck every week, shouldn't take long. I've streamlined it. But, dammit, I have no desire to even begin.

"Not in the slightest. It's the freakin' weekend, babe." She puts her arm around my shoulder in an awkward side hug, smushing my floral print-rimmed glasses. "Think of the little free libraries we'll pass on the way to town. They need to be restocked."

I push my glasses back onto my nose before throwing my hand over my eyes as if I am a damsel in distress falling into Nova's shoulder.

"The public needs my worn romance novels," I proclaim in a breathy, Southern accent.

"Damn straight they do!"

I cross the room, gathering the four books I finished this month that sit in front of my over-stuffed bookshelf. The middle-aged Wilfred jumps in excitement, his tag creating a happy tune. This brown-and-white pup knows it's time to go for a walk when I put the pile into my tote.

"I do feel guilty about leaving, though. I have two more updates I didn't get done on my latest project."

"And when are they due?" She perches her hand on her protruding hipbone.

We are the definition of opposites attract in every aspect. Her tow-ering, slender body is the reverse of my compact, curvy one. My chest-nut curls are short and bouncy, while her hair flows straight, hitting just above her waist. Even our personalities differ. She's the *everything happens for a reason* to my *everything happens, what the fuck do I do now?*

"Tomorrow… but I want to make time in case I screw up."

Nova hops off the bed and grabs my Chuck Taylors and tosses them at me. "Mazey…"

"Nova…" I slide on the shoes.

"You're going to be fine." She pulls me up by the hands.

"Yeah, I know. The universe will work itself out," I say, not certain I mean it. Fine. I'm always fine. I would love to be more than fine. More put together, maybe? More happy in my career for sure. If that's even possible. Nova loves her job. So do my parents and brother. Mine? My career path is just a path to a paycheck. Nothing more, nothing less. I like helping my customers, sure, but I'm not passionate about managing software projects for construction companies.

With a heavy sigh and a shake of my head, I pull myself back to reality, grab my bag, and clip Wilfred's leash on and head out the door.

The air is like an overripe melon—moist and floppy. I can almost taste the disappointment as Nova and I follow Wilfred on the path that leads to downtown Honeyville, North Carolina. The suffocating August weather is nothing like the beautiful autumn decor that adorns the porches of the familiar houses along the way.

"You gotta remember, you don't always screw up," Nova says as she digs through her tote bag, pulling out a water bottle covered in stickers with mantras like *you got this* and *screw Mercury's retrograde*. I should have realized she wasn't going to drop the topic. She's like that—she'll push the conversation until that poor self-talk flies right out of you.

"Three write-ups." I hold out three fingers as if I'm explaining to a toddler how to count. "I have three write-ups for turning in the wrong report."

"The reports were right, though." Nova defends my honor for the millionth time. "They were just on your laptop still."

"I love that you will defend me no matter what dumbass thing I do." I put my arm around her narrow shoulders. Nova has been my person since I was seven, defending every choice I've made and vise-versa. She's the type of friend who not only will help me hide the body (figuratively, of course, but also probably literally), but she will talk about my feelings to resolve the root of the problem. "But emailing my boss the wrong quarter's project budgets will never go over well. She didn't catch my massive error until—"

"Mazey, stop. You've retold that story a million times. You messed up, apologized, and took your… What's it called?"

"Disciplinary notice."

"Yes, *that*. You took that like a champ. Besides, it's not like you aren't qualified for the position. You just hate it."

The MBA degree and PMP—project management professional certification—that hangs in view of my webcam in the home office of our apartment screams my qualifications. Being a project manager at Pixel Perfection wasn't something kid me dreamed of. There were no gnat charts or project plans scribbled in the back of my algebra notebook.

There was, however, a notebook filled with other dreams that kid me dreamed up. But those are far more scary to execute than a secure paycheck with guaranteed benefits, no matter how much I wish they were real.

Nova side-eyes me. "You know, if you actually cared about what you were doing, you'd probably review the attachments a bit more instead of hurrying at the last minute."

"Nova…" I sigh, knowing what conversation is coming next.

"What? You know I'm right. Your *secret*"—she uses air quotes—"savings account you opened the minute Dawson died proves you've been stowing away cash for over a decade."

When my brother died, a spark of motivation hit me with the urge to finally bring to life what we had filled *that* notebook with. I opened a savings account, putting every penny away for the moment I could open the doors of the business that we created only on paper. But year after year, those plans took a backseat to the reality of life.

"You have the money to chase your dreams." Nova stills, the wind catching her maxi skirt, sending it streaming behind her. Like a starlit priestess with amethyst hair on a journey to remind everyone of their importance in the universe.

"Not everyone loves their job the way you love yours." I close the door to the little free library, which sits next to some picnic tables along the path, leaving a couple of the gently read novels inside.

"Ahh yes, designing book covers and doing marketing campaigns for independent bookstores is the dream." Nova smiles that only people that truly love their job can do.

"Especially when your cover gets named The Golden Bookmark's *best cover design of the year.*"

A lump of jealousy sits next to the pride I have for my bestie. Nova has been designing covers since graduating with her digital design and marketing degree, fulfilling her younger self's career ambitions.

I, on the other hand, have been coasting on a job I hate, too afraid to do what will make my heart happy.

"Let's go by the lake." Nova squeezes my hand, an act of solidarity.

"I'm pretty sure that path is so worn because of us," I say, thankful for the shift in conversation we've had far too often. Wilfred tugs at the leash, leading the way along Sugar Lake towards downtown Honeyville with the grumble of an old man angry at the children on his lawn.

Sugar Lake, our quaint town's biggest draw from spring to early fall, has always been my safe place. Growing up in a two story on the lake's shore with my mom, dads, and two brothers was every introverted book-lover's dream. My afternoons were spent curled up in a worn-down beach chair, reading with the picture-perfect background. Breathing in the freshwater air and soaking up the warmth of the sun was my favorite thing to do. There was no pretending I wasn't the girl that was teased for having one friend or preferred books over sports, while I lay in the sun-soaked moss and clear water.

"How was your date last night? The one with…"

"Lilly…"

"Yeah, Lilly." Nova dates more than I change my clothes. In between her freelance jobs, she crams a series of first dates. How she balances her social calendar alongside paying for chronic medical bills is beyond me. "Sorry."

She scrunches her face. "Sparkless. She doesn't think crystals have spiritual properties. She told me all about how silly I was for wearing my lapis lazuli necklace last night. Jokes on her though. She showed me exactly who she was."

"No second date, then?"

"Not a chance." She shakes her head.

"Probably for the best. Maybe you should send her some amethyst. Help open her mind to the world a bit."

"Maybe." She shrugs. "Anyway, how's the old vagina? Still dry as ever?"

"Nova!" I sputter, opening the little library that my dad's coffee shop sponsored. The thing is even coffee cup shaped.

"What? It's been a while since you've gone out, let alone been laid." She throws her hands up palms to the sky.

Ignoring everything that just came out of her mouth, I quicken my steps. There is a good chance she'll be interrogating me the entire walk. And it hasn't been that long since I've been on a date, has it?

I rack my brain. There was that twenty-four hour read-a-thon over Valentine's Day at the bookstore, but my nose was in between the pages of a fantasy trilogy the entire time. Definitely didn't bang one out there, though I think that was the entire point of the event. Over the summer Verne, from book club, tried to set me up with one of his line dancing partners. The setup sounded fun in theory, but I politely declined. I'd rather shove toothpicks under my fingernails while Nickleback plays in the background than be set-up with one of Verne's *he's perfect for you* acquaintances. When was the last time…

Shit. I think it's been almost a year. A year without dating. A year without human connection in a romantic—or even just a physical—sense. How did another year pass by without me noticing?

The last person I dated, a guy I met at the comic shop the next town over, wasn't terrible. I still talk to him from time to time after we—*I*— decided we'd be better off as friends. There wasn't a spark in his eye when I went on about a new novel I was reading. No tingle in my lower belly when our lips touched, not even for the first time. I'm not saying the lack of fireworks was the reason I called it off with a perfectly nice guy, but I'm not saying it wasn't either.

When I fall in love, like real, true love, I imagine there will be more than fireworks. There will be skywriters scribbling our names in big, loopy letters. Acrobats filling the background of a kiss that will cause world peace. Being apart from my love will cause physical pain, an ache that won't settle until I see their gorgeous face again.

Until then, I will live vicariously through my books. Within the pages are the real love stories. Book boyfriends who listen intently to the heroine as she rambles on about her latest hobby. Where consent is practiced at all times, and it's clear from the first chapter who will fall in love.

Nova's phone pings seconds before mine with a new text.

Nova clears her throat. She's part of my family group chats and loves reading the texts aloud. "From Jonathan: *Mazey, send me a recipe for those lemon cookies.*" She smirks at me. "Your brother's bestie thinks you made the cookies we brought yesterday."

"Ugh, I'll send him a link."

"A link to the grocery store where you bought them?" Nova scoffed.

"You hush your mouth." I grin, googling a random lemon cookie recipe. It looks more complicated than it should, but I send the link anyway. "There. Now he can make these for next week's family dinner. They look better than the ones from a plastic container."

"You know he won't." Nova gives me a knowing grin. "He's going to make your favorite, like he always does. He is one of the sweetest people I know, and he has those caramel eyes set on you."

"Ha! Get real. I'm his best friend's little sister." I run my fingers through my hair. "I don't understand how he has a standing invitation to our family dinners every Saturday anyways."

"The same reason I do. Your mom takes in strays."

My family has the biggest open arms in Honeyville. Jonathan has been coming to the potlucks ever since my brother, Elliott, claimed him as his life-long confidant at the age of seven. Unfortunately for me, they are basically attached at the hip. With the two-year age gap, I was often thrown in the same play dates and kids tables as them. I'd marvel at the way he'd reattach the barbie heads that Elliott pulled off my dolls with concentrated precision and laughed at the nonsensical jokes I made, attempting to fit in. When he smiled, I knew everything was going to be alright. The more time we spent together, the more I kept my crush on him close to the chest. And the more I knew what unrequited love felt like.

"Some strays are better than others, that's for sure," I say. "Like you and your dad."

"Larry and I thank you." She glances down at her pinging phone again. "Jonathan says thanks and asks if you're feeling okay. Said you looked a bit tired last night." Nova shoves her phone back into her pocket. "When will he learn that you stay up all night reading? I swear he asks that every week."

I shrug, not wanting to think about Jonathan today. I'm already annoyed about work. I don't need to add the confusing feelings he inspires into the mix.

Inhaling deeply, I smile at a woman jogging past us and laugh lightly at the golden Lab mightily tugging its owner. My attention drifts to the bed and breakfast we pass on our treks to the town square. Peeling white shutters. Overgrown hydrangeas. Nova routinely jokes she can spot ghosts in the windows.

Today, it doesn't have the eerie vibe I associate with the place. Maybe it's the golden halo around it, or the way the lake sits behind it in a forgotten fairytale sort of way, but it looks like it's filled with magic.

Before I can think twice, I'm lured in the direction of the cottage, the jingle of Wilfred's tags chiming with each step. The need to investigate the cottage overcomes me, a tingle in my toes pulling me to the creaky steps of the wrap-around porch.

"What are you doing, Mazey?" Nova hollers, footfalls trailing me.

I honestly don't know. The moment is surreal. I'm aware of the absurdity—searching for something without a clue as to what it is. I just can't seem to stop myself. A force stronger than myself is coaxing me to find *it*—whatever *it* is.

I cup my hands around my eyes, pressing them against the front door's ornate glass window, and I peer inside.

Rays of light spill through the other windows, illuminating the dust motes floating lazily in the air. A once-polished banister lining a half-twisted wooden staircase sits in the middle of the foyer. Faded wallpaper peels at their edges. In the corner of the room rests a small, round table with a cracked vase. Bits and bobs scatter the nearly empty shelves against the walls.

I drop my hands to my sides. It's not here. I don't even know what *it* is.

"Have the urge to visit the spirits?" Nova adjusts her shoe. "These sandals were not made for dilapidated lake fronts."

"Sorry, I don't know what came over me."

Nova raises her eyebrows, interest piqued. She shoves me to the side and cups her eyes to see inside the window. "All I see is cobwebs and dust."

I peer through the window again. A wall filled with books stands out. The corner of the main entry way has an antique coat rack, like the one from *Beauty and the Beast*—sans the human soul—is filled with jackets. Bright colors and soft lighting. Chairs with cushions that are perfect for curling up with a book. New friends laughing as they walk down the staircase, gossiping over their latest book boyfriend crush.

"Yeah, cobwebs and dust." I drop my hands, the fantasy fading.

I walk along the porch toward the back of the house, the wood planks groaning with each step. Nova follows, petting Wilfred as I peer into each window. The views inside are captivating, the winding staircase showcased from every angle—the type of architectural design that takes time and consideration. It's the vision of someone who dreamed in curves and light, who poured love into every angle so the house itself could hold on to it. More than just a place to hang your hat, a place to live. A once-loved space.

Still, the unease of something missing hasn't settled within me.

I pace the bare porch—once, twice, three times—scanning between the balustrades, into the corners, my stomach doing somersaults in anticipation of finding a surprise that only the cottage knows is waiting for me.

Instead, there's nothing.

Nova plops down on the steps leading down to the beach. She

leans back, holding herself up with her arms, and starts her breathing routine. "This place isn't as bad as I've always made it out to be."

"No, it's not. It's beautiful, really." I wrap my arm around one of the ornate pillars, scanning the property for whatever drew me in this direction. I frown at something tucked in the corner of the porch. "What's that?"

Wilfred charges the angular object with a little yap. I creep behind him, his sniffs loud in the silence. I feel Nova's presence behind me.

"It's a book." She squats to pick it up. "The Story of Daisy and Jonas. That sounds cute."

"I swear there was nothing there a moment ago." I scan the area again, checking for other missing relics.

"I'm sure it was. Maybe you just missed it when you were pretending to be Sherlock Holmes." Nova stands, handing me the paperback.

"Do you see an author? I don't see an author on this." I flip from the front to the back cover before fanning the pages.

"Someone could have bound it themselves or something."

"Right, but a professional publishing house could have made this." I point to a tiny icon on the spin of the book. "Is that…"

"An outline drawing of this cottage?"

We lock eyes before sprinting off the porch. I pull the book closer, studying the tiny image embossed at the bottom of the spine—a delicate illustration of a sprawling cottage with a distinctive wraparound porch.

I hold the spine up against the view before us. The silhouettes align perfectly: the generous porch that encircles the cottage, the peaked gables, the clusters of rounded bushes along the railing. There's no doubt—we're standing in front of the very building etched into this book, right down to the hydrangeas blooming in full, billowing masses along the porch's edge.

"That's so weird. How much do we know about this place?" Nova asks.

"Apparently, not as much as we thought." I study the mysterious novel. Teal, beige, and pink, accented with pops of yellow and coral, make up the muted color scheme. In the center of the cover is a cartoon drawing of a blond woman. She stands outside a bookstore holding a coffee cup and loosely crossing her arms. A guy with brown hair stands by the store window. He has a soft smile and holds a book. He stares at the blonde nearby. "It doesn't look old. The artwork on the cover looks modern, right?"

Nova nods.

I flip the book over and read the summary aloud.

"Daisy Jane has always followed the rules. She sticks to her family's expectations, society's standards, even her own rules scribbled into notebooks at thirteen. They told her who she should be by thirty. At twenty-nine, she's back in her quiet coastal hometown after getting fired. Now, she's working to build a life that finally feels like her own, following the dream that hibernates inside of her.

Jonas Brooks has never cared for rules. He runs the local bookshop. Quiet, observant, and deeply patient, he lives life on his terms. When Daisy stumbles into his store and into his world, he sees the spark of someone who's spent too long trying to please everyone but herself.

But Daisy isn't ready for love. Not yet. Not until she figures out what she truly wants and who she's meant to be.

And Jonas is willing to wait."

"The best stories begin when you stop pretending," Nova reads the last words out loud over my shoulder. "Aren't those the perfect words for you to hear right now?"

A familiar *ping* comes from her pocket. Nova pulls out her phone, already walking. "Come on, your dad just texted. He has new syrup flavors he needs tested." Nova heads back to the path and toward my dad's shop, Gus's Grounds, Wilfred prancing behind her.

"Yeah, you're right," I whisper, still looking at the book. After a quick glance over my shoulder at the abandoned home, I slip the book into my bag. I curl my fingers around it like it's a secret and jog to catch up.

Chapter 2

The Story of Daisy and Jonas

*"The best stories never have just one author, kiddo.
They collect people along the way." - Gus Lane*

As we sit in my dad's shop, *The Story of Daisy and Jonas* radiates through my bag, begging me to dive into its pages. I bounce my knee under the round, wooden table.

Dad moves through the little shop, greeting customers, balancing a tray of espresso cups filled with Dad's new coffee concoctions. If this were a Hallmark movie, my dad would be cast in this role, with his signature shaggy grey locks and soft cardigans.

"Alrighty, here you go. Make a list from favorite to least favorite." He claps his hands, the rings that adorn his fingers sparkling. "Shoot, I forgot a notepad. Be right back."

"Thanks, Gus!" Nova shouts at my dad's back, bringing a cup to her lips. "What's up with you?"

"Nothing," I blurt, sweat beading on my forehead. Likely from basically stealing a book and then hiding it from the person who would drive the get-away car, no questions asked.

Nova raises an eyebrow, licking the foam from her top lip.

"Okay, something. I took the book." I put the book on the table with a thud, sliding it toward her. "I couldn't resist. It's so weird. The way I had to go see what was going on at the cottage, the book randomly showing up… It's freaky, right?"

"Well, that took all of two seconds for you to spill." She chuckles, holding the book at eye-level. She can read me like one of her monster romances.

I'm a terrible secret keeper, even worse when it comes to Nova. Our sophomore year of high school, I tried to keep the crush I had on Ryker Miller to myself. When our science teacher announced Ryker was going to be my partner for the year, she caught me blushing profusely. I gave up keeping things quiet after that.

"You probably just over-looked this guy." She shakes the item in question. "Or someone—or *something*—is trying to send you a message."

"Send me a message?"

"Yeah, you know, a push in a direction you're too afraid to take," she says this with ease. As if I have a secret decoder for the events of the day.

"I suppose the universe works in mysterious ways."I shrug her off. "But what do you think it means?"

"Let's find out." Nova, the spiritual creature that she is, pulls out the pack of tarot cards she keeps in her crossbody. My best friend keeps a pack on hand at all times, pulling them out for any decision or confusing situation.

She begins to shuffle the cards, periodically holding them out for me to split the deck. I obey her silent request. This isn't my first rodeo.

"Here we are." Dad bustled back to the table, notebook and pen in hand. "Sorry about that-Bobby brought over a snack from the diner."

"Is he still here?" I ask. "I'd love to get his opinion on the branding for a bookshop I'm working on."

Nova organizes the cards into what I recognize from the years of being a tarot card enthusiast's best friend, and occasional dabbler in the craft-a three-card spread: past, present, future. "Your husband has an incredible eye for color coordinating," she tells Dad.

"He does, but he left. Had to head back to the studio. He's doing a photoshoot for a newborn in an hour. He popped in on his way to the florist to pick up fresh Aster flowers."

"September's birth flower?" I pick up a striped cup, bringing it to my lips.

"Yes, the couple are botanists from a couple towns over." Dad points to the table. "You two doing a reading or a *reading*?"

"Good one, Gus." Nova laughs, pushing the novel towards dad with her free hand. "We're trying to figure out if this book is one-of-kind."

"Hmm, I've never heard of the title. Who's the author?" Dad examines the cover, landing on the spine. "Is that the old, creepy cottage on the path?"

"Yes!" Nova and I say in unison. The cottage has a reputation with the residents in this town.

I stand, sliding out the mismatched chair, and point at the bottom of the front cover. "There isn't an author listed as far as we can tell."

"What do you know about that old place? Was it a small publishing house at some point?" Nova puts her hand on her chin, narrowing eyes laced with mischief. "Maybe something more scandalous?"

"What could possibly be scandalous in this situation?" I ask, genuinely curious.

"You know... Like an underground smuggling ring or something. Or..." She waggles her eyebrows. "A brothel. It could be anything."

Dad rubs his eyes under his frameless glasses, head tipped back, holding in a laugh. "Not that I know of. It went through owners faster than Mazey goes through coffee during a twenty-four hour reading session."

I lower to my seat and study the book's logo again. People would pay a pretty penny to stay in a lakefront property that's practically a hotel. Not to mention, it's walking distance from downtown. I don't understand how something with such potential can't keep an owner.

"Try this one." Dad slides a shot-glass-sized coffee cup with orange polka dots to me. "It's a cherry almond blend with notes of cinnamon and Tahitian vanilla syrup."

I feel like a giant sipping from the minuscule cup, but damn, Dad's twenty years of owning this shop has paid off. "Hate the cherry, love the Tahitian. Maybe a more citrusy blend would pair nicely? But back to that old cottage—do you know why it can't keep an owner?"

"Ohh—citrus. Good thinking." Dad pulls a tiny notepad from his shirt pocket that I know is full of the random combinations that pop into his head for menu items. He scribbles down my notes.

"From what I can remember, that place is in decent condition. The place gets bought, owners start to fix it up hoping to turn it into one thing or another. One time it was going to be a vet with a dog groomer in the garage. One family wanted to turn it into a vacation house. They only lasted two months." Dad pulled a chair up to the table, joining us. "Hell, Bobby looked at it for a photography studio. Said the cottage didn't give off the vibe that it wanted to be a studio—whatever that means. I'm sure there's more I'm not remembering."

"Can I?" I gesture to the notebook Dad wanted us to use for our coffee flavor rankings.

"Sure, kid, you can have it. Just make sure to leave your top picks before you head out."

I flip to a blank page and start to list the oddities from the book and the tidbits Dad just told us about the cottage. I scribble down question after question. How old is the cottage? What's the longest it has ever held an owner? Has anyone else been drawn to it the way I am? Who designed the elaborate spiral staircase in the middle of the first floor? If I were to redesign the space, I'd paint the entryway walls light blue, lining one side with soft yellow bookshelves. The color combination would bring out the grain of the wood perfectly.

"I always thought it should be a bed-and-breakfast situation. Something cozy and inviting." Dad taps on the table, indicating he needs to attend to customers. "Welp, you two have fun."

"Thanks, Dad."

"This one for sure, Gus." Nova holds up a tiny coffee cup covered in vibrant stripes. Dad pumps his arm in a *cha-ching* motion, celebrating his victory.

Nova turns to me. "I think it's made with real lavender."

"I wouldn't be surprised. Dad's ingredients are always top notch." I don't look up from the notes I'm scribbling down.

"Hmm." Nova holds up her hand as if she just remembered something extremely important. "Check out the cards. Past. Present. Future."

I stop, examining the spread between us. "The empress, the hermit, and the ten of cups?"

Nova has the ability to look at a card and know exactly what it's trying to say without having to reference anything. Once, she explained that she examines the card with her intention in the forefront of her mind, paying close attention to the items that stick out to her, seeing how they could relate to the other illustrations around it. That's why a card has so many meanings.

I'm distracted by the beautiful woman in Nova's past spot. She sits enthroned on the riverbank. I'm shocked by the sheer abundance surrounding her—lush wilderness, golden wheat fields stretching endlessly in every direction. A starry crown rests on her head, and her nurturing figure is draped in a flowing gown. But what truly captivates me is the love radiating from her, warm and all-encompassing, like sunlight itself.

Nova taps the card, an indication that her reading is about to begin. "The cottage used to be a safe place for creative minds. Like a mother fostering her child's artistic side." Nova taps on the card again. "That's what I'm gathering from the empress."

"The hermit makes sense, since the cottage is empty." I hold up the second card.

"It does. You can see by the way this guy holds the lantern with his head down that he's searching for something. In the cottage's case, it's likely for someone. Patiently waiting for the right person to walk through its door." She grins at me. "Pun intended."

"Ten of cups." My eyes move to the last card. Four people—two adults, two kids—doing what can only be described as frolicking in a field with a farmhouse surrounded by trees in the background. A rainbow soars above them, lined with ten cups. "To me, this represents the cottage finding the owner it's supposed to have, living happily ever after."

"So, the new owner has to be a tiny, picture-perfect family?" I raise an eyebrow at her.

"It could be, but it's more symbolic. It just represents happiness. For whoever owns it next." Nova holds up the card. "Maybe it represents your happiness."

✦

"I'm going to go read," I shout to Nova as I race to my room as soon as I crossed the threshold of our apartment. Jingle pup trails behind me. Every minute at the coffee shop dragged on and on, anticipation growing for the moment I could dive into the mysterious novel.

"I expect nothing less." Nova laughs. "I want to read it at some point too."

"Yeah, sure. That's fine."

I crash into the corduroy chair-and-a-half tucked in the corner of my room with my laptop, a notebook and pen, and the book. Wilfred jumps onto the ottoman, his paws shaping the fuzzy blanket he's claimed into a nest. He spins before settling sprawled out on his back, feet in the air.

"Should I research the cottage or read the book first?" I ask no one in particular, holding up the laptop and the book like a weighted scale going from one to the other. Dropping the two to my lap, I sigh. "I also need to work on Pixel Perfection stuff for tomorrow's meeting."

According to the cat-shaped clock on the wall, I could investigate the cottage a bit, eat supper, and then work on the reports for my presentation. Or I could read the mysterious novel before the necessities of food and work.

I raise the laptop higher. Researching the oddity that is the formally creepy cottage could provide insight on where the book came from. Or why it doesn't have an author. Maybe explain the cottage drawing on the spine. There's a chance it could even explain why it suddenly went from the spookiest place in Honeyville to a place that I couldn't wait to return to.

On the other hand—I lowered the laptop while raising the book—*The Story of Daisy and Jonas* may be exactly what I need.

Lately, every time I crack open a much-anticipated novel, my interest is lost within the first few chapters. There has only been a handful of times I've experienced reading slumps, always right before a major life event: my twin, Dawson's, death; my parents separating; the first time I endured a broken heart. It's like my body knows something bigger than me is about to happen, and it has no idea how to react. Unfortunately for me, it leaves me an unsettled mess.

Reading isn't my only hobby, it's just my primary source of joy. Getting lost between the pages of a far-off land fulfills something in my soul. It's like the rest of the world disappears—mundane jobs, heartbreak, loose ends. In my favorite novels, the protagonist always learns the lesson they're supposed to learn—tied up in a perfect little bow. I pretend I'm the main character, following their internal struggles and celebrating their wins as if they are my own. Finishing the most impactful stories leaves a hole in my heart, knowing I'll never be able to visit that world for the first time ever again.

"Book it is."

I hold the book up in victory, placing the laptop on the table next to the seat. Goosebumps trickle over my arms as I train the spine of the paperback, keeping it from cracking while reading. Energy surges from the pages as I firmly press along the spine. Tottie, the former owner of The Story Porch, taught me this trick. Every time I brought in a used book to trade in for a percentage off my purchase, she'd roll her eyes at the worn spines. Eventually she sat me down, showed me the proper way to "train" a paperback.

I settle into the cushions, pillows all around, Wilfred on the thick blanket over my lap. We lock eyes. He does his signature micro-sneeze of approval then goes back to sleep. With a deep breath, I turn to page one.

Daisy always did what was expected of her: MBA no later than twenty-four, corporate job secured at twenty-five, penthouse apartment by twenty-seven. The only problem was that her heart called to an unexpected, yet not surprising, path. Anyone who knew Daisy Jane would tell you her storytelling abilities were unmatched. The detail she weaved through the tale was a gift of the world she described. Love poured through each sentence she spoke, enthusiasm highlighting each word.

Daisy Jane was meant for something bigger, she just didn't believe.

Damn. I guess I'm not the only one that feels the pressure to hit all the *right* milestones—education, career… Okay, so I don't live in a penthouse, but I have a really nice apartment. I've always prioritized security over passion. Too often when I've taken risks, it backfired right into my face.

My achievements, as impressive as they appear—like the degrees line my wall—are hollow. The accomplishments I'm most proud of are the ones that I kept quiet while waiting for the other shoe to drop. Like starting the book club at The Story Porch and advocating for the installations of the Little Free Libraries around town.

Those were low risk though. Nobody could get hurt. Not like when Dawson and I got into the car accident on our way to school junior year.

"Hey, I'm heading to bed." Nova appears in my doorway. "Did you eat anything?"

"What time is it?" I check the time on my phone. "Holy shit. It's almost nine?"

So much for my brilliant plan.

"Yeah." Nova yawns, stretching her arms. "Need help with your presentation? We could tag team it."

"No, I got it. Thanks though." I shoo her away. "Get to bed, you look exhausted."

"Thanks, my blood sugar has been wonky today. I'll be better in the morning, I'm sure."

"I'll check on you in a bit." I promise as she turns down the hallway. Nova's type 1 diabetes has never stopped her from doing anything she wants in life, but it does leave her exhausted if her blood sugars aren't cooperating.

Should I continue the story and then work on my presentation? Page after page I felt more connected to Daisy's journey to happiness, and I don't want it to end.

I have a couple hours of work left. Which primarily consists of mapping out this project around the availability of all the key players. If I start now, I could create a high-level plan and still make it to bed by midnight. The projections may be something that *resembles* a high-level plan. Very high level. You might have to jump on a plane to get high enough to see it.

I look over at *The Story of Daisy and Jonas* longingly, resisting the urge to say *fuck it* and finish the novel. Instead, I open my laptop and begin working on the reports.

How am I only a quarter of the way through this shit? I glare at my new enemy—my laptop with the former love of my life, Excel, on the screen. The hope I held for racing through this project plan with time to spare to read more of *The Story of Daisy and Jonas* has faded into a whirlwind of pivot tables.

I look over at the novel that has been consuming my thoughts for the last hour and a half. It's still there. Part of me anticipated it disappearing as quickly as it showed up.

That's ridiculous. As much as I'd love to believe that it randomly appeared out of nowhere like some sort of gift from the cottage or something, I'm sure it was just left behind by the previous owner. For six months, leaving it in perfect condition on the porch despite the rain storms we got over the summer.

That has to be it. Right?

Maybe I could refocus myself if I researched the cottage a bit more. Just for a little bit. Then I could jump right back into this project and head to bed.

I jump up, not letting myself second guess my decision to scour the internet for whatever information I can find on the place that I have a sudden and unexplainable connection to.

Before I know it, the clock in the corner of my laptop reads 1:12 a.m. I type the cottage's address into the search bar and hit enter for what has to be the dozenth time tonight. I even include a few descriptions here or there like it's going to magically produce something new. It doesn't.

I click through the same thin threads—a real estate listing with photos so aggressively staged they look like a fever dream, a local tourism blog that dedicates exactly one sentence to the cottage before moving on to a lobster shack—nothing that explains why the place has cycled through owners the way it has. I even dig through the location tags on Instagram, squinting at the backgrounds of strangers' beach pictures hoping to catch a glimpse of the porch, the garden, anything. The only thing I glean from them is that people really should turn off their location settings.

I snap the laptop shut and move to the bed, lugging a drowsy Wilfred with me.

The novel screams to me where it's still sitting on the edge of the table where I left it, spine up, splayed open to the page I shoved a hair tie in before telling myself I'd only take a quick break. I pick it up without thinking.

Welp, I'm about to find out how much you can get done in the eight hours you are supposed to be asleep.

I settle into my bed, positioning the pillows into a nest-like cocoon of warmth and comfort. Daisy pulls me under the same way she did when I opened to page one. I'm not reading so much as I'm living inside the sentences, feeling the weight of every choice she makes settle somewhere in my chest.

Around three am, with Wilfred kicking his little legs at my feet, her logic doesn't just make sense—it feels inevitable. The suffocation of a life built around everyone else's expectations. The way a dream can survive years of neglect, quiet and stubborn, waiting.

I get it, Daisy. I really do.

I slow down when I hit the Jonas chapters, though. My eyes keep snagging on the same details—his chaos against her order, his dog-eared paperbacks shoved into a jacket pocket, her color-coded shelves. The only thread between them is books, and even that they can't agree on. He reads to escape. She reads to understand.

I set the novel down on my chest and stare at the ceiling.

The opposites attract thing has never sat right with me. It's a good story. It's a terrible plan. In real life, the things that seem charming in the first chapter become the things you're fighting about in chapter twenty. You can't build something lasting on the thrill of being different—can you?

I pick the book back up before I can answer my own question.

Chapter 3

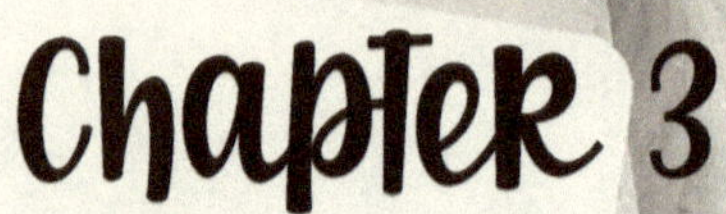

Risk Assessment

The home office feels extra gray as I crash into the wing-back chair in front of my desk. Nova has a matching set-up a few feet down the same gray wall.

I rub my eyes, trying to wake myself up. The report I'm working on glares at me from the screen. The first page, then the second, possibly the third roll by in flashes of outrageous numbers and color-coded projections for a new construction business the sales team landed a couple weeks ago. For whatever reason, the overly ambitious timeline of six months to go-live landed on my desk mid-last week. Strategically planning every configuration of the system and coordinating each training session between each area expert and the client's stakeholders requires weeks of planning, organizing, and tedious attention to detail—even for a "teeny implementation" like this. Those were the sales team's words, not anyone with any sense.

"Anyone in need of some caffeine?" Nova hands me a cup of much-needed coffee, topped with whipped cream. "I'm going to run to the bookstore for a few. I need to deliver a few design concepts for the new logo for the bowling alley. Should only take about an hour. Then I have to work for a few hours, but I shouldn't interrupt your meeting."

After living together for years, Nova's announcement no longer feels like a competition of the day's tasks or some weird proclamation of her productivity. It's her way of being respectful to our shared office. My job requires more sitting in front of a screen or three. Her job has more face-to-face interactions since the majority of her clients are local. We've learned to schedule our virtual meetings around each other to eliminate the background noise.

"Oh my God, give me that." I gulp the coffee, licking away my fluffy mustache. "It's delicious."

"Bobby dropped it off on his way to the studio. I just poured it into a cute cup." She gestures to the gnome-shaped mug. "What flavor did you get? Mine was shockingly delicious. I think it was some kind of peanut butter chocolate situation."

"I think it's toffee." I take another sip. "Maybe Butterfinger? I have no idea, but it's so good. I really needed it."

"I heard you up last night. Everything okay?"

"Yeah. Just had to finish up this report for the company meeting today. Took longer than expected."

Not to mention I had to finish it as quickly as possible before the sun came up when I woke up to Wilfred nudging me to go to the bathroom.

"And?"

"And… I might have been distracted by—"

"*The Story of Daisy and Jonas?*"

I nod, laughing. I can't hide anything from Nova.

"I couldn't stop thinking about the cottage either," she says. "I wasn't up all night, but I definitely fell asleep with thoughts of weirdness dancing in my head."

Nova flipped her pocket watch necklace open. "Shoot. I gotta go, Tottie." She hurries past Wilfred as she races through the door.

Wilfred curls into a ball on my lap, warmth radiating through the blanket. The fluff ball is basically an honorary project manager as often as he takes this position. From time to time, he pops his head into view of the camera, creating a chorus of laughter from whoever I'm on a call with. He's a great ice breaker, especially when I have to deliver bad news regarding budget.

During my last employee review, my scores were devastatingly low, with ample amounts of notes to push me closer to my full potential. Margot, my boss, created a project plan for my career that includes presenting my latest project during the company updates meeting.

The slide deck is ready. Notes are in front of me. I flip my phone to *do not disturb* for the next ninety minutes. I'm as ready as I'll ever be. The only issue is that my eyes keep growing heavier and heavier. Twenty minutes until the meeting starts. Sixty minutes for the meeting. My presentation is around forty-five minutes in, takes about five minutes. I can be in my bed by eleven for a nap, since I rearranged my schedule today, pushing most of my work to the evening.

I scroll through my phone for more information on the cottage, hoping someone posted the chronicle of the place online sometime in the last six hours. Unfortunately, no such luck.

A high-pitched ding indicates our meeting is about to start. I throw on the black blazer I keep on a hook next to my desk, adjust it over the plain green scoop neck in the video preview before clicking "Enter."

Tiny boxes with my co-workers from all over the country pop up, their greetings bumbling over one another. Lincoln's cat jumps on his keyboard turning him into a cartoon character of himself, and the virtual room busts into muted laughter, bodies shaking, hands covering mouths.

"Hello, everyone! I'm so excited to see so many smiling faces. Thank you for remembering to keep cameras on during this call." My boss's voice booms with tender authority.

The first ten minutes consist of going from person to person, introducing ourselves for the thousandth time, our role with the company, and a fun fact about ourselves.

"Mazey Lane, project manager for four years." I hate the fun fact part. If I say I read over two hundred books a year, I'm met with looks of *yeah right* or *you read picture books, right?* My other hobbies are that of an eighty-year-old widow: hand embroidery and quilting. Both I do while listening to audiobooks on the couch.

I stick to a cute fact instead. "My dog Wilfred insists on wearing clothing or a bandana. He picks his outfit everyday from his basket and brings it to me. The vet said it could be a form of comfort for him—feeling something wrapped around him—since he was a rescue, but I think it's more that he enjoys being stylish."

More bouncing shoulders.

The meeting drones on about the key updates, goals from the leadership team, forecasting for upcoming quarters. With every slide, my eyes grow heavier and heavier. Somewhere during the sales team goals, I prop my head on my hand, shaking my head every couple of seconds to keep myself from nodding off. I rhythmically scratch Willy's ears, his soft snoring a smooth melody behind the monotone voice of the current speaker.

"Mazey!" Nova's voice jolts my eyes open.

"Where am I? What time is it?" I wipe drool from the corner of my mouth.

"It's five after eleven. How long have you been asleep?"

Horror flows alongside the blood in my veins, hot and vibrating. My eyes dart to the computer screen.

"This meeting has ended" in bold, white font displays on a black background in front of me. The chat is going crazy, my name tagged in almost every message. My phone buzzes, lighting up the screen to show forty-two text messages and sixteen phone calls from my co-workers. And my boss.

A meeting invite pops onto the corner of my computer screen for today at one o'clock. The only people invited are my boss, Human Resources, and me.

Fuck.

Chapter 4

Unemployed, but Hydrated

"Dollar drop night exists for two reasons: celebrating the good stuff and drowning out the bad. Tonight qualifies for both." - Elliott Lane

"Then she said I wasn't living up to my potential and have become too much of a risk to the company at this point." I gulp my third lemon drop. The wooden barstool is making my ass numb. "Because I could have fallen asleep during a client meeting."

Nova dragged me out of the house after witnessing my termination from Pixel Perfection off screen. As Honeyville's only bar, The Bee Hive is thankfully within walking distance of our apartment. Lucky for me, tonight is dollar drop night.

Nova rubs my back and motions to the bartender for another round. "You really weren't living up to your potential. You hated that job."

"But now I have no job." I hiccup, wiping snot from my nose. "What am I going to do?"

She tilts her head at me. "I know this is rough, babe. But at least you have that killer savings account. That should get you by until you figure out your next move, right?"

"That money is for Reading Lane, not because I can't keep a job."

A fresh drink appears in front of me, and I chug the remains of the previous one. The prospect of opening Reading Lane now isn't possible. Not when I screwed up so badly. I'm not sure I'm qualified to open a new business. The chance of failing is just too high. A dream this big. A dream that isn't just mine, but also Dawson's, has to have perfect timing. I have to have all my shits together. Who knows when that'll happen. The best I can do is plan for the moment I feel ready—if that ever happens. By saving the money I will need to open Reading Lane's door someday. The funds I've saved so far can sit in the high-yield savings account, collecting interest, until I *am* ready to move forward.

"You can keep a job. The universe is pushing you in a new direction since you refuse to go there yourself," Nova says in a comforting voice.

"Fancy seeing you ladies here!" A voice booms behind me.

I push off the bar to swivel the barstool. Elliott and his *bros* are standing right behind me. This is exactly what I need—to display my new unemployment to this group.

Elliott and Jonathan met Brody in college. He's not so bad. Morgan, his adorable wife, convinced him to join our book club a few years back when he moved to town after a career-ending injury. His participation in discussion is always fascinating—not at all what you'd expect from a former linebacker-turned-realtor.

Jonathan is everything you might think of when you think of a successful, intelligent man. He is so considerate to everyone he meets. One time, he nursed a baby squirrel back to health because the thing's mom turned her nose up at it. How did he find out the squirrel needed help? One of those squirrel feeders with corn on it, except this one looks like a picnic table. It sits next to the shelter he made for them. With a camera on it so he can observe them.

I hate how much I find that attractive. Especially when he sees me as family and not his best friend's hot sister.

Jonathan Kirkwood is the last person I want to see while I'm tumbling towards rock-bottom.

"Hi, Elliott. Brody, where's Morgan?" I chirp. Then, with a deep breath to gather courage and not to jump on the man, "Jonathan."

"Home with the kids. Insisted I come out with the guys." Brody's eyes crinkle with his grin. "She's the absolute best."

After a few minutes of small talk and a fresh round between the guys and Nova—I zone out, too busy debating when I should rip off my *I got canned* bandage. It's only a matter of time before Mr. Perfect finds out anyway.

"Listened to any terrible music lately, Mazey?" Jonathan asks with a grin. He's always teasing me about my music, but I've caught him jamming out to emo that demands you line your lower lash line in thick black eyeliner and rage scream the lyrics into your hairbrush. And Taylor Swift. But everyone loves Taylor Swift.

"Always. It's the only soundtrack of my soul."

Jonathan's effortless confidence makes me want to put my lips all over his stupid face. Give him a hammer, he builds a Pinterest-worthy bookshelf. I'd give myself a concussion. Don't get me started on his pancakes. He has the flip precision of an Olympic gymnast. The first pancake theory doesn't even apply to him. Even Wilfred refuses to eat mine, and he scarfs down Mom's potato salad. It's like he's too perfect to even be a book boyfriend. Not that I'd know anything about that. The night I blurted my true feelings for him at a house party freshman year in college, he shut me down with a harsh, "You're my best friend's little sister." Never mind what I overheard him saying about me afterward.

And yet, even though he was uncharacteristically mean back then and has no interest in me, I still scan every room, hoping he's there. Which is ridiculous. He's perfect, and I'm still figuring out how to be a person without apologizing for it. He is too much. Actually, too much isn't fair. He's *exactly* much. It's just that I'm not enough.

"I lost my job," I sputter before emptying my cup with a hard gulp. "It was… I had… There wasn't…"

"Mazey has decided to pursue new opportunities in the workforce." Nova explains on my behalf, grinning. "She's brave."

"Makes sense." Jonathan takes a sip from the glass bottle he holds loosely between his fingers. His tongue licks up the stray drops lingering on his full lips.

"They fired you? Or you quit?" Elliott asks, his protective big brother showing.

"Fired." I down my lemon drop. "It was for good reason though. I fell—"

"There is not a good enough reason, Mazey. You are smart. They made a mistake. What's your boss's number? I'll give her a call and straighten this out." Elliott already has his phone in his hand, ready to call my former Pixel Perfection boss.

"Calm down, Wild Card." Jonathan claps Elliott on the shoulder. The nickname fits—Elliott can go from laid back to "fuck around and find out" in a heartbeat. Especially when the people he cares about are in trouble.

"How about we get a booth," Brody shouts over the music.

"And celebrate!" Nova adds, swaying her hips towards the back of the bar.

"Hey, did you guys hear me? I have no job."

My brother and his friends have lost their minds. I have failed. There is no income, no prospects. Nothing. Just me. Unemployed.

"I got fired. For falling asleep. On camera. In front of the entire company." I throw my hands up displaying the *what the fuck is going on* vibe to no avail.

Ignored, I weave through the packed dance floor. No one seems to notice the mess I have made out of my career. Someone crashes into my side, and liquid sloshes over my fingers. A warm pressure steadies me, a palm pressing against my back.

I whip around. "Hey, buddy. I'm not—"

"Whoa, Mazey. Just me." Jonathan lifts his hands in surrender. "Wanted to make sure you didn't fall."

"Oh, uh, thanks." I shout over the blaring music, missing the pressure of his hand. Stupid warm hand.

"No problem." Jonathan gestures for me to walk ahead of him.

By the time we finally reach the booth—did it really take me that long? Maybe I should slow down on these drops—Brody has distracted Elliott with sharks. My brother is explaining the importance of teaching the impact of climate change in relation to shark habitats, an argument I have heard so often, I can recite regardless of the amount of booze flowing through my body. I slide into the booth next to Nova and boop her on the nose. She grins back at me, sliding a glass of water my way. I slide it back in front of her.

"It's crazy," Elliott goes on. "These kids have no clue that ocean temperature directly impacts the embryo mortality rate."

"Does *anyone* have that clue?" Brody asks.

Jonathan tips his beer bottle towards Brody in agreement.

"What about the acidity in the ocean? That does something too, right?" Jonathan encourages. This isn't the first time Elliott has rambled on about this topic. My brother downs a couple drinks and the only thing he can think about is educating the next generation. I suppose that isn't a bad thing since he's a high school biology teacher. He talks about his job as if he's in love with it.

That's not how work is supposed to be. I mean, it's called *work*. You go there, do the job, and go home to do the stuff you love while trying not to think about the crap you have to do for money the next day. My day-to-day responsibilities don't have to be something I love, as long as I get a paycheck at the end of the week.

Would I love running the retreat, though? It's obvious I didn't love being a project manager for a software company. At a retreat, I could talk about books all day with the guests. Curate themed craft nights for new releases. Meet authors who need a space to put pen to paper. My heart races at the possibilities, but then I quickly remember I'm a fuck-up, and making that move right now is a terrible idea.

"You're right, Jonathan. The acidity does so many things to the sharks. Thanks for reminding me," Elliott says around a mouthful of community pretzels he brought with him from the bar. "Impairs their sense of smell, interferes with navigation. The list goes on and on."

"My next cover design has a shark on it." Nova saves us from another ocean acidity rant. "And a scantily clad lady."

Brody perks up at the topic change. "Oooh, shark shifter?"

Nova nods in slow motion, grin growing with each dip.

"Fuck yeah. Count me in." Brody claps his hands.

Nova goes on about the premise of the monster romance and her design. She showed me her progress last night. It's a breathtaking cover. It mimics the traditional bodice-ripper-style romance book cover but as an oil painting, the two main characters intertwined, shark mostly in water, the heroine's naked body wrapped around the creature's slick form.

Since I already know the cover details, I swipe open my phone, navigating to a career site. Might as well look at some job boards. I switch my employment status to *excited to explore new opportunities within project management,* but I frown. Am I excited to explore new opportunities? I'm not sure. Daisy didn't entertain the thought of a different life until she was forced to. After some coaxing from her best friend—and a dwindling bank account—she turned her life into what she wanted it to be. Sure, it took time; writing a novel is not something that happens over night. But she figured it out. Got a job at Jonas's bookstore—a place she could read and write until her heart was content. She started a writing group, made friends along the way, one of whom connected her with an agent that helped get her book published.

But real life doesn't follow a three-act plot structure.

"How's the hunt for the property going?" Elliott asks Jonathan.

"You're looking for a new place... to live?" I ask. "I thought you were living above the Phoenix offices."

"I am living there. It's for work." Jonathan sips his beer, avoiding eye contact. "Katie wants to do this marketing thing. I'm not sure I'm going to go through with it."

"Katie is the best thing that's happened to Phoenix. You got really lucky finding her to be your Marketing Director. You should probably listen." Elliott throws a couple pretzels into his mouth. "Especially since your revenue is down."

Phoenix Construction's revenue is down? Since his grandparents retired, Jonathan runs the company, and I thought his decades-old family business had consistent streams of business coursing through it. There are signs stuck in yards all over town with "Back from the ashes thanks to Phoenix Construction. Call for your free renovation quote today!" written all over them. Everyone in Honeyville uses them. Probably because it's the only one in town, but they do solid work too. Jonathan's grandparents built the place from the ground up while raising him. And they offered employment and training to those down on their luck.

Jonathan's gaze doesn't leave his beer. He twirls the bottle in a circle on the table. His thick brows are creased, forming a furrow so deep you could go canoeing through them. The space under his chocolate eyes is tense and colored a faint purple I've never seen on his olive skin before. I can't see his jawline through his black beard, but I'd put money on it being clenched.

"I know Katie is the best," he finally says. "There are just a lot of things to consider. Like, is this vlog project that she wants me to do actually going to work? Or is it going to cost more money in the long run? Where am I even going to find a place to convert into something that will win the hearts of the cyberverse? Speaking of which, who is going to run said business that is going to benefit the community?"

I'm lost in the choppy sentences he's running together. Did he say *vlog project*? What does the Spider-Verse have to do with it? I know my brother and he are obsessed with Spider-Man, but I'm not sure how that relates to a family-owned construction company.

"Slow down. What are you talking about?"

Elliott wastes no time answering for Jonathan. "Phoenix needs more customers. Honeyville is only so big, so Jonathan here needs to cast a larger net." He slaps Jonathan on the shoulder. "Katie suggested working with Brody might get more views if his name is trending."

"Retired hall-of-fame running catcher living a mundane life." Nova rainbows her hands. "I'd follow that story."

"Running *back*. Running catcher isn't a position in any sport," Brody corrects. "Starting a realtor business is no joke. Tying my name to this type of project would be huge. For whatever reason, my name still pops up with rumored stories of my dating life."

"You're married to Morgan!" I slam my glass to the table. Lemon drop sloshes over the side. "She's a dime piece!"

"Oh, I know. I have no idea how I got someone so out of my league." Brody's eyes sparkle. "The media doesn't see it though. Small town elementary teachers don't usually marry NFL players."

Brody met Morgan six years ago at Honeyville Elementary. Morgan had somehow convinced Brody's old team to visit, sharing inspirational stories, doing crafts, and playing flag football with the kids in the playground. If you ask Morgan, he was annoyingly adorable with his determination to take her on a date, sending her flowers and much needed classroom supplies.

If you ask Brody, it was love at first sight.

"Go back to the vlog thing." I finish my drop, sliding the empty glass across the table. It tinks against Jonathan's bottle. He looks at me through dark lashes. "What the frack is that?"

"Frack?" He quirks an eyebrow.

"Frack. It's a thing."

"Oh yeah, totally." He chuckles, gaze dropping. "Katie wants to do a HGTV thing on Phoenix's socials with the hopes of it going viral. Buy a cheap property. One that needs a ton of work. Film the repairs."

"Thanks so much." Nova says to the back of the waitress that dropped a trough of nachos on our table without a word before walking back to the bar. Nova wiggles her fingers in delight, selecting the first chip victim, popping it in her mouth. "What happens once the repairs are done?"

"Then Honeyville will have a brand-new business." Jonathan shrugs.

"Seems sketchy," I say.

"Well, there would be a vetting process since we'd be co-owners of the property for a bit. The prospective owner would need to provide a business plan. Need to make sure it won't go belly-up in the first year," Jonathan says.

"How does that even work? You'd just be part of this unknown business?" I ask through a mouthful of cheesy goodness.

"Once the project is done, Phoenix would hand it over to the new business owner." Jonathan says this as if this plan is common knowledge instead of an elaborate PR stunt his marketing specialist dreamed up. "Take my name off the mortgage."

"None of this makes sense." Chip crumbles tumble out of my mouth. "What about the down payment? Or the cost of the renovation?"

"Phoenix would be sinking the majority of our marketing budget into the project, since social media is free. We'd have to sit down with the new owner and come to an agreement. There's a lot to think about." Jonathan takes a long drink. Eyes closed, tilting his head back. His loose waves tumble backward, bit by bit. The collar of his open flannel brushes his Adam's apple.

Damn, his neck is thick. Like a wrestler or lumberjack. Lumberjack Jonathan. Lumber-Jonathan.

"What are you doing?" Nova whisper-yells, elbowing my side. I realize my eyes are tracing his neck as I lick my lips.

"Nothing," I hiss back, straightening. "Just trying to wrap my head around Lumber-Jonathan's crazy idea."

"Lumber-Jonathan?" Jonathan smirks.

Our stupid eyes meet again. Linger longer. My stomach becomes a gymnastic studio for toddlers with all the somersaulting. Why am I not climbing on top of this dude? He's gorgeous. Oh, that's right. I'm his best friend's little sister.

"Is that me?" he asks.

"Mind your business." I scowl as my phone pings. New job posting. I save it to my Notes app, half-heartedly promising myself I'll apply tomorrow.

Too bad the cottage isn't for sale. As much as I'd hate it, I could partner with Jonathan to get it into book retreat bliss. I shake away the thought as quickly as it enters my brain—these lemon drops are going straight to my reasonable thinking.

There is no way Jonathan and I would be able to work together long enough to renovate an entire cottage. Ever. He'd be too close to me. I'd be able to smell him too much. And what if the feelings I've pushed down for the last decade bubble up to the surface, and I touch his gorgeous, full beard? The amount of time I've spent avoiding being in close proximity to him in an effort to steer clear of the decade-long crush is embarrassing.

Chapter 5

Potato Salad

*"He kept showing up. She kept having explanations for it.
She was running low on explanations." - The Story of Daisy and Jonas*

"**M**om, that potato salad is a culinary catastrophe of epic proportions. Please spare us the torment of that dish again! I'm begging you!" I plead, sitting on the counter, swinging my legs.

My mom cooks like a Michelin-star chef. Growing up, there was always an elaborate home-cooked meal at six on the dot. Some dishes were generational, passed down in a busted-spine recipe book. Others Mom tossed together with whatever was left in the cabinets. Meals were always planned for the week with detailed grocery lists, utilizing every close-to-expiring item in the cabinets. She'd even make fresh muffins or granola bars for the week, since "breakfast is the most important meal of the day."

The only exception to mom's cooking is her potato salad. She tortures us every single week at family dinner. If culinary crimes were a thing, this lumpy mush would serve life without parole. Wilfred doesn't even like the monstrosity, and I once saw him try to eat the goose poop off the beach in the backyard.

"Listen to me, Mazey Bug." She squints at me, x-raying my intentions. Her finger wags so hard that her greying curls bounce. "This is your father's great-great-grandma's recipe. It's award-winning." She stirs the sad potatoes in a comically large bowl. "Anyway, Larry loves this recipe. He asks for it every week for family dinner. I can't let that man down."

Larry takes scoop after scoop of the stuff, choking down each bite with a water chaser. He once sided with her during a recurring debate on the side dish, her only ally on the topic. Mom decided that day, a decade ago, that it was Larry's favorite thing in the universe. It's not. My *mom* is Larry's favorite thing, but she hasn't figured that out yet.

"The recipe was developed before flavor was invented, Mom."

She sticks her tongue out at me like she's five. I grin at her, eyes catching on a photo of my parents when they were seventeen, shoulder to shoulder on the hood of Dad's beat-up truck, both holding cherry slushies and grinning like they just pulled off the world's best prank. That's how they always looked—like best friends. While I was growing up, they finished each other's jokes, raced to answer Jeopardy questions, and tag-teamed bedtime stories like seasoned improv partners.

Love was never in short supply in our house. My parents functioned like a well-oiled machine, complementing each other. The same way Nova and I do. Dad's *whatever happens, happens* attitude balances out mom's logic and giant color-coded calendars. They are a good team, but not as a married couple.

Dad moved next door when I was six. I wasn't sad. None of us were more excited for the seemingly obvious choice. Mom and Dad were honest about the life-changing decision, explaining that they loved us unconditionally but were better as friends. My brothers and I shared a look like *duh, we already knew that*, but we didn't say that part out loud. We did ask why they got together to begin with if they weren't in love. Mom smiled and said, "Because there was a time when loving who you really are was scarier than hiding it. I love your dad. He will always be my best friend. And we got you and your brothers out of the deal, so I'd say it was the best decision of my life."

It wasn't long before Bobby came around. He melted into our family as if he was always there, bringing blueberry scones and laughing at

Dad's terrible jokes like he'd waited his whole life to hear them. Dad looked different too. Like he could breathe. Like he could finally be himself.

"Speaking of your dad, run next door and grab my cookie sheet. Bobby borrowed it last week to make oatmeal raisins." Mom gestures wildly with her spoon. "I'm gonna need it for one of my desserts. "

"Yes, Mom." I slide off the counter, swiping a pig in a blanket and popping it into my mouth. "Shit, that's hot," I say, flapping my hands by my face.

"That'll teach you to wait. Now get going." Mom swings the wooden spoon from me to the door, potato salad spattering the floor.

I step forward to help clean it up, but Mom hits me with *that look.* I rush out of the house.

I make it ten feet off the porch before I hear Elliott call, "Mazey daisy!"

Within seconds, I'm floating in my giant brother's arms. "Hi, Elliott smElliott. "

"How's the job search going?" He drops me, pursing his lips. "You doing okay?"

"I have to grab something for Mom," I quickly deflect. "We'll talk later, okay?"

I beeline for the cottage next door, avoiding eye contact with my brother. He means well, but I don't want to dissect my lack of employment anymore today. Mom already presented me with a list of jobs she found online the second I walked in the door. If I'm being honest, I haven't been able to focus on anything except the creepy cottage and the novel. I've combed over each page, over and over, with a feeling that the words are trying to lead me to something.

I also keep toying with the idea of the bookish retreat. Random thoughts about how I'd decorate the house or special events I might hold pop in my mind. I can't stop myself from pulling out the old Reading Lane journal from my nightstand, recording the ideas. The project manager side of me has started creating a project plan, mapping out a renovation of a standard bed-and-breakfast-style cottage, according to google. Last night, I went into the financials of the business. I blame drinks last week for putting business plans in my brain.

Halfway across the yard, a voice much gruffer than my brothers sneaks up behind me. "Mazey Lane."

I stumble on an invisible rock in the yard. "Hi, Jonathan."

"Saw you walking over to your dad's and thought you might need some help." He's at my side now. Through my peripheral vision, I spot the emerald platter he brings every week that usually has my all-time favorite dessert on it. Only I can't see what is on it thanks to the foil covering the contents. "I also wanted to talk to you about the—"

"What are these?" I point to the platter, stepping closer.

"Oh, these?" He waves what I hope is the blondies under my nose. "Thought you might need your favorite dessert."

My heart does something stupid in my chest. Damn him and his genuine thoughtfulness.

I curl my lower lip in-between my teeth as he leans towards me. His rustic scent causes a slow-blink situation that I usually reserve for one of Nova's meditation sessions.

"I know Judith hates it when we sneak food early."

"No kidding. I about lost my tongue on a pig in a blanket on my way over here." As the words leave my mouth, Jonathan's eyes dart to my mouth as if he were checking for injury. "I'm fine though. No need to worry."

The corner of his mouth ticks up. "Would one of these help?" His voice hums as he slowly pushes back the foil revealing the blondies. His thick arms flex with each tug, defining the muscles that come from swinging a hammer.

"I always need these little pieces of magic." I swipe the top golden square, begging my eyes not to trace his outline. He has the type of body that I would call "realistic perfect." He doesn't have a six pack, but he doesn't have a Homer Simpson body either. It's somewhere in-between. Jet-black tousled hair that does the floppy curl thing when he's been working outside for too long. His olive skin glows, like he returned from a week on a yacht. In reality, he probably spent the day fixing his truck or rescuing an orphaned animal.

And the beard. My god, *the beard*. It's a combination of "polished masterpiece" and "dangerous mess." More times than I can count, I've had to stop myself from running my fingers through it. Straightening out a rogue tuft. Keeping it from tickling his cheek.

Watching this man uncover my favorite dessert is like reading the dirtiest erotica.

I bring the buttery, caramel sweetness to my mouth, letting the fudgy texture melt on my tongue. Jonathan watches with his mouth slightly agape as I shove the entire thing into my mouth. A snort creeps out of him as I shake the crumbs from my shirt. Heat creeps up my neck.

I have to get out of here. I just ogled this guy over a blonde brownie.

"Mazey, I wanted to talk to you about—"

"I have to get to my dad's. Mom sent me over to get something." I scurry out of his proximity, certain that he's working with Elliott to find out what's going on with my job search. Besides, with the sugary goodness coursing through my body, there is a high chance I'll do something impulsive. Like find out how soft his beard is.

"I really think you'll want to hear what I have to say!" His shout fades as I bound up the porch steps, taking two at a time.

"Later, okay?" I shout, swinging open my dad's front door. "Dad, Bobby! I need mom's cookie sheet."

Bobby rounds the corner, drying his hands on a dishtowel before tossing it over his shoulder. "I tried to keep the damn thing until after today. That woman always makes too much when we get together."

"But it's all so good. Other than the potato salad, I'm not sure what I'd tell her to skip. The leftovers feed Nova and me the entire week. The snack mix is great while I'm reading."

Bobby chuckles. "Oh, that reminds me, I found a limited edition *Anne of Green Gables* at a thrift store the other day. Wanted to see if it's the missing one. It's in the office."

For a graduation present, I received a limited edition Anne of Green Gables… from Jonathan. It's not that it was *from Jonathan*, necessarily. It's the book itself—mostly—with its bonded leather binding on a textured cover with rose gold embossing. Inside the front cover was a hand painting of the original cover, while the back featured a modern rendition of Anne in her signature boater hat.

As far as I know, there are only five hundred of the edition in existence, and they go for a pretty penny. The fact that Jonathan got it when it first came out, remembering how it is my favorite story in the entire world—well, maybe I keep that close to my heart. Especially after the distance that had grown between us.

When I read *Anne of Green Gables* for the first time, I discovered the power of letting a book take over. Each sentence could transport me out of the world that pinned me as the weird kid and into a world that celebrated flaws. Anne taught me resilience—a trait I've cherished my entire life.

I lost the treasure when I moved back from college years ago. Dad's old Dodge hit a bump, sending a couple of my boxes across the interstate. Most of the stuff I got back or replaced, but no one ever found the book. Bobby and I have been searching for it ever since at flea markets and used bookstores. We've only been able to find a couple, and none of them are The One, but we keep trying. I think he feels guilty since he was the one driving. But just like Jonathan, the book wasn't meant to be mine.

"I'm not sure we'll ever recover *that* one." I follow him into his office. A desk is centered on the wall opposite the door, with giant double monitors lined on top for photo editing. I plop down on the plaid couch in the corner as Bobby opens a file cabinet drawer.

"Maybe not, but I will always continue searching for it." He hands me the hard cover with a grin.

"Thanks, Bobby." I flip to the inside cover, eyes closed, heart racing. If this is the copy, there will be a choppy hand-written note on the top left corner. Slowly, I open my eyes to see the standard inside cover. My shoulders drop. "It's not the one."

"Next time, kid." Bobby pats my shoulder. "I'll go get the cookie sheet. I'm sure Judith is chomping at the bit for it."

Chapter 6

Three Feet to the Left

"She had been living three feet to the left of everything she wanted. Close enough to see it. Far enough to pretend she didn't." - Don't Say It Out Loud, Sawyer Storme

When I'm back from my dad's, Nova has arranged our matching bright floral lawn chairs, angling them toward the lake where the grass meets the sandy beach. The late afternoon sun cuts through the massive oak trees overhead, dappling everything in shifting gold. I can hear the water lapping at the shore, the distant hum of a boat motor, someone's laughter carrying across the inlet.

I flop into my chair. Nova arches a brow at me, the corners of her mouth twitching like she's fighting off a smirk.

"Saw Jonathan catch up to you," she sing-songs.

"Yep," I grumble, contemplating the choice of coming to dinner this week knowing I'll be grilled on my future plans. "Kept saying he needed to talk to me. Probably trying to find out what my next career move is."

"Maybe. Or he wants to confess his love for you," Nova says, batting her mascara commercial lashes at me. She doesn't even wear makeup most days.

"Get real. He's just a good guy. Elliott is probably driving him nuts talking about my lack of income," I say. "You know, my brother has called me every day on his way to work since I told him?"

"He's a worried big brother. Totally normal, especially after Dawson. Losing your twin in a car accident puts a toll on a guy, I'm sure."

"Right, but he also calls on the way home and texts me endlessly throughout the day."

Thirteen years ago, our normal Thursday morning ride to school—with a slight detour to the bakery for cinnamon roll donuts—became the worst day of our lives. Elliott was a sophomore at Blue Ridge University. His groggy voice told me he hadn't even rolled out of bed when I called to tell him Dawson died on impact and I'd survived with a broken arm and some scratches.

I know why Elliott hovers. That day changed all of us. I completely get it. It's the reason I can't stop thinking about opening Reading Lane but am too damn afraid to do it. That doesn't make Elliott's constant check-ins less suffocating.

"Well, I know something you don't know." Novas drums her fingers on her knees, antsy, waiting to fill me in on some kind of gossip.

"What do you know?" I ask, thankful to talk about something new.

She gives me a mischievous grin. "Guess who took your mama on a twelve-hour hunt for the antique plates she's been searching for."

Mom's mix of thriftiness, rigidity, and nostalgia keeps her from making any drastic changes—especially when it comes to gatherings. She insists it's the reason she can feed half the neighborhood without breaking a sweat.

"She got the plates? Where did she find them?" Every so often, Mom brings up breaking her *any plates will do* rule and splurges on a specific set of dishware. It was her favorite thing about her childhood, helping her grandpa set the table with those plates. We've been able to spot one or two, all in terrible condition over the years, but it was never enough to feed the army on the weekend.

"Charleston," Nova blurts, excitement all over her face.

"Wait, who took her?" I ask, remembering the original question.

She straightens her back. "My dad," she says, overenunciating the words.

We squeal in unison. "Tell me it was a date."

"When I questioned the old man, he told me to mind my business." She shrugs. "So, your guess is as good as mine."

"They'll figure it out eventually." I sigh.

"Speaking of which…" She narrows her eyes on me.

"I know where you're going with that meddling face, but there is no *speaking of which*. Jonathan and I have nothing to figure out."

Nova has it in her head that Jonathan is secretly pining for me. She knows almost everything about me, including the crush I once had on the tall, bearded man—okay, the crush I *still* have. She insists his rejection was a misunderstanding. That I should confront him. How do I approach the person I compare all the others to, feel most myself around, and ask him why he didn't want to kiss me? Yeah, no thanks.

"I was going to ask about that rom-com you picked up. Finished it yet?" I ask.

"No. I've been—"

"Reading *The Story of Daisy and Jonas* for the millionth time?"

Nova smirks. "It's a good one."

Nova read it the day after we found it. I was reluctant to let it leave my side, but I was desperate to have someone to discuss the story with. I watched like a creep, pretending to search for a job as she devoured it in less than a day. The mark left on her by those words was faint compared to what was carved into me.

"It's the *best* story," I say.

"Food!" Mom hollers to no one and everyone. Plates and bowls teeter along her arms as she navigates to the long table she insisted we make as a family the summer before Elliott's senior year of high school. She was tired of setting out the card tables every weekend. She wanted something that would be more permanent. Dad brought home a huge black walnut slab, and we got to work one weekend. The six of us—Mom, Dad, Bobby, Elliott, me, and Dawson.

Our fourteen-year-old-selves were no help. We spent the entire time asking for outlandish things like a cut out in the center for an ice cream machine and a throne. I was so annoyed to be pulled away from my novel—a riveting story about a couple of middle schoolers defying the odds in space. But Dawson made it fun. He always made it fun. I wish I knew I'd only have three more years with him. I would have spent every minute by his side. Taken more pictures, slammed fewer doors in his face.

Everything reminds me of my counterpart lately.

"Mom, let us help you!" Nova and I sprint to her, scooping dishes out of her arms.

"Thanks, girls." Mom blows a gray curl out of her eyes. "Just line them up along the middle of the table."

She says this to me as if our patchwork family dinners are a new thing and not something you can set your watch to.

I snag the seat beside Nova, across from Elliott. Jonathan plops down on my other side. I shift my body just slightly to make room, hands already occupied with another blondie.

This week, the table is littered with the conventional cookout foods, typical of our family squeezing out the last bits of summer. Everything from the hot dogs and hamburgers Larry's been grilling for the last two hours, to bowls of potato chips and fruit salad. Arms reach across the table, plates clatter as they're passed hand to hand. Someone's already stolen the majority of the sour cream and onion chips before they make it past the halfway point. A fork clinks against glass. Napkins get tucked into collars and spread across laps.

"So, Jonathan." Larry scrubs hot dog mustard off his fingers. "How's Phoenix going? Heard a couple of rumors about the Pathways Program being in a bit of a pickle? Need any help?"

"Well, the crew misses you an awful lot. Care to come out of retirement?" The table chuckles. Larry spent years as foreman for Phoenix. "Nah, we're fine, really. Couple small hiccups. Need to cast a broader net for new customers. Only so many construction projects available in Honeyville, you know?"

"Don't worry, we have a plan." Elliott wiggles his eyebrows.

"Did you decide to do it then?" I find myself asking. "The vlog?"

"Yes. You'd know that if you would have talked to me earlier." Jonathan's words are a low rumble, the intensity in his gaze making my stomach do backflips.

"What do I have to do with it?" I shake my head, shoving mac and cheese into my mouth.

"I would love to tell you—"

"Miss Mazey." Larry chews with his mouth slightly open and points a finger coated in ketchup across the table. "How's the job hunt going, Miss Maze?"

I swallow hard. Along with everyone else, my parents—and Larry—weren't shocked when I delivered the news of my departure from Pixel Perfection. Their sentiments were the same as everyone else's: I can now pursue things I would enjoy more.

"I figured I'd look into becoming a professional sign-spinner. The deli had a help-wanted sign in the window for a sandwich mascot." I grin. Larry barks a laugh at my joke. "There's probably a whole world of opportunities in sign-spinning, if I learn how to flip it over my shoulder."

He throws his hands up before slamming them onto the table in excitement. "You'd stop traffic. Someone would crash into the bakery across the street."

Elbows on the table, I pick at the roll I'm holding at eye level. "That would be their fault. I'd have been hired for enthusiasm, not road safety."

Mom leans forward, her fork pointing across two salad bowls. "Mazey Lane. You are not going to wave a sign like one of those teenagers in front of a cell phone store. You are not a pop singer. You are not trying out for Broadway."

"She's not going to sing, Mom," Elliott chimes in. "We all know she can't carry a tune."

I went through a phase in my pre-teen years with Nova, both of us swearing we were going to be the next big pop duo. We practiced everyday in the garage until my brother stormed in and begged us to stop. He wasn't wrong when he told me that I couldn't hit a single note. Or that the melody was about four beats slower than it should be. Our dreams of stardom were shattered that day, and I'm so thankful he stopped me before I could make a fool of myself at the school's talent show.

"I've been putting my resume out there," I say, ending the conversation.

Everyone's gazes drop to their food, except Jonathan's. His focus stays locked on me for a few extra beats. Heat expands in my chest. A bowl of fruit ends up at his elbow, and he hands it off to Nova without looking away from me. God, why is he being so weirdly intense today?

"Mazey," Mom says, breaking my trance, "Nova said you were talking about that book place the other day. The retreat you've always wanted to start. You should do that instead of wasting time thinking about being a hot dog."

I almost choke on a roll.

"Reading Lane? It was something we—" I coughed and pounded my chest. "—used to talk about when we were kids. Just a made-up place," I lie.

It's easier to downplay a dream than admit how much you still want it. Only Nova knows I have a savings account dedicated to actually opening the retreat someday and am too afraid that if I said anything, I'd have to do it.

"You and Dawson would go on for hours about it," Mom continues as if her voice doesn't catch. His name isn't foreign in our house, but it's always paired with the heaviness of what his life could have been. "Wrote down every room in that notebook." She nods at the table, pride radiating off her. She'd support her children if we decide to sell bags of turds on the highway. "With colored tabs."

"I thought about making a retreat." I trace a circle on the table, watching my thumb create wet circles from my drink's condensation, pretending the words don't mean as much as they do. "Like a house people could visit. Readers. Mostly romance readers. It was our— Dawson's and my—favorite genre." I laugh at the memory of my twin brother rambling on and on about his favorite tropes—always roommates to lovers—and how miscommunication in novels was annoying because of how realistic it is. "I wanted it to feel warm. Comfortable. Somewhere you didn't have to pretend you were too cool to care about happy endings. It was stupid. I probably wouldn't be able to do it even if I wanted to."

"The creepy cottage would be the perfect place," Nova whispers, elbowing my side.

"Maybe. But it's not for sale," I mumble. "And I'm not doing it."

The table erupts with conversation about the cottage. Rumors zoom across the table about its history and the last resident to abruptly depart. I shove sour cream and onion chips into my mouth and keep my thoughts to myself, listening closely to various versions of the cottage's lore. I'm not sure how to explain how I felt when I saw the cottage when I found the book with Nova. How do I tell them that I have a magical connection to a building and it just happens to have a book that mirrors my life? They'd have my head examined for sure.

"I'm going to the beach," I say. Mom gives me a knowing nod, and I slip away to my favorite place.

Chatter swells behind me as I go, bag slung over my shoulder. I drop into my usual beach spot, dig into my bag, and pull out the now-familiar book with no author. I rest it in my lap, pages fanned, and I can already feel the tension in my shoulders loosening. Every turn of a page undoes a knot I didn't know I was carrying.

I trace my finger along the edge of the bookmarked page, imagining if the fantasy room would have velvet armchairs and twinkling fairy lights. I sink back into the story, time disappearing as I reread about the time Daisy rushes into the bookstore looking for a job, only to be met with a gorgeous rule-breaker.

A throat clearing. I glance up, blinking.

"You're still here?" Jonathan settles into the chair next to me. "I figured you left."

I shove the book into my bag, worried I'll have to explain the story to him. "Yep. Still here. Really good book."

"I wanted to talk to you about the Vlog project." He leans forward, resting his forearms on his knees. "I want to use Reading Lane."

"What?" My mouth hangs open. "You want to use my idea? *Dawson's and my* idea? Who would you even want to run it? And where would it be?"

He chuckles, rubbing his hands over his face. "No, I want *you* to open the retreat. Elliott goes on and on about the brilliant concept. It would be incredible to have a place like that in town. Honeyville's seasonal visitors would love it."

My heart speeds.

"You have great ideas. You know the free library boxes you organized around town have new books in them daily during tourist season."

"You mean the ones I bullied businesses—including Phoenix—into building because so many tourists talked about not wanting to buy books at The Story Porch because they didn't want to haul them back home in their suitcases?"

"Luggage fees are no joke." He smiles.

"That doesn't mean I know how to run a business," I say as a picture of myself standing in the foyer-turned-lobby filled with eager guests. I crush the image. Every time "the perfect" place goes up for sale, I come *this* close to buying it, only to back out at the last second, claiming it isn't the right time.

"You do. Not only do you have the education, you're clever." He meets my eyes, desperation mixed with his undeniable confidence in me swirling into a tornado of hope.

I tug my sleeves over my hands, my teeth skating across my lower lip.

"You were made to do this," he says, softer, tender almost. "Just think about it, okay?"

He walks to his truck before I can respond. My legs give out, and I sink back into the lawn chair, staring at the space where he stood.

Was he fucking with me? Why would he think I'm suited to run an entire business? He's smart enough to know I'd fail—just like I failed at managing projects for a software company. And Reading Lane isn't something a new person could swoop in and fix. It's too personal, too tangled up in everything.

Dawson had the idea when we were in seventh grade, scribbling floor plans on notebook paper during study hall. We spent years dreaming it up—the cozy reading nooks, the coffee bar that would smell like cinnamon and old books, the events we'd host. It was supposed to be ours. And now it's just mine—a half-finished dream I can't seem to let go of, but can't seem to convince myself to move forward with.

And Jonathan thinks I can do it?
What the fuck?

Chapter 7

The Story Porch

Love 'Em and Read 'em Book Club—Unofficial Rules:
1. Show up.
2. Bring snacks or emotional support. Preferably both.
3. Don't yuck someone else's yum. Try it instead.
4. There are no other rules. Show up.

The following Tuesday night, Nova and I push open the door to The Story Porch, the best independent bookshop in North Carolina, in my opinion. There's something special about an old house that's been converted into a store that adds a layer of pizzazz.

Tottie didn't stand a chance. After weeks of shameless begging—and a bribery scheme involving fresh scones—she surrendered and let us launch Love 'Em and Read 'Em. We meet every single week. Do we finish a book every week? Most of the time, just not the ones that we are reading for book club. But we do show up to trade paperbacks, spill tea (literal and metaphorical), and remind ourselves why we love stories in the first place.

"Beat you to the good seat," Nova challenges, not waiting for my response.

"Dammit, Nova. You know Tottie will ban me for life if I knock over another tower of books." I jog through the towers of new releases and back stock piled in front of the shelves.

I've tripped over the stacks before, and Tottie shows no mercy when it comes to her chaotic organization. She refused to let me buy any new releases for two weeks. It was agony to be loyal to her, especially because Sawyer Storme's latest was sitting on the shelf, taunting me.

"You two better not be breaking anything," Tottie yells from the register.

"We aren't!" We laugh, crashing into the same chair. It feels so good to laugh.

A few weeks of unemployment will do that to a girl—forget what it's like to have fun. My brain is constantly focused on the lack of potential employers. And the prospect of having to use the retreat fund to survive. I started treating my unemployment like a nine to five. Wake up, get dressed, scour the internet for jobs, read articles about the best way to score your next position, go to bed, rinse, repeat. It's the stuff dreams are made of.

"Do you have the discussion questions? I forgot mine at home." Nova throws pity my way and moves to the seat next to me.

"Yeah, they are in my bag somewhere. Can you grab them? I need to check something on my phone before we get started." I say, checking my inbox for a job offer to magically populate. There is nothing.

"And what is this, Miss Mazey Alice Lane?" Nova holds the notebook at eye level.

"Nothing." I snatch the book from her grasp and clutch it to my chest. I've shoved Jonathan's request to partner with him for the vlog to the back of my mind. I know he's going to want an answer sooner rather than later. Nova, of course, thinks I should do it. She started looking up every available property in Honeyville about twenty seconds after I told her. I played along, but the twirling knots kept growing in the pit of my stomach. I blame the lack of interest on my period—the monthly visitor really does affect everything. Honestly, though, I'm too scared to agree. Scared of failing. Scared of succeeding. Scared of Jonathan.

"Can we get started?" I say, desperate not to talk about Reading Lane.

"We are still waiting on the *club* part of book club." Nova arches an eyebrow. "Are you going to open the retreat?"

"Doris! Hello. Our first member to arrive." I greet the older lady. "Well, besides Tottie."

"That's not all six of us." Nova's playful glare cuts through me before she gives the older lady a genuine smile. "Hi, Doris."

"Hi there, girls. I brought this for you." Doris slides a paperback towards Nova. Her giant beaded earrings dance at the movement below her silver bob. "It's the big foot erotica from that author I told you about."

"Thanks, Doris. Can't wait to read it." Nova grins as she reads the summary.

"So, what are we talking about?" Doris digs her latest knitting project from her purse: a pair of socks with penises stitched on the cuff. Socks are her favorite thing to knit, especially with inappropriate designs decorating them. Last Christmas, each member of the book club, including Brody, received a pair with stick figures going at it up the side.

"Mazey was just telling me how she decided to open a book retreat," Nova announces.

"A book retreat?" Morgan asks, lowering herself into the chair Brody pulled out for her.

"I did no such thing." I shoot Nova a glare before panning to the table. "Everyone here? We should really get going on this week's discussion."

"What kind of things would happen at the retreat?" Verne asks as he removes his cowboy hat and hangs it on the back of his chair. He's not a cowboy, he just loves a themed outfit.

"Picture this." Nova leans forward, lacing her fingers in front of her. "A cozy book-themed getaway with curated reading nooks, author panels, and writer weekends. A community for every book lover."

I let my forehead hit the table with a dull thud, muffling my protest in the crook of my arm. Nova's intentions are from the kindness of her heart. She butts in when she really believes in something and tells everyone she knows with the enthusiasm of a puppy learning to play fetch for the first time. Her caring soul wants the best for the ones she loves, even if that means bulldozing their fears with her excitement for the greater good. But damn—I'm not sure it's time to tap into this ludicrous dream.

"What do the suites look like?" Morgan asks, flipping to a fresh page in the notebook that she usually records the discussion in. Her pen scribbling creates a background soundtrack to the conversation. "Oh, is there a fantasy room? I'd love to sleep in a room filled with magical creatures."

"What about book bingo?" adds Tottie as she kicks her feet up on the empty chair next to her.

"Will all genres be included?" Brody leans across the table, clutching his iced tea. "Romance is my favorite, but I also love a good thriller. You could host a mystery dinner party!"

"Those are great ideas!" Nova chirps. "Morgan, can you snap a pic of your notes and send it to me? Mazey has been working on this for years. She has sketches, color-coded lists. Everything."

I peeked through my arms just in time to catch Nova smirking at me.

"Then why does she look like you just exposed her deepest, darkest secret?" Doris pokes my head with her knitting needle.

My deepest, darkest secret. Is that my deepest, darkest secret— wanting to open Reading Lane? It's not really a secret if my entire family knows about it. If Jonathan knows about it.

Jonathan.

The way he makes my heart squeeze and my knees go weak might be my deepest, darkest secret, but not the cottage.

"I'm not sure that it's a secret that I'd love to open a literary retreat," I hedge, "but the risks are so high. I'm not sure if it makes sense for me to do it. The chances of me failing are way too high." I smooth out the pages of this week's talking points. "I've already put my name in for a couple PM positions."

"Any interviews?" Tottie asks. "You did a nice job getting me on track with the bookshelf construction last spring. Use me as a reference."

I flash her a forced grin. "Thanks. Nothing yet though. I'll keep you posted."

"We should really get started on the book conversation. We are already twelve minutes behind." Morgan gives me an understanding look. I've known Morgan almost as long as Nova, though we've never been as close. Our friendship only truly blossomed when the book club did, and I'm forever grateful for the way she steps in to redirect conversations that get uncomfortable.

Collective grumbles come from around the table, but we dive in anyways. The conversation quickly splinters into the usual chaos. Doris swooning over the morally gray hero, Brody defending the twist ending, Morgan pulling out her notes to prove that the foreshadowing was obvious all along, and Tottie declaring she'll never forgive the author for making us think the dog got injured. By the time Nova and I are laughing so hard our sides hurt, I can't even remember what page we were supposed to start on.

"How's it going with Phoenix? Find any properties yet? Mazey told me that Jonathan's going to do it." Nova asks Brody during what Verne has deemed *book club intermission.*

"Actually, great. I got an email this morning from the owners of that old cottage by the lake—the one that can't keep an owner." Brody pulls up a picture of my cottage. Nope, not my cottage. The creepy cottage. "They decided to sell. It's been vacant for about a year, kept up by a property management company since they live out of state."

"Why are they selling?" I blurt. Maybe he has answers about why this place has such high turnover. It's not like the internet explains the purchasing history of a property, and the people of Honeyville have very little information about the previous occupants. There's been a lot of *it just wasn't the right fit for them, I think* or *no clue, they just up and left* from the couple people I brought up the place in casual conversation.

"All they would say was there was something off with the place." He shrugs, taking a drink from his soda.

"Their kid told me that weird stuff would happen. Nothing bad or dangerous. Just weird." Morgan is sitting on the edge of her seat, face animated. "Like one time all the toilet paper went missing from all the bathrooms."

"There has to be like ten bathrooms or something in there, right? And none of them had toilet paper?"

"Seven. And a half bath," Brody says. "No T.P. in any of them."

"So, it has ghosts? Is that what I'm hearing?" Verne throws his hands up as if he were surrendering. "No thank you."

"That's the weird part. There has never been any recorded"—Brody uses air quotes—"sightings or orbs or anything like that. Just odd things that happen from time to time… Enough things to weird out the occupants to the point that they don't want to stay."

"Seems about right." Doris's head shoots up for the first time since the beginning of the conversation. "If I remember correctly, it's been a few things. Well, *tried* to be a few things. Mostly along the lines of a hotel or bed and breakfast type. It's got to be huge. How many bedrooms is it?"

"Doris. Do you know anything about when it was built?" I ask before Brody can respond to her question. Doris has lived in Honeyville her whole life. She has to know more about the cottage, but I haven't had a chance to talk to her since she got back from her sister's house in Florida a few days ago.

"You are full of questions. Let me see." The seventy-something year old woman pushes up her thick red glasses. "Well, my mama talked about a beautiful house on the water that was once owned by two best friends that never married, but thrived through the written word." She sways her knitting needle between Nova and me. "Not unlike you two."

Nova and I look at each other, grins spreading across our faces.

"How did they have it? I mean, they couldn't own it since they already owned a vagina and everything." Nova rolls her eyes at the patriarchy.

"Well, from what I understand—mind you, this could be wrong— is that one of them took a lover. He was head over heels for her. Would do anything for her, including building her that oversized cottage." Doris goes back to knitting the socks. "The women created a place for everyone—no matter their gender, social status, race, who they liked to fuck."

"Oh. Ok, then. My kind of ladies," Verne says. All seven of us are captivated by the story.

"Honeyville has always had people coming and going for a spell. The lake is a huge attraction, and it was even back then. I believe there were five rooms. Two, sometimes three beds in each one, and they were constantly filled.

"The biggest draw to the place was the parties they hosted. According to my mom, they threw one once a month, themed to a book."

"They threw literary costume parties?" Tottie asks. "Damn. That's a great marketing idea."

"Supposedly," Doris says. "Could just be rumors. My mom would have only been one around the time it was built, so most of what she told me was just hearsay."

"Did she tell you their names?" I ask. "The friends."

"Daisy and Savvy."

Daisy. One of the original owners was named Daisy. But how…

"So, when can we see the place?" Nova asks a little too casually.

"Ooooh, I want to go," Verne says.

"Are one of you going to buy it?" I ask, knowing that neither of them have any plans on moving forward with a real-estate purchase anytime soon.

"This book sucked. We're calling it quits on this week's book club. I'm closing early," Tottie walks over to the shop door and flips the sign.

"I could really go for a walk," Doris gives Tottie a conspiratorial look, and she gathers her knitting supplies. "Mazey, dear, would you mind walking with me? I'm afraid to go alone, you know. On account of my being old and all."

Doris has more energy than the entire book club put together. If it wasn't for her wrinkles and shaky voice, you'd think she was the same age as me. Last spring she ran—yes, ran—a 5K to raise money for type 1 diabetes in honor of Nova. Did she tell anyone? Nope. Just went out and did it. We only found out because she popped up on our Instagram feed for being the oldest person to run the entire race.

"Doris, didn't you walk here?" I ask. "Alone?"

Verne stands as he puts on his cowboy hat. "A walk sounds nice. Maybe we should all go."

"To keep Doris safe." Morgan winks at Brody.

Brody clears his throat, tugging at his collar. "Yes, Doris. She's old. Can't walk alone. What if she falls and dies and no one is there to see it?"

Morgan leans over to mutter in his ear. "Too far, babe. Too far."

I see right through these people. Somehow, they have telepathically joined forces to get me on a walk to, no doubt, lure me to the cottage. Judging by the way they are staring at me, I know there is no way I'm going to win.

God, I love these people. They are complete nuisances, especially when curiosity takes over their sense of boundaries. Their conspiring comes from the most caring of places, and I can't say I haven't participated alongside them a time or two. Ask Verne. I'm one-sixth of the reason he has embraced his ostentatious style.

On the edge of their seats, my people wait for my next move. A notification illuminates the inside of my bag as I search for an answer. My stomach drops as I see the invitation for an interview. I close my eyes, count to three, and the only thing I can focus on is the creepy cottage's gift to me. What could it hurt to take a peak inside? Maybe learn a bit more about this novel or the cottage's history.

"Listen, I'll go." The group throws out a collective cheer. I put a finger up, quieting them. "It's just a tour of the place. That's it. Got it?"

They're nodding, but I know it's just to get me out the door. And we do just that. A combination of excitement and vomit settles in my throat as I clear away the interview notification.

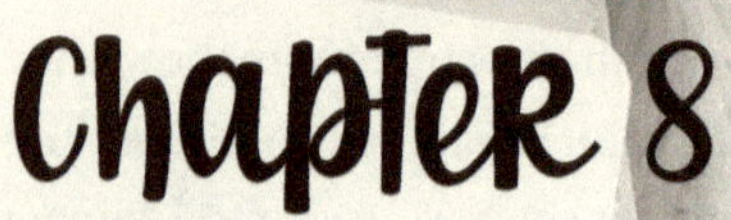

"She didn't decide all at once. She decided one inch at a time—one room, one window, one what-if at a time." - The Day the Deed was Done

The looming dread of trudging through the trenches of figuring out my next corporate career move lessens to a more tolerable pressure.

The gravel shifts and crunches beneath my feet, but I barely hear it. I barely hear anything. The cottage pulls at me the same way it did weeks ago, and I surrender to the comfort it brings. I slow without meaning to, letting the others move ahead, their voices dissolving into background noise.

This is the first time I've been near the cottage since I found the book. I was too afraid the magical moment I felt that day was bigger in my head than in reality. Like the way you anticipate a new release of a movie or the food at a four-star restaurant, building it up to something life changing, only to feel a bit let down at the actual experience.

It was not bigger in my head.

"Can we be clear on something?" Tottie stomps up the steps. "This place is no damn cottage. Cottages are supposed to be small and charming. This place… this place is anything but small. This thing is ginormous."

"You're acting as if you haven't seen it before, Tottie." Verne says through a laugh as he struts down the path leading to the steps of the wrap around porch. "You've lived in Honeyville longer than any of us."

"Yeah, I know. But I've never been this close to the thing." Tottie huffs, following Verne. "I thought Doris was kidding when she told us the number of bedrooms. Now I'm thinking she was under the actual number."

I'm the last one to the porch, the group parting as I approach to reveal the front door. It's even more beautiful than the first time I saw it—dark mahogany carved with climbing vines and roses so detailed they almost look soft to the touch. A brass lion's-head knocker sits at the center, worn warm by years of use, with two elegant curved handles on either side. Decorative stonework frame the doorway, while a half-circle window above the door throws patterns of amber and gold light across a threshold that's been worn smooth by countless feet over the years. Next to the door, a narrow window lets me catch a glimpse inside. It looks the same as it did last time, but I'm more excited by the potential that lingers past the threshold.

"Your castle, Madame." Brody opens the door with a flourish. I follow as the group funnels through the worn doorframe into the foyer, eyes darting in all directions.

Nova spins, her hair fluttering out. "Should we wander around or are you giving us a tour?"

"Why don't you look around," Brody says.

Tottie, Doris, and Verne take off through the apparent living room to the back of the cottage like they're on the hunt for the best bargain in a department sale.

The deeper into the cottage I go, the stronger the musty scent hangs in the air, curling into my lungs. Sunlight catches on the dust the book club's footsteps have stirred, turning it into a glittering haze. Beneath it all, the hardwood's faint shine fights to peek through the grime.

Morgan pulls out her notebook, opening to a blank page. She pulls the pen from behind her ear and scribbles something down. She looks up at me with a soft smile. "I don't want you to forget any details."

"Thanks, I really appreciate it." Morgan records everything. No exaggeration. I've never been to her house, but I wouldn't be surprised if she has an entire room dedicated to just notebooks—in chronological order. She's been able to prevent numerous rereads when we select our books every week, organizes snacks to include everyone's favorite options at least once a month, and is the best secret Santa. You will not receive a back-of-the-closet candle if she draws your name. A personalized gift bag will be carefully placed in your spot before your arrival, filled with all the things you love the most. Even if you said you liked a thing in passing four years ago, it'll be in there.

I envy her organization and attention to detail.

"No problem." She smiles.

"But don't feel obligated. You should roam around." My stomach suddenly hollows at her obligation to take notes on my behalf. "There might be some cool stuff in the nooks and crannies."

"True. I'll record what I find." Her face brightens as she bolts through the doorway the rest of the group disappeared into.

"Should we start from the top and work our way down?" Nova asks.

I nod, leading the way up the wooden spiral staircase, a flurry of sensations coursing through my body. Am I really considering using the Reading Lane savings account for its intended use? Changing my entire career, banking on a dream from my childhood?

And why do I constantly feel the need to question my every move?

Taking a tour is not committing to signing my name on the dotted line or opening myself up to running a business. It's just a tour. Maybe the universe brought the cottage, and the book, into my life—to give me something to do, knowing I was going to get fired. Like it knew I was going to need something to pass the time until I settled into my next job as a project manager.

We make our way to the top floor turned studio apartment—converted from the attic, judging on the odd slants of the ceiling. *If* I were to open Reading Lane, this space would be all mine. And it is dreamy.

Well, it had the potential to be dreamy, with exposed beams and large windows overlooking the lake. Right now, dust balls poofed up with every step leaving a musky scent in my nostrils.

Nova jogs to the lowest part of the ceiling. "Your king sized bed could go here."

"What about my reading chair?" I fall into the *what if* game. It's just a tour. What can it hurt?

"Over there, duh." She points across the room. A built-in bookshelf would look fantastic lining the slanting wall, filled with mismatched volumes and little—fake—plants positioned toward the light. I'd kill real plants in approximately twenty seconds.

She points to the corner of the room farthest from the simple staircase. "Imagine a little kitchen situation over here. With a mini-fridge and coffee maker."

"Sounds like the set-up we had in our dorm room freshman year of college." I laugh, remembering how excited we were to move in together. I've lived with Nova my entire adult life. If—and that's a big if—I bought this place, could I really move here? Without her? What would that even be like, being alone? My stomach swirls at the thought. Big dreams mean big risks… Which usually turn into big losses.

"I love this place!" Nova spins again.

"Are you sure you aren't actually a ballerina and not a graphic designer?" I stop her mid-spin. "You know I'm not going to do it, right? I can't buy it and partner with Jonathan."

"And why not? Everything is lining up perfectly, Mazey. Just let it happen. The universe is begging you."

"Where would I live? Where would *you* live? What will my income be during the renovation process?" I rattle off my questions, saving the biggest to ponder myself. What if I fail? What if I disappoint Dawson? What if I lose my best friend?

"You'd live here, you goof. I'd probably keep the apartment. It's so cheap, thanks to Doris not believing in inflation." Did I mention Doris is also our landlord? She owns the only apartment complex in town. With six apartments—three on the first level, three on the second—it's the cheapest place to live in Honeyville. "And it's literally within walking distance of this place. We'd see each other every day. You cannot get rid of me."

"What about Jonathan?" I search for more reasons why this is a terrible idea.

"What about him? He wants to work with you. You are the only one standing in the way."

"I'd be working with him daily. How is that going to work?"

"You're the only one who has an issue with being around the guy." She starts down the stairs. shouting over her shoulder. "The dude is the nicest person ever, especially to you."

He is. That's part of the problem. Being around Jonathan every day for months sounds like a dream and a nightmare tied into one. A whirlwind of confusion. One minute he's providing blondies week-over-week and complimenting my appearance when I know damn well I look like I just rolled out of bed. The next minute, he's reminding me that I'm his best friend's little sister.

I look around the apartment before following Nova downstairs.

On one side of the staircase are two bedrooms and a storage closet. The other side has three more bedrooms and a sitting area that's open to the hallway. Each bedroom, including the two downstairs, has a full bathroom.

I could transform each suite into a genre-themed escape with various-sized beds to accommodate various-sized individuals. A bookshelf or two could line the wall with a cozy chair and snack cart, for when peopling wasn't an option.

I find Nova in a weird space on the second floor. The room's too small to be a guest room but too big to be a storage closet. The walls are narrow with enough space to put a chair and maybe an ottoman, possibly a side table. I can't imagine what it once was or what it could be. I suppose I'd figure it out at some point once construction was underway.

If construction begins.

I join Nova at the window that consumes the entire wall that sits opposite of the door. My hand instinctively reaches into my bag, fingers wrapping around a now-familiar spine.

This view is breathtaking.

Outside the window is a perfect view of the lake. It stretches wide and still, the kind of stillness that provides comfort rather than unease.

The water is a deep, muted blue-gray, the color of old glass. It mirrors the sky so cleanly that, for a second, it's hard to tell where one ends and the other begins.

A combination of weeping willows and sycamore trees crowd right up to the edge all the way around, dark and thick, roots disappearing into the water. There's an old dock that stretches from the beach into the water with a rowboat tied to the end, bumping softly against the post like it's got nowhere better to be. It doesn't look like anyone's touched any of it in a long time.

There's just something about it. The whole thing feels like it means something.

"How many rooms have you decorated in your head?" Nova's words startle me.

"A couple," I admit, biting back a smile.

"Good," she says. "While you're running the retreat, I'll get the website and marketing designs together. I'm sure Katie will be working on the promotional stuff, at least in the beginning since she does Phoenix's. That's something to check on. I want to make sure the whole world knows about it. I'm talking promo reels, guest interviews, themed weekend live streams. People will be begging to book a room before we even open."

My chest warms at her offer, but I can't let her take on another project. Nova has been managing digital campaigns in between designing book covers for independent authors for years while managing a chronic illness. That's too much to put on my bestie's plate.

I point out the window. "Did you see that shed just off the beach?"

"Awe, It looks like a miniature version of the cottage." She turns to me. "How cute would it be to make it an office?"

"So cute." Involuntarily, I beam at her. "Let's check out the rest of the rooms."

As I turn to leave, my bag slips from my shoulder, the contents spilling across the floor.

"Dammit," I say, dropping to my knees, shoving things back to their place.

Nova does the same. "Holy crap, you have everything in this bag."

"I don't want to forget something."

She holds up a tube of glucose tablets. "Do you really need this? I have those in my emergency kit that is always on me."

"What if your blood sugar drops and you can't find them?"

She shakes her head, but I see the grin.

"Hey, wasn't the porch book in your bag?" she asks.

"Yeah." My heart thuds, searching for *The Story of Daisy and Jonas.* "It's gone."

"Is it still at the bookstore? You could have left it there." Nova thrusts her arm into my bag, digging around inside.

"I was just touching it. My fingers were touching the pages." My voice is higher and faster than normal.

I grab the bag from her, dumping the contents we just picked up onto the floor. Wallet, keys, charger, e-reader.

We stare at the last thing to tumble out.

"That's not the book, is it?" Nova asks.

"No, this is a different one."

"It's gone. *The Story of Daisy and Jonas* is gone." My gaze bounces from Nova to the new novel in my hands.

The Day the Deed Was Done

And we burst out laughing.

"So, where did this book come from?" Nova asks.

"I haven't the slightest." I examine the new book. "There's no author."

"Mysterious." Nova twinkles her hands.

"It's fucking weird, right? This place has to be haunted. That's the only explanation. I'm sure if I had toilet paper in my bag, it'd be gone."

Would it though? Let's say, for arguments sake, that the cottage gifted me the first book. And now this oddly named, new book. It's doing the opposite of what Brody described at the bookstore. Those actions were trying to get the owners out of there. Is it trying to get me to stay?

"How are you not more weirded out by the fact that two books have randomly appeared when we are at this cottage?"

She shrugs. "Sounds like the Universe is shoving this opportunity at you."

My heart tugs at Nova's free-spirited optimism. With everything she's been through, she could've easily turned out to be an asshole of a human, but instead, she shines. Her mom, if you can even call her that, peaced out when Nova was in sixth grade. Just a month after her type 1 diabetes diagnosis. Larry had to start working doubles to cover the cost of insulin, snacks, and everyday life. That's when my mom—a nurse—stepped in, offering a safe place to go when Larry had to work.

Our backs against the wall, we read the novella in silence, Nova's head resting on my shoulder. Three chapters in, I know what I need to do. It's right there in literal black and white. This story isn't a romance like the first one. *The Day the Deed was Done* is about making bold choices. Being terrified to your bones, but doing the damn thing anyway. About doing the deed. In the case of my life, and the novel, it's an actual deed. It's enough to convince me. The title alone is a sign I needed to see. Excitement tangles with nerves in my belly, but I've never been more certain.

"I think I need to put together a business plan," I whisper.

Chapter 9

The Overalls Decision

"The universe doesn't hand you a feeling that strong just to watch you talk yourself out of it." - Nova

The bulb over the chipped porcelain flickers as I twist toward the mirror. The strap of my overalls dangles behind me, resembling a question mark. I tilt my head. I reach back with fumbling fingers before finally catching it and snapping it in my place.

I study the outfit I picked for the first official day of the cottage renovation.

"I look like I'm twelve. Not the owner of a pristine bookish retreat." I violently spin to get the other strap, fastening it into place.

I am definitely a two-buckled-strap kind of girl.

Loose tendrils of hair tumble at my temples, refusing to stay in the messy bun on top of my head. I decide they can do whatever they want.

Wilfred yips, tail wagging.

"Hey buddy." I scratch him behind the ear before grabbing the basket of dog bandanas. I pull out a green kerchief with little yellow flowers scattered across it. "Should we match today?"

His tail wags increase to full speed.

"There, all set. Ready for today?" I say, tightening the knot. He yips, and I take it as confirmation.

I grab my canvas tote with the inside zipper that perfectly holds a paperback. Nova surprised me with a new notebook and a pack of my favorite pens. They're the smooth kind, the ones that make whatever I'm writing make sense. I toss them in. Gummy bears, emotional support water bottle, snacks for Wilfred, and his water dish. I toss in a few other essentials and pause when I reach for the last two items.

The Reading Lane journal—Dawson's journal. And the latest book the cottage gave me.

For a breath, I just stand there, pressing them to my chest, grounded by the weight, and by everything that the combination of these pages mean. Then I tuck the two most important items I own carefully into the bag.

I am putting my entire savings—no, my entire future—into a gut feeling from a random book. What the fuck am I doing? Technically, the savings is for this very reason. I'm not convinced it's the right time to play Evil Knievel. The plan has always been to open the bookish retreat, but it has never felt right. Maybe it's the void inside me, the one that was filled until I was seventeen and my twin was taken from me forever.

My entire life I have played it safe, avoiding the dicey paths in favor of a safe option. There was no dream of being a project manager when I was a kid, I picked it after I learned how reckless behavior can take everything away in a matter of seconds.

And now I'm deciding to throw all my eggs into a basket on a plan that may or may not play out.

I collapse on the bed, dropping my head between my legs as far as it'll go with my belly, gripping the journal to my chest. The entire room feels like it's spinning. Like I can't catch my breath. Wilfred whimpers at my feet. His tiny paw runs down my leg, trying to get my attention.

Honk. Honk.

Shit. Katie's here to pick me up. No turning back now. I adjust my glasses—today's frames are a round purple plastic that makes my olive eyes pop—stand, and swing the bag over my shoulder.

"It's time, Willy." I secure his green leash to the matching collar.

The air outside is brisk, the kind that sends a chill through your entire body with a deep breath. Katie's bright pink Jeep sits next to the curb, music humming from the cracked window.

I take a deep breath, adjust the strap of my bag on my shoulder, and charge forward adventure.

"Here you go!" She hands me a paper cup with a Sharpie drawing of a house sitting on top of books. Wilfred jumps in, beelining for the pupachino in the cup holder. "I stopped by the coffee shop. Your dad wanted me to tell you how proud he is of you."

My heart warms at the support. Dad, Bobby, and Mom—they've been like this since I signed the paperwork three weeks ago. I'm not sure why I expected practical questions, gentle redirects, or a slew of *are you sures*.

Instead, I got Bobby showing up with a tape measure and opinions about load-bearing walls during the inspection. I got Mom sending me listings for vintage light fixtures at eleven in the morning with no context and advising me on paying ahead on the utilities to reduce the to-do list during renovations. And Dad, who has never in his life used the word "proud" sparingly, finding new ways to say it every single time—mostly through delicious coffee with cute drawings on the cup.

And now, Katie is picking me up, her car loaded with recording equipment and snacks, and handing me the breakfast I forgot, including a pup cup for my favorite pup.

I look down at the little house sitting on top of its little stack of books.

"He drew that himself," Katie says, reading my face. "Took him three tries. He made me watch."

I press the cup to my chest for a second.

"Don't," I warn myself quietly.

"Too late," Katie says cheerfully. "You're already doing the face."

"I'm not doing a face." I argue, turning my head away from her, wiping a stray tear.

Wilfred chooses this moment to sneeze whipped cream all over the middle console.

"Ready?" Katie nods aggressively, knocking her sunglasses from the top of her blonde hair to her nose.

"I think so," I say honestly. Part of me, the part that gushed over the retreat idea when Dawson and I first came up with it, is bursting with excitement. The *when I grow up I want to be…* finally coming true. Ask a random person on the street what they wanted to be when they grew up and what they are now. I doubt they are the same. But today—today, mine are a matching pair.

As we pull away, butterflies thrash in my stomach, their wings charged by energy that is impossible to contain. The other part of me bubbles to the surface. Am I really doing this? My bank account reflects that I am, that's for sure.

"Jonathan will meet us there," Katie says.

"Wonderful." My stomach flips at his name. "How much interaction will we have?"

"Well, I'm leading the project since it's a marketing promotion, but he's the face of Phoenix. He'll be in all the vlogs." She rambles.

"But I don't need to be in the vlogs, right?"

"Not often. I mean you'll be in the stuff that highlights the retreat. The goal is to keep Jonathan the face of Phoenix and you recognizable when it comes to Reading Lane. Jonathan insisted on making sure there is plenty of footage covering Reading Lane, not just Phoenix." My brain is slow to keep up with the fast pace of her words. "Before he was the CEO, he worked alongside the crew. Don't tell him I said this, but he's better at the designing and construction part than he is the business part. Just doesn't seem to love it as much, you know?"

I knew. I've seen what Jonathan can do with his hands.

Back when we were kids, he and Elliott would vanish into the old workshop for hours during play dates. Elliott was the idea guy, flipping through comics and tossing out wild suggestions for Jonathan's next project. He'd just nod, quietly gather his tools, and get to work.

The funniest part was when he'd try to teach Elliott how to build something. The two of them were both the teacher to an empty classroom—until they'd catch me watching through the crack in the door and force me to be their student. Elliott often had no idea what he was teaching, but he provided the comedy. Jonathan supplied the lesson. He was patient and kind as he taught me how to build trinkets and small pieces of furniture.

"Yeah. Makes sense," I mutter, looking out the window.

She giggles and turns up the radio, blasting some pop song I don't know the lyrics to. I hum along off-key, the melody buzzing in my chest—nervous energy with nowhere to go. It's a short drive, barely enough time to finish the song before we pull into the gravel lane.

Katie slows as we crest a small hill. "There she is."

It's like the first time seeing the cottage.

The cottage appears in the sunlight, glowing like an old friend waiting at the end of a long road. The butterflies in my stomach soften to a flutter.

The porch wraps around the front with that gentle slouch. A gutter hangs loose, swaying slightly in the breeze, but even that has a kind of charm to it, a little offbeat welcome. Front steps tilt at an angle that I make a mental note about, but I'm already moving past it. My eyes travel up the facade, taking inventory with the particular focus of someone who sees the potential of this place.

Someone loved this place once, and it shows in the way the paint held on, in the original windows still intact, in the porch columns standing straight beneath their slow crown of vines. It wasn't abandoned so much as it was left to wait.

Daisy and Savvy.

I smile.

"She's got character." Katie grins, undoes her seat belt, and jumps out of the Jeep, "Don't worry. Phoenix will make it look mind-blowingly awesome."

"I'm not worried." And oddly, I'm not. The dread of failing that greeted me when I woke up this morning lingers, but the anticipation of creating Reading Lane pushes it to the foreground.

I climb out of the Jeep. Wilfred bounds out, tugging me along to explore the grass. To the right of the lane is a beat-up two-car garage. Between that and the lake is the shed that will become the office. To the left is the cottage. Oak trees polka dot the yard—Wilfred is determined to pee on each one.

I'm less concerned about it looking *mind blowingly awesome* and more concerned about keeping the project on track. I'm not ignorant to the repairs that need to take place, tracking each flaw in the beautiful structure as I take it in. With the business plan, I mapped out the project's plan based on the inspection report, the suggestions from Phoenix, and a basic design each room should look like when completed—all of which Jonathan signed off on. What if more work is required? I have to keep the renovations on the strict timeline or immediate failure is not outside of the realm of possibility.

"What time is Jonathan supposed to be here?" I holler at Katie. She's bouncing towards the porch snapping pictures of the *before.*

"Any minute," she says. As if on cue, the sound of an old work truck crunching over gravel fills the air.

Jonathan parks next to the Jeep. He swings the door open and drops to the ground. His boots hit the rock with a solid *thud.* He has on a sun-faded navy t-shirt that clings to his chest and shoulders. It's unclear whether the shirt sleeve had shrunk or if his muscles are just that giant. Soft-looking cargo pants hang on his hips, and I swear, they are bespoke the way his ass looks in them. A cap shadows his face, making the curve of his smirk feel dangerous.

"Mazey, you ready?" He asks as he walks towards us, hands on his hips.

"Oh shoot, I forgot the ring light in the backseat," Katie says, scavenging through her bag. "I'll be right back."

"As I'll ever be to make this baby mine." I wave my hands in front of the cottage.

"Damn straight." Our eyes meet. His phone rings. "Gotta get this."

Jonathan walks toward the cottage, answering his phone with a swift *hello.*

"Where is he going?" Katie reappears with the ring light in hand.

I shrug. "Phone call."

"He's on the phone all the time since the Pathway Program has been in jeopardy. I think he's doing too much. Feels like it's all his fault," Katie says with a heavy sigh.

I shift from heel to heel. Why would Jonathan feel like that? He can't control the cost of supplies or the lack of customers in Honeyville. I guess he could have projected his revenue differently, prepared his marketing strategy gradually instead of this Hail Mary vlog project. Hindsight will do that to a person—make you see where you could have done better. Make you feel like a failure because you didn't see the writing on the wall at the moment.

His grandparents, as wonderful of people as they are, handed him the keys to the business and hopped on the next cruise ship. Elliott said there was very little in the way of training. Jonathan had to rely on his business degree to guide his way. Education is fantastic, the perfect foundation to a successful career. Nothing compares to on the job training though. No matter how many times the curriculum is combed over and revised, life happens. Twenty-twenty is enough to prove that.

"It's not. It's no one's fault." I find myself whispering, eyes fixed on the front door of something that has to work. Not just for me, but also for the Pathways Program.

Chapter 10

Hands

"The best things always take longer than you want them to. That's how you know they're worth it—and that you're probably being impatient." - Tottie

I can't look away from his hands.

There's something hypnotic about them—broad, confident, completely unbothered by the fact that I'm staring at them. His knuckle catches a loose edge of paper and smooths it back against the plaster like he's done it a thousand times, gentle in a way that doesn't match his size.

It has been fifteen days of constantly being around this man—bouncing ideas off one another for the cottage's design, creating lists (he loves a good list as much as I do) of materials to order, and inhaling the intoxicating combination of citrus and biceps.

"I think this stuff is from the forties," he says as we stand in front of the breakfast nook's back wall. It's covered in a paisley print that resembles a handkerchief from the seventies, peeling at the edges. "Maybe earlier."

I mean to respond. I really do. But his thumb drags slowly along the seam, leaving a slight indent under his touch, and suddenly whatever I was about to say just disappears.

Working man's hands. Calloused, thick-veined, lived-in. They don't match his low and calming voice. No, those hands mean business.

"The layers underneath are probably original." He peels back a whisper of the edge to show me the stack of cream, then green, then something the color of old honey.

I lean in closer, examining the wallpaper. Thankfully, these walls are the only ones that have a stack of the paper as thick as an encyclopedia pasted to it since I have no idea how to remove wallpaper.

"Uh huh." I bite my lip. "Layers. We need to remove them."

Jonathan crouches down behind me, close enough that I feel the shift in the air. He steadies himself with a hand on the wall above my shoulder—not threatening, but not safe either.

"It's not a fast process." My hair flutters with his words. "People want it to be, but it isn't."

"Slow, then…"

"Very"—a pause that has no business being that long—"slow."

I swallow. I keep my eyes on the wall, examining each layer of paper as if they might tell me what my next move should be because hell if I know. I can barely stand straight with his body so close to mine.

Cool and ordinary air rushes into the space where he was, and I have to stop myself from reaching back for something that isn't there anymore. He drops into a crouch at the baseboard in one easy movement, forearm resting across his knee, head tilting toward the wall like it asked him a question. The loss of his warmth is so sudden and so complete that it takes me a full breath to remember I'm just his best friend's little sister.

"You'd start here." His voice is quieter at this level. "Score it first. Small pressure. You're not trying to force it—you're just giving the water somewhere to go."

"Water." I kneel next to him.

"I find fabric softener works best. Leaves a nice smell. " He glances sideways at me. "Mix it warm to loosen the adhesive."

I nod slowly. We're both looking at the wall.

"And then?"

"Then you wait." The corner of his mouth moves. "That's the part most people get wrong. They don't wait long enough and they tear it and then they've got a mess on their hands instead of a clean pull."

I gulp.

"So, that's the slow part." My voice is shaky.

"Sure is."

"How do you know when it's ready?"

He's quiet for a moment. Considers the layers way longer than necessary, as if he's pondering something other than wallpaper.

"You just learn to read it. The surface changes." His eyes meet mine. "Stops resisting what's right in front of it."

The afternoon has gone very still. Somewhere outside a car passes, but neither of us look up..

"And if you do it right," he continues, "the whole thing comes together. Everything underneath, exactly as it was."

I look at the old honey color. At the green beneath it. At all those years of careful covering.

"Should we remove this part of the cottage's history?"

"There could be moisture trapped. Could cause mold."

"That sounds worth doing," I say.

A beat passes.

"Tearing off the old layers," he says quietly, "makes room for new ones." His voice comes out lower than before, and for a second his eyes drop to my mouth before snapping back up, jaw tightening like he surprised himself with it. I turn back to the wall. The plaster. Anything. My heart is doing something embarrassing, and I'm fairly certain he can hear it in the silence that stretches between us—just long enough to mean something. Neither of us moves to close it.

I stand, flapping my shirt for air.

"You okay?" Jonathan rises, takes a step in my direction. I step backward, running into the kitchen island. He reaches out to steady me, those hands on my upper arm in a careful, solid grasp. "Whoa, Mazey."

I tilt my chin up, eyes catching his. Honey darkened to amber, rimmed in lashes too unfair for someone who owns steel-toe boots. Gold specks dance in his irises. Standing in front of this man is like standing in front of a fortune teller. Part thrill, part fear. Possibilities doing laps around your frontal lobe before the psychic tells you what your life is going to be.

Did he really just make me weak in the knees because he touched me?

I need to refocus. I need to stop thinking about his hands… and what he can do with them.

"Is Phoenix really in that much trouble?" The words tumble out.

He drops his hands, the absence of it heavier than the touch itself.

"Let me put it this way, if this project doesn't do what it's supposed to do, we have to close our doors in the next year." His head drops. "It's not just the Pathway Program. It's the entire company."

"You said it was just Pathway."

"Lumber costs keep rising, and business keeps dropping. The benefits we provide aren't something we are going to cut back on, health care sucks enough. I can't imagine not providing it for my team, but the cost of that is increasing as well. It doesn't look good, Mazey." His face grows more and more pale with every harsh piece of reality he lays in front of me.

The entire company is at risk. The company that Larry retired from. That so many of Honeyville's residents depend on. Not to mention the Pathways Project that provides so many opportunities for growth and opportunity. My stomach turns at the new layer of pressure that has been added to this project. There is a lot riding on an idea that came from my childhood.

I want to say more—offer something useful, something hopeful—but the look in his eyes stops me. He's already been everywhere I might try to lead him. "What colors do you think for the counters?"

He nods. "The same as the background?"

"I think you are right, sir." I rock on my toes.

He leans in, our breath mingles. "Mazey Alice…"

"Jonathan Austin…"

Did his face just get closer?

"Are we doing this?"

I don't remember how to take a breath.

"Doing what?"

Did *my* face just move closer?

"Reading Lane." A lop-sided grin sneaks across his face.

"Yes, we are." I drum the kitchen island, pulling my body away from Jonathan.

I have to get out of here.

"I'm going to check on—" I turn on my heel, slipping away before I have to figure out what just happened and how my focus shifted so quickly from the cottage to man hands and thick arms.

The hallway narrows, guiding me into a room I haven't paid much attention to. The light is dim through lace curtains browned at the edges. Against one wall, a broken down end table sits at a slant, its drawers closed except for one slightly ajar.

I brush dust from the top and notice something wedged between the drawer and the frame. Tugging it free reveals a slim hardback, the deep green cover softened by time, its gold lettering faint but still legible. *The Keeper's Guestbook.*

Inside, the margins bloom with handwriting, some in faded ink, others fresher. One page underlines a line about hospitality. Next to it, with a giant arrow, written in neat cursive, is a note.

Start with the bones, then you'll hear the moans. Build it for you, fuck everyone else. If they don't like it, you don't want them here anyways.

I close the how-to guide gently, fingers still tingling, and tuck it into my bag. Whatever this cottage is doing, I'm here for it. I just wish that working with Jonathan was going to be simpler than I know it will be.

When he asked me to do this project, I saw a flash of him the way I always do—the version of him I've been trying to talk myself out of for over a decade. Jonathan is infuriatingly, exhaustively good. The kind of person who remembers how you take your coffee and holds doors open for strangers and means it every single time. The kind of person who makes it very difficult to stay professional and remember that he's my brother's best friend. I was optimistic enough to think I could keep things clean between us, focused. Work is work. That's all this is.

My curls flutter from my exhale. I just spent the last ten minutes staring at his hands while he peeled wallpaper.

His *hands*.

The frustration curls inside me. How quickly I unravel around him without him even trying? It tangles with the warmth of the cottage and the holy-shit-what-have-I-gotten-myself-into feeling that has taken up permanent residence in my chest.

A bit less than eight months. I just have to stay focused for that long.

This stubborn, inconvenient feeling for Jonathan that has outlasted everything isn't going to be the thing that stops Reading Lane from happening. I won't let it.

Chapter 11

Camera Shy

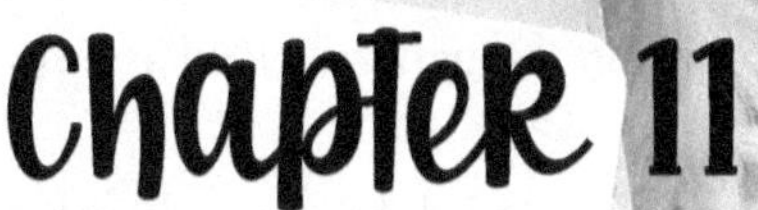

"Places everyone. It's almost time!" Katie hollers, jumping over a rogue power cord. Her long pony tail bounces behind her, blond highlights glowing under the umbrella lights.

"Think she'll notice if I run? I do not want to be in front of the camera." Jonathan creeps up behind me. A delay in the insulation delivery delayed the project by almost a week. Jonathan promises that he'll make sure the time is not lost, and I know he'll try his best, but what other setbacks lurk behind these walls?

We are starting this today whether Jonathan is in front of the camera or not.

"She'll notice," I whisper over my shoulder. "During one of the promo shoots, she found a stray nail in the dirt in the front flower garden."

"That's not hard. Nails are silver."

"This one was rusted brown." I turn, facing him.

"Damn. Guess running is out of the question."

"Sure is. We have way too much to do for you to bail now. What's the problem? There isn't even an audience."

"I had to take the required public speaking class twice in college." He rocks back on his heels. "Still only got a C plus. Hurt my GPA."

"I'm sure that happened." I cross my arms. I have held myself together since the hand fiasco—only a few glances at the broad palms with thick, capable fingers. Rough-knuckled and strong, built like they could fix anything.

I've been pretending that I didn't know him before this project. It helps, slightly. Not enough to remove my attraction to the man that's never failed at anything in his life.

"Oh, it did. Ask your brother. He tried to tutor me but gave up." He puts his hands in his pockets with a shaky grin. "I had to beg for extra credit to get that grade. Wrote a twenty-five page paper on the importance of learning how to speak in public that I did not have to present as a speech. I suspect the professor didn't want to endure my speeches and threw pity on me."

Jonathan is truly nervous, a side of him I'm certain I've never experienced before. The overly-confident man, the one who I have seen firsthand bullshit his way into buying beer in high school by radiating the essence of a person of booze-buying age. The owner of the liquor store didn't even ask for an ID. Rang out the underage con-artist and wished him a good week. But for some reason he's afraid to talk to a camera lens?

Another thought hits me. "Wait, don't you teach at the community center?"

"Yeah, but that's completely different. It's basically hanging out with friends." His cheeks are pink.

"Think of the camera as your friend," I suggest. "I bet I could put a hat on it. Maybe some pants over the tripod legs."

He adjusts his flannel, fighting a smile. "I'm not sure it works that way."

"I'm glad you're behind the camera and not me." I hold up a hardcover. "Book club. I have seven chapters left on this bad boy. If I don't get it done before Tuesday, Tottie will have to run the discussion questions. Who knows what the topics will be if that happens."

Jonathan's eyes sparkle. "Mazey, I wanted to—"

He's cut off by the bubbly marketing-slash-vlog manager sing-songing. "Jonathan! It's time."

"Wonderful." He rubs the back of his neck, walking to his place.

"The face of Phoenix Construction." Katie does a theatrical sweep, presenting her words in lights when he gets into position. "Are you ready, boss?"

"Sure." Jonathan groans, shooting a pleading look at me.

I giggle. "Best of luck, Kirkwood."

"This is her bedroom. Hell, this is her suite," Jonathan grumbles with a grin. "Why isn't she in it?"

"We've been over this, Jonathan." Katie tries to scold with the same impact of a toddler telling you to answer the banana phone when she calls—effective, but in a cute way. She rummages through a backpack covered in sparkly stars, pulling out a folder with a neon cartoon unicorn jumping over a rainbow. She presses the folder to Jonathan's chest.

"Here is another copy of the schedule details. Yours are in pastel purple and Mazey's are in vibrant green. It matches her gorgeous eyes."

Katie is terrifyingly efficient in the most pleasant way. Never rude. More matter-of-fact—anticipating needs, keeping the project on track with the biggest smile on her face, and a snack table to match any dietary need.

I curl up on the old velvet chaise we dragged up here. Nova and I stumbled upon it at a thrift store and knew it needed to be part of this journey. Larry taught Mom how to reupholster it—giggling throughout the cottage with every instruction—and now it's covered in plush blue fabric. Add some oversize pillows and it's the ideal reading spot.

Nova flops down next to me, waving a design magazine. "I'm telling you, emerald walls with matte gold sconces. That's main-character energy."

"Every inspired idea starts with a little havoc," Jonathan says in robot monotone. He is holding a hammer by the metal claw end with both hands.

"You just want me to live in your dark academia fantasy," I mutter, my eyes on an awkward Jonathan getting into position. "Hey, do you think Jonathan's okay with being on camera? He said he hates it."

"You're the one building a romance retreat. Lean in, babe." She doesn't look up from an article that claims it can tell what your room color should be based on your zodiac sign. "He's fine. I mean, he agreed to it."

"Yeah, he did…" My voice trails off. I open my book to the marked page.

Jonathan's robot voice fills the air. "A community renovation project? Sure. A full-on documentary-style vlog chronicling said renovation? Absolutely."

Bang! Jonathan jumps back as the hammer hits the ground. "In this series, I'll help you learn basic skills that'll help build your skill set, not get injured, and expose the way Phoenix Construction really works."

He swipes a blueprint off the sawhorse table, tossing it between his hands. His eyes squint. "Dammit, I can't read that. It's so small. Who wrote this shit?"

Nova and I lock eyes, muffling our laughter behind our palms.

"Hold on," Katie says over the squeaking of the permanent marker. "Better?"

"Yeah, thanks." Jonathan fumbles. "So, uh… Welcome to Phoenix does Reading Lane."

Jonathan stands with his hands on his hips, still gripping the blueprint.

"That's the name of the vlog," Nova whispers.

"Katie says it'll spark interest."

"It sounds like a porno." Nova's laughter catches a *you better quiet down* look from Katie.

I mouth "sorry" on behalf of my best friend.

"This week we are going to be tackling—" Jonathan shifts his weight, knocking into the sawhorse. His cheeks flush as he moves forward as if nothing happened at all.

"I can't take this," I whisper to Nova before running over to his side, plucking the blueprints from his hands.

"Uh, the attic," I finish, showcasing the space with jazz hands. "My studio apartment. I'm so excited to move into this place. Living onsite will allow me to be readily available for guests once we're open."

Katie lifts her brows behind the camera, the debate between yelling cut or keeping it rolling written all over her face.

"This is, uh, Mazey. She owns… Reading Lane. The—" Jonathan stutters.

"The first bookish retreat in North Carolina." I flash him a smile. "I have it on good authority that Jonathan will be building me approximately a million bookshelves and adding a rainwater shower situation to every suite."

"A million? Now, wait a damn minute." He shoots me a wink and tosses a pack of paint swatches at me. "You're gonna learn how to do some of it yourself."

"Hmmm. I was planning on letting you do all the upkeep, but I suppose it would be nice to learn some basic repairs and maintenance." I tap my chin, considering the importance of learning basic home care. "As long as we can take reading breaks."

"Deal." The weight of his look is heavy, and I am afraid to turn to him. If I mess this up, we can rerecord it, right? From the corner of my eye, I see him turn to Katie and the camera.

I play into the part, smirking into the camera. "You are gonna teach me?"

"Yelp. You better buckle your tool belt," he draws, sounding like a cowboy from a 1960s western. "It's gonna be a bumpy ride."

A laugh bursts out of me. "That's what you went with? Of all the things you could have said?"

"Uh, I guess so." He runs his fingers through his hair. "It wasn't that bad."

"No, it was great." I wipe a tear from the corner of my eye. "Is there something specific we are working on today?"

"Oh, hmm." He shuffles around the work area. "This."

Jonathan hands me the plans for the attic. I show the sketch to the camera. "Are we able to accomplish all of this today?"

He breathes out a laugh. "No way. It'll be about two weeks to turn this around. The most important thing is to make sure this space is insulated."

"So, it needs a winter coat?" The corner of his mouth ticks up, and he dives into the logistics of insulating an attic.

The rest of the recording is much the same—Jonathan showing me the correct way to hold a tool or explaining why a certain material is used. Me pulling every piece of information from him while providing comedic relief. Working alongside him is not as terrible as it should have been. It should have been a whole lot of me getting caught up in the way he treats every question as if it is the most important thing anyone has ever asked and not the ridiculous bait I set whenever he skimmed over obvious instructions, or how his hand brushed mine every time we passed tools to one another.

"Cut!" Katie yells after we wave our *see you next times!* She rushes to us, arms open to gather us in a three-way bear hug. "I was wrong. Totally and completely wrong. New angle."

"Whoa." I hold my hands up. "I thought I was going to be doing separate recordings. Maybe cameo with Jonathan *occasionally*."

"The chemistry between you two is unreal." Katie bounces around, gathering the recording equipment. "You make Jonathan sound normal."

"I have so much to do. Carving out time will be impossible. Once the attic is done, we have all the guest rooms and the outside." I search for every reason why I cannot co-star with Jonathan. Why being around him even more than I already am is the worst idea ever.

"Oh, and the shed. Not to mention all the prep for the grand opening. Planning an event like this is going to be *very* time consuming."

Katie stares at me. "You good? Done telling me why you can't do the vlog with him?"

"No. Not at all. We don't have chemistry. We have last resorts and that's all. That was all fabricated nonsense to make this one," I throw my thumb over my shoulder at Jonathan, "less of a weirdo on camera. No offense."

"None taken." Jonathan kicks an invisible soccer ball, hands shoved in his pockets.

"Well whatever it is, it's perfect. It was informative and entertaining. Exactly what we are looking for. Exactly what will get new customers for both of you."

My head rolls in Jonathan's direction, and I look away just as fast. Co-hosting means more time with him. More of whatever today was.

But new customers.

I pull at a loose thread on my sleeve. It's a business decision. A practical, logical, completely non-complicated business decision. People co-host things all the time without it meaning anything. Partners. Colleagues. People who are nothing more than last resorts to each other.

"Katie is the scariest ray of sunshine I have ever seen," Jonathan says.

"That's a fact." I laugh before I can stop myself, which is exactly the problem. "But I was talking about being co-hosts of the vlog."

He shifts his weight. "I'm game if you are."

I look at him then. Really look at him—hands still tucked in his pockets, completely unbothered, like the answer is obvious. Like it's simple.

Maybe it is simple. Customers. Business. Grand opening.

I stick my hand out. "Strictly professional."

He glances down at it then back up at me with that barely-there almost-smile. "Obviously."

I ignore the way my stomach does something stupid when he finally shakes my hand.

"Here you go." She hops over to me and places a folder similar to Jonathan's, but with a tiger on it. "Had some extra shooting schedules, just in case. Let me know if you have any questions or need to rearrange anything. And all the stuff you have to do, it'll get done. I promise."

"You promise?" I open the folder and examine the schedule

"Yep." Before I can argue—not that I would—she's out the door with all the recording equipment strapped to her back.

"Mazey, thank you," Jonathan whispers and walks down the attic stairs before I can reply.

"We gonna talk about that?" Nova immediately says.

"Never," I blurt. "But check out your dad."

Larry, bless his handy soul, is crouched near the window, measuring the frame while humming along to a Fleetwood Mac song that's barely audible over Mom's singing.

I shake my head and whisper to Nova, "Do you think they know how adorable they are?"

Nova mutters, "Nope. Some people don't see what's right in front of them."

Chapter 12

Orange Ones

"The first night in a new place is always the truest. You find out very quickly whether you belong there—or whether it belongs to you." - The Keeper's Guestbook

It took approximately a million days—or Jonathan's predicted two weeks—to finish the attic and get me moved in. This is the first time I've ever lived by myself. I went straight from my parents' house to sharing a dorm with Nova in college, then to the apartment we rented after graduation. I tried to talk Nova into coming with me to the cottage, but she insisted the tarot reading guided her to realize she would benefit from some independence.

Wilfred is folded into a dog ball as close as possible to my side. His tiny back feet are practically touching his floppy ears. A grumble comes from the fluff, but his eyes stay closed.

"Whatcha dreaming about, buddy?" I ask, giving him a scratch behind the ear. I would love to know what goes through this pup's mind.

I've been combing through the latest book I found, trying to figure out how it ended up in my possession. The thing is full of useful tips and insightful notes. It's almost as if it were curated for a thirty-something who decided to purchase a cottage to turn into a retreat and who has no fucking clue what they are doing.

"Mazey?" A yell rumbles through the cottage. Did I lock the doors? I know the doors were locked because Elliott tested the lock's strength when he stopped by earlier for dinner.

Only a few people have a key to the cottage. Nova, who has been on a first date for the last hour with a journalist for the news channel a couple towns over; my mom, but she's working a night shift for a co-worker with a sick kid; and Jonathan.

Jonathan.

"It's way too late to be showing up at someone's house," I grumble, checking the time on the vintage alarm clock on my nightstand. How is it only seven in the evening? I'm in my button-up shorts pajama set. The ones with tiny tacos all over a purple background. My hair is in a ball on top of my head, and I have three zit patches on my chin. *Thanks, stress acne.* After Elliott left, I sprinted upstairs with big plans to work on an embroidered pillow for Verne's birthday and trying to figure out the mystery behind the cottage. My body was not made for the physical labor I've been putting it through the last few weeks.

"Uh, Mazey? Can I come in?" Jonathan knocks softly.

"Yeah, sure," I say, pulling off the zit patches with the speed of a cheetah and plaster on a smile. "Why are you here?"

The attic door creaks as Jonathan steps inside, fiddling with something in his hands. "Sorry, I can come back another time if now isn't good. I used my key. I was hoping you'd be downstairs, organizing books or reading or something." He examines the room as if it's the first time he's laid eyes on it. We've recorded three more episodes of the remodel shenanigans since we accidentally became partners on day one.

The vlog is getting serious traction, viewers ranging from homeowners to book lovers to scrollers. The comment section has been equally as interesting as our viewer base. There's a solid amount of comments asking for specific tips on various DIY projects, loads of book recommendations, and—the most awkward type of comment—speculation about whose bed we're spending the night in.

After Nova read the fifth comment out loud the other day, I rewatched an episode to determine how delusional our "fans" are. There was teasing, laughter, learning. Perfectly platonic. Then I caught it—what the viewers have clearly misunderstood as something more. The way his eyes crinkle when I look over at him, that stupid genuine grin spreading across his face like he can't help it.

We may have insane chemistry in front of the camera, and working with him has been as easy as working with Nova, but for the sake of this project, there is no way I am revisiting my grade-school crush. I don't have time with planning the grand opening, making sure the business side of things are on track, and the vlog.

Why would Jonathan show up after work hours? I assumed he'd be out on a date or picking up women at the bar with Elliott. Does he date? Is he in a relationship? It's not like anyone's love life comes up when we are tearing down walls. He's never brought anyone to family dinner, but that doesn't mean that he doesn't have a girlfriend.

Stop it. I do not care about Jonathan's relationship status.

"I wasn't sure if you were an early-to-bed kind of lady still." He tracks every slanted wall, taking in my space from the deep teal walls to the charcoal bookshelves.

I pull my knees up to my chest and focus on the tiny hearts on my favorite socks. "I am. Early riser too. What brought you this way on this fine evening?"

"You know socks with holes in them are pointless, right?" He quips, stepping closer to me.

"They're lived in." I wiggled my toes at him. These are the only pair of socks that have a hole in them, but I can't fathom getting rid of them—they're fuzzy and soft and just the right height.

"Brought you something." He stands next to the bed facing away from me, head turned to the side as if avoiding his own kind gesture head-on in case it goes south. "As a thank you for… saving me on that first day. And every day since."

"I love presents." I nudge his leg with my foot, excitement buzzing through me at the thoughtfulness behind it. There are few things more exciting than being given something that someone purchased because it reminded them of you. It's like getting a glimpse into their true thoughts. "What is it?"

He tosses a bag of gummy bears and a hardcover next to me, lowering his head to his chest as he sits on the edge of the bed. I've been too busy to stop by The Story Porch to check out the new releases, even skipping book club in lieu of getting all my stuff moved in. But I know this book was released this week. It's been on my *to-be-read* list since the release date was announced.

"Oh, I've been really excited to read this." I pick up the new release, examining it. "Thank you."

"Tottie helped me." He nods at the wall. "I still think we should've gone with sage green in here."

I pretend I'm offended, tossing the book down to grasp my imaginary pearls. "You mean instead of Exotic Mermaid Teal? Never."

"Mermaids aren't a color." He deadpans.

"It's a vibe," I say with a shrug. "You wouldn't get it."

He rolls his eyes. "Nope. Don't get it. Just painted the damn thing."

I laugh, but Jonathan only manages a thin smile that doesn't reach his eyes. His fingers drum against his thigh, and I notice the way his jaw keeps clenching. Is Jonathan Kirkwood nervous again?

"I like that you didn't argue about the chandelier." I reposition my legs into a pretzel. "I thought you'd say it was impractical."

"It is impractical."

"But you still put it up."

He shrugs. "You wanted it."

"Still didn't have to." I study him for way longer than necessary. "So, thank you."

"I'd do anything you asked," he says so softly I'm not sure if he meant to say it out loud.

Jonathan's eyes meet mine.

The room is filled with nothing but Wilfred's sleeping grumbles for an awkward amount of time. I grab the gummies, ripping them open.

"Want one?" I offer the bag to him. "Just don't steal—"

"The orange ones, I know." He reaches into the bag, pulling a cluster out before holding two orange ones out to me.

"So, uh..." He runs his hands through his hair. "What are you doing?"

"What are *you* doing?" I ask, crinkling the bag closed, tossing them on my nightstand. Wilfred, who hasn't moved through this entire interaction, lifts his head only to harrumph at Jonathan before rolling over.

"I mean what are you reading?" he asks, twisting to see the cover better. "*The Keeper's Guestbook*?"

"It's to help with the whole running a retreat thing." It's just not on the shelf anywhere, and I'm pretty sure the cottage gave it to me because it's obvious that I have no idea what I am doing. I don't say that part, though.

"Oh, not a bad idea. Good to get a bunch of opinions and then decide what works for you." Jonathan's forehead wrinkles a bit as if he were debating letting something else escape his lips. He shakes off the words, raising off the bed. "Welp, I better go. Just wanted to bring you the gummy bears and the book."

"That is the way to my heart." I immediately wish I didn't say it.

"I'm aware." He crosses the room to leave in slow motion, grinning.

"Jonathan?"

He stops in the doorway. "Yeah?"

"Thanks. Again." I sound like a broken record. *Wonderful.*

"Right. I'll leave you be, then." He taps the doorframe, walking away.

Thoughts jumble my brain. Did Jonathan Kirkwood just come to my bedroom at night? Granted, my bedroom is also my living room, and he basically rebuilt the damn thing. This was different, though. It was more intimate than even earlier today when he helped hang the canvas of a giraffe wearing bright red glasses over my bed. And to bring me a thank-you present? A very thoughtful thank-you present. That book was a new release from my TBR. It was on the pricier side with its hardcover and sprayed edges.

I sit, staring across the room at nothing in particular.

Working with Jonathan, avoiding any type of more-than-coworker feelings, is going to be harder than I thought.

Chapter 13

Book Challenges and Author Idols

"Next to trying and winning, the best thing is trying and failing."
- Anne of Green Gables, L.M. Montgomery

"Okay," Jonathan releases a sigh so strong that his hair flutters across his forehead. He checks his watch. "Katie should be here any minute."

"You in a hurry or something?" I ask, following him into the book shop.

He looks up, eyes wide as if he were caught with his hand in the cookie jar. "No, no. It's work. A lot of work stuff."

My heart settles heavy. I have noticed the normally easygoing Jonathan has been wound a bit tighter the past few weeks. Even more than when he asked me to do this project. It's not that he's been short-tempered or rude, or even on edge. He's been more distracted. Frazzled, maybe? I can't place my finger on it, but I definitely don't enjoy this look on him.

"Do you need to leave? We can probably reschedule." I pull out my phone, open my calendar. "What about—"

"Mazey, I got this. Don't worry." He gifts me a grin that makes me go weak in the knees, and I momentarily forget where I am. "Everything at the office can wait. This is more important."

"Are you sure? I bet I can talk to Tottie about opening up after hours. She'll grumble, but I think she likes having people owe her favors. I'm convinced that's how she gets so many advanced copies of books."

He chuckles and places both hands on my shoulders. Shivers race up my arms. "I'm sure. Now, do you want to go first or second?"

Before I can answer, a voice pipes up behind us. "Nope. Same damn time."

Tottie loops around the display with the ease of someone who's lived among teetering book towers for years. She tugs on the turtleneck that sits under her pumpkin-covered dress. "I'll be timing you two. That Katie girl called earlier and filled me in. Said something about enemies-to-lovers trending or some shit. Talks like her mouth's trying to win a race."

Jonathan grins. "Yeah, she's a chatter-box, but one heck of a worker."

He does that a lot. Talks up his employees. The other day I overheard him talking to the foreman about the high schooler who picks up hours on his school breaks. Went on and on about how the kid has shown real potential in the construction industry. Even said something about creating an internship for him so he'd get some college credit.

"Alright! Let's do this. Oh, Sawyer Storme will be in shortly to sign her back list. Apparently, she's into tiny touristy towns with charm. I guess Honeyville has that. Said she seeks them out. Who the hell woulda guessed?" A ring from the counter interrupts her. "Ah, hell. Hang on, let me ring up this customer."

"Did she just say Sawyer Storme is going to be *here*?" I spin to Jonathan.

"Yeah, why?" He's flipping through the pages of a book.

I swipe the book out of his hands. A chunky burgundy hardcover with gold lettering—*The Mortician's Art & Science: A Complete Guide to the Preparation of the Deceased*, London, 1887. The cover has ivy and delicate skulls bordering an engraved illustration of a suited figure standing next to an embalming table, instruments all neatly laid out.

"Are you thinking of becoming a mortician from the Victorian era?" I say, raising an eyebrow.

"Possibly. Backup if Phoenix goes under." He shrugs. "So, who is this Sawyer Storme?"

"That woman…" I whisper, grabbing his beefy arm and bouncing on my heels. "That woman. She builds the heroines I've spent years waiting to become. Smart. Lovable. Deserving. Do you understand how rare that is?"

"You are all those things," he says simply, no question in his tone. Our gazes meet.

The words land somewhere below my ribs and stay there. I'm used to compliments that come with a little laugh attached, or a "you know what I mean" tacked on the end to soften the vulnerability of having said something true. But he offers nothing like that. No escape hatch. He just looks at me with those steady eyes like he's been certain of it for a long time and simply waited for the right moment to say so. Something in my chest does a slow, helpless turn.

I want to deflect. I want to make a joke, figure out a way to circle back to preparing bodies in the eighteen hundreds, look back across the room at anyone else.

But I can't move. I stand completely still for once, held in place by the frankness of being told that I'm loveable, smart, and deserving.

"So," his mouth tugs upward, "you're excited?"

I gasp so hard I almost inhale my tongue. "Excited? You're kidding, right?"

"She's just a person, Mazey." He snorts. "No different than you or me."

"*How. Dare. You.*" I whisper-scream. "She is a literary *icon*. A goddess among mere mortal romance writers. If the book world had a Nobel Prize for making women both emotionally and intellectually fulfilled, she would win every single year."

"What's the plan?" Jonathan lowers his mouth to my ear. "Ask for an autograph? Get on one knee and propose?"

I clutch my chest. "I don't know. What if I embarrass myself? What if I lose the ability to form complete sentences and just make high-pitched dolphin noises at her? What if—"

The door flies open and Sawyer *Freaking* Storme steps inside. I swear a burst of wind, gentle enough to blow wavy copper hair off her face, dances through the bookstore at that exact moment. Her tailored skinny jeans are paired with a pale yellow baby-doll t-shirt. She floats to a display, ignoring a giant stack of books sitting on the floor. Her sparkly blue flats catch on a copy of *Wuthering Heights* and she tumbles to the floor. Lying on her back, she bursts out laughing at the ceiling.

"Sawyer!" Jonathan and I race to her aid. "Are you okay?"

"Oh, I'm fine. A bit mortified, but fine." With red cheeks, she accepts my outreached arm and stands. "I'm a bit on the clumsy side. Sorry about that."

"Tottie always has stacks laying around." Jonathan squats down to re-stack the books. "You are not the first to crash and burn because of it."

"Thanks for that." She juts out her hand. "I'm Sawyer"

I grab her hand and bow.

"Okay, that's very formal of you." She giggles.

"I am not a knight. I'm a normal person. With a normal job—definitely not protecting a far-off kingdom or upholding a code of chivalry. I guess I have a kind of normal job? We are doing this thing for a vlog for Jonathan's construction company." The words tumble out in a rush as I point at Jonathan. "That's Jonathan."

"And, for *your* Reading Lane. Mazey is opening a bookish retreat." Jonathan winks in my direction.

"Book retreat? Oooh, that sounds incredible. I love books." Sawyer beams. "Obviously I love books. I'm in a book store, and I literally made a career out of writing them—books, that is. I'm an author."

"Me too!" I blurt. "I mean, not the author part. The book loving part."

Tottie—thankfully—doesn't let me finish embarrassing myself.

"Okay, let's get started. I have shit to do," Tottie booms, tossing something from hand to hand. "Where's that Katie girl? She's supposed to be recording this nonsense."

Jonathan stares at the object in Tottie's hand. "Is that a replica of the stopwatch from Season One, Episode 14 of *MacGyver*."

"What?" I ask, the quivering in my stomach easing at Jonathan's confession. "How do you know the exact episode?"

"I have so many questions," Sawyer pipes up. "Are you obsessed with *MacGyver*?"

"Are you a MacGyverite?" I quip.

"Are you part of The Mac Pack?" Sawyer asks with wide eyes.

"This thing? I don't know. It was in the lost and found." Tottie shrugs as she examines the device in her hand. "No one claimed it for years. Figured it'd come in handy."

"Can I see it?" Jonathan puts his hand out, but Tottie shakes her head. "*MacGyver* is incredible," he continues. "In episode 14, he synchronized his wristwatch with the bomb's timer to measure the exact delay between the two and—"

"I'm here! I'm here! Sorry I'm a bit late—traffic," Katie says in a huff, hands full of recording equipment and a very familiar latte cup from my dad's coffee shop.

"Traffic? In Honeyville during the off season?" Tottie puts her hands on her hips, stopwatch wrapped around her hand. "Isn't your office like three blocks down the road?"

"Ok, yes, but Gus's just released a new flavor, and I had to try it." She holds her cup up in the air, the tripod that was wedged between her body and elbow tumbling to the ground. "It was basically a traffic jam with how many people were in line."

"Gus's?" Sawyer asks.

"Story time later., Tottie says before I can answer. "Ready? You two have exactly three minutes to get however many books as possible. Whoever gets the most, wins. Don't try to grab multiples of the same one, I won't count those. Each book needs to be a different title."

"I'll fill you in after," I say to Sawyer, then turn to Jonathan. "And you'll have to tell me more about your obsession later, MacHead. I need to kick your ass."

"Pause. Is that Sawyer Storme?" Katie says. She has somehow miraculously set up the tripod and ring light, and now clips microphones to our shirts.

"Yes, I'm Sawyer." Sawyer throws her perfectly polished hand out to shake Katie's.

Katie, genuinely matching the enthusiasm, smiles as she pulls her into a Southern hug.

"Oh, this is perfect!" Katie claps her hands, releasing a dazed Sawyer. "You should totally be a part of this challenge!"

"That's a great idea!" I blurt. My shoulders drop. "You'd have to be okay being filmed for social media, though."

Tottie taps her toe. "Get whatever you need to do done. I have inventory to get out and customers to charm."

We are the only customers in the shop right now.

"Umm, sure?" she stammers. "What are the rules?"

Jonathan starts to list the rules like he's reading from a guidebook.

"Basically," Katie, thankfully, cuts him off. "The point is to get as many books as possible. They will all go to the book retreat."

"I've built approximately fifty-million shelves to fill there, so every bit helps." I say.

"*You* built them?" Jonathan raises a brow at me.

"Jonathan might have helped… a bit." I give him a side grin.

Sawyer nods her head. "What does the winner get?"

"Bragging rights, mostly," I say.

"I've been thinking about that." Jonathan crosses his arms. "Maybe we should make it a bit more interesting."

"Oh, yeah?" I mimic his stance, moving in front of him. "What were you thinking?"

"Loser has to bring the winner coffee for a week?" Katie shouts over her shoulder from the recording equipment.

"That's good, but not great." Jonathan shakes his head, takes a half step closer to me. "I was thinking of higher stakes."

"Sounds like you have something in mind." I inch in his direction.

Jonathan bends forward so we're eye level. "Winner gets to pick the costume—"

"Costume? Halloween came and went, Jonathan."

"—that the loser has to wear to a family dinner."

"Oh, interesting," Katie says.

"And buys lunch," I add, locking into Jonathan's competitive side.

He's close enough now that I have to tip my chin up to hold his gaze. There's something satisfying about watching the corner of his mouth pull into that slow, deliberate smile—like he's already calculated three moves ahead and is waiting for me to catch up. I refuse to be the first one to blink.

"Deal." He extends his hand.

"Deal." I shake it once, firm, and neither of us lets go, holding on a second longer than necessary.

Behind Jonathan, Katie leans toward Sawyer. "Tell me I'm not imagining that," Katie whispers.

"You are absolutely not imagining that," Sawyer whispers back. "It's like a scene from one of my books."

"They've been like this since Mazey hit high school," Tottie says at full volume, unbothered. "It's exhausting."

"Tottie!" I lean around Jonathan.

She holds both hands up, the picture of innocence. "I said what I said."

"Are we ready yet? I don't have all day, Mazey Lane." She plants her hands on her hips, the warmth in her eyes betraying the bark in her voice.

"Yes, ma'am." All three of us answer as we line up, giant wooden baskets in hand.

"About damn time. Ready. Set. Go!" Tottie hollers.

I make it to the romance section just as Jonathan reaches for a box set of historical novels. I slam my hip into his side. He stumbles and knocks into a spinning rack. Books fall to the floor. He catches one before it hits the ground and looks down at the cover.

"This guy's holding a goose." He turns it over in his hands. "I think this is in the wrong section." He examines the back cover, standing close enough that I catch something warm and woodsy drifting off him— something that definitely wasn't there when we were kids.

I lean in without thinking about it. "Are you wearing—"

"What are you doing?" He glances sideways at me.

"—cologne?" I finish, taking a half step back like I didn't just have my nose near his shoulder. "You smell different."

"You smell me enough to know my baseline scent?" The corner of his mouth ticks up, slow and unbearable.

Heat crawls up my neck. "Do you have a date after this?" I grab a book I don't even want off the shelf. "Are you trying to impress some-one?"

Jonathan sets the goose book down and looks at me for a moment—really looks at me—in that way that makes me feel like I've asked a question he's always known the answer to.

"I'm always trying to impress her," he says quietly, turning back to the shelf.

I blink. "Her who?"

"It appears a human falls in love with a goose shifter."

I grab the book from him, our fingers brushing as I yank it away and drop it into my basket. "Oh, Nova loves that one!"

"She's read it?" Jonathan asks, arms to his side, mouth agape.

"Of course. She said it's excellent." I say, shoving a five book series into the basket while very deliberately not stepping back. "What do you read exactly?"

"Two-minutes and fifteen seconds!" Katie squeals from behind Tot-tie's shoulder.

"Shouldn't you be recording or something?" Tottie shrugs the blond off her shoulder, crossing her arms. "I'm the timekeeper here."

"I know what you read." I block his path to a shelf. "Nonfiction. Auto-biographies about past leaders and how to make an impact on your employees. Books that have something you can extract and apply to your work ethic. The joyless stuff that turns a carefree hobby into secret work."

"If you think you can, maybe you should make me a list of books that are Mazey approved then."

My stomach does a little flip. The idea of Jonathan reading books I recommend, of him thinking about me while he's turning pages, of having that kind of inside joke between us—it sends a thrill through me that I absolutely should not be feeling.

"Minute-thirty," Tottie bellows.

I glance in the timekeeper's direction. "Maybe I will."

His eyebrows lift slightly, like he wasn't expecting me to agree. There's something in his expression—surprise, maybe, or interest—and the corner of his mouth twitches up just enough that I notice. "Yeah?"

"Don't sound so shocked, MacHead. I'd actually love to curate a list of must-reads for you." I clutch the basket tighter to keep my hands busy, suddenly hyperaware of how close we're standing in this narrow aisle.

"I'm not shocked. I'm…" He trails off, running a hand through his hair. "I'd actually like that."

He shoots me a look, and for a second neither of us moves. Then he turns toward the next shelf. I step in his way and block him with my wicker basket, my shoulder pressing against his chest.

"Excuse me," he says, voice low, grin widening. "I need to obliterate you at this challenge."

"Oh, get real." An unexpected laugh escapes me.

His eyes drop to my mouth for half a second before he reaches over me. I'm acutely aware of how close he is, his arm extended above my head as I grab three paperbacks and dump them into my bag before he can react.

"You're not playing fair," I say as he hovers over me.

"I'm winning."

I tilt my chin up to meet his gaze, refusing to be the one who backs down first.

My jaw tightens. "We'll see about that." I dart under his arm and dash to gather some classics by Jane Austen. My fingers fly across the spines—*Pride and Prejudice, Emma, Persuasion*—tossing them into my basket without a second thought.

Out of the corner of my eye, I spot Sawyer working through the displays with surprising efficiency. She's hitting sections Jonathan and I haven't touched yet—true crime, travel memoirs. A small stack of thrillers is already tucked under her arm, and she's moving with the quiet confidence of someone who might have thought this through before jumping right in. She's not rushing like Jonathan and me. She's being strategic, checking each spine carefully before adding it to her pile.

Smart. Duplicates don't count.

She straightens up with a small stack, catches my eye, and gives me a thumbs up. I return the gesture, loving how my idol is a normal, book-loving nerd just like the rest of us. Honestly, I don't even care about winning. It's fun to play with Jonathan, getting him all flustered at the thought of losing.

"One minute left!" Tottie shouts from the counter. "Move your asses!"

Chapter 14

One of Everything, Please

*@sunlitspines: new here and i need someone to explain the dynamic because i feel
like i'm missing context and also i feel like i'm not missing any context at all
@mugsandmargins: replying to @sunlitspines you are not missing any context.
you see exactly what you think you see.
@readsbythelake: the way he went still. he went STILL.
@fernanddfiction: elliott texting in real time is sending me into orbit
@tealandtattered: "that's… something." jonathan kirkwood you are not as neutral
as you think you are*

The bell over the diner door jingles as we walk in, Jonathan muttering something under his breath about "pointless competitions" and "fluke wins."

"Tottie did the final count." I slide into the booth by the window.

"And eighty-three is higher than forty," Sawyer adds.

"You're going to look so cute dressed up as a chicken at family dinner."

"It's a shame I won't be in town." She turns to me with a small smile, and I remind myself that she is just a person. A person who has written eleven books that I have read a combined forty-seven times. "You'll have to send me a picture."

"Oh, no problem." My voice comes out even. Breezy, even. I slide my phone to her on the new contact screen like I do this every day—like handing my phone to my favorite author so she can type in her number is a completely unremarkable Tuesday.

She enters her name without hesitation.

I watch her fingers move and think very hard about not grabbing

Jonathan's arm under the table.

"I could have him dress up as a pirate or a sexy vampire," I add, because my mouth is still working even if my brain has fully left the building.

"That's a good one. Or Luke Skywalker. I'm a sucker for *Star Wars.*"

Sawyer and I stare at Jonathan, who is intensely examining the menu that hasn't changed in twenty years. "I let you win."

I snort. "Yeah, and I'm the Queen of England."

Sawyer sits across from me, hiding her smile behind the laminated menu. "Should I be worried you two are going to start throwing silverware?"

"Depends," I say. "If he tries to skip out on paying, I'll start with the forks."

"Hey, folks." A waitress with a ponytail on top of her head and bright blue eyeshadow stands at the edge of the table, pencil to her notepad. "Whatcha havin'?"

"Burger and fries. And whatever these two want." Jonathan waves in our direction.

"I'll have one of everything, please," I say. Jonathan glares at me. "Mushroom Swiss burger, extra mushrooms, hush puppies, and the apple crumble pie."

"Damn, that sounds perfect." Sawyer drools. "I'll do the same."

I leaned back. "So, Sawyer, what made you decide to come to Honeyville?"

She lights up the way people do when they get a new gadget and all they want to do is talk about it. "My best friend convinced me to get away for a bit to write. She came through Honeyville last summer with her kids and husband and knew I'd love the small town, touristy vibes." She pauses, turning her phone in her hands.

"I've been in a bit of a writing slump since my divorce finalized back in May." She said it quickly, like she was hoping it would land softer that way. Then she looked up and winced. "Oh, I'm so sorry. I tend to overshare when I'm nervous."

"You don't have to apologize," I said.

"We've known each other for what, four hours?" She laughed,

clearly a little embarrassed. "You did not need to know that."

"Honestly," Jonathan said, "you'd fit right in here."

"That's good because I'm meeting a realtor named Brody, I think, tomorrow to look at houses. Evie and I need a fresh start."

"Brody is a buddy of mine. He's in her smut club." Jonathan nods at me. "Hell of a guy."

"It's not smut! It's literature!" I jab his shoulder.

He drops his head, chuckling. "Yeah, okay."

"You two sound like an old married couple." Sawyer laughs.

My heart seizes and it takes me a beat to suck in a breath again. I open my mouth to correct her—to say something easy or dismissive—and find exactly nothing waiting for me there.

"Nope." Jonathan saves me. "Can't afford her taste in throw pillows." He smirks at me over his coffee cup.

I point at him. "That is fair, and I resent it."

Sawyer is still smiling at us like we are something to figure out. I busy myself with my menu.

"Can I ask who Evie is?" I murmur.

"Of course," Sawyer laughs. "Evie is my daughter. She's eleven. My husband—ex-husband—and I are divorced… Finally."

"Thank you. This looks delicious." I rub my hands together as the waitress plunks down our meals. "Did she come to Honeyville with you?"

Sawyer shakes her head, cheeseburger puffing her cheeks out. She swallows. "No, she's with my best friend. I didn't want her missing any more school than necessary."

"Makes sense." I dunk a hush puppy into honey mustard. "Honeyville is a great place to raise a kid. We both grew up here and loved it."

My phone vibrates against the table.

Elliott: Just watched your vlog. Are you into Jonathan?

Mazey: What? No! Why would you say that!

"Apparently Katie already posted the book challenge vlog. How did she do that so quickly?" I release a hair-shifting breath. "And Elliott has feelings about it."

"I'm not sure who Elliott is, but I want to watch." Sawyer pulls out her phone and stares at the screen for a few. "Oh, wow. He's not the only one with feelings. Look at these comments."

She turns her phone toward me. I scan the screen.

"The way he looks at her!!! 😍"

"This is the slow burn forced proximity we NEED"

"Get you someone who looks at you like Jonathan looks at Mazey"

My throat goes dry. Jonathan leans over to see, his shoulder brushing mine. The comfort from his brief touch dissolves when he goes still.

"Well," he says, voice carefully neutral. "That's… something."

My phone buzzes again.

> Elliott: Seriously, Maze. Don't go there. He's my best friend, and you are my little sister.

I flip my phone face down, deciding to do the adult thing and ignore the entire situation.

"Elliott is my older brother," I say to Sawyer.

"Actually, he teaches at the school. He could give you some insight on getting Evie signed up, I bet," Jonathan says, encouraging the shift in conversation.

I gulp my tea. "He's harmless unless you're trying to date me. Over-protective brother and all that. But I doubt you're trying to get in my pants, so you're safe."

Jonathan chokes on a fry.

"What? She's not." I say.

Sawyer laughs behind a napkin. "No, certainly not. I'm not in the market for a partner of *any* kind right now."

I give Sawyer Elliott's information as she continues talking about her decision to move to Honeyville. She's been struggling with writer's block since her divorce about a year ago. Thought a new environment would help reboot her storytelling.

"I'm ready for my fresh start." She shrugs. "That's why I'm here. Promoting my newest series by doing the dart thing, going to independent bookstores, signing backlists. But this place is unlike anywhere I've ever been. I'd bet money that magic floats through the air."

"It's a magical place for sure." I gulp my drink. Is my cottage the only place in Honeyville with magic coursing through its walls?

"Speaking of new things, tell me about Reading Lane. I want to hear everything." Sawyer's eyes sparkle.

We spend most of the afternoon talking about the retreat and vlog. Sawyer offers to send signed books and merchandise for guests and promises to promote the grand opening on her socials, certain her author friends and fans will be eager to attend.

When we part ways, I walk away with a bounce in my step and my chin held high.

Chapter 15

I'll Go Get Sandwiches

"The spaces people remember are never the ones that show you everything. They are the ones that make you feel like you found something that was waiting, just for you." - The Keeper's Guestbook, Chapter 12: "The Room Behind the Bookshelves"

It's late by the time I finally get into bed. I reach for *The Keeper's Guestbook* on the nightstand and something stops me.

My bookmark is in the wrong place.

I know where I left off. I've read this book so many times the spine cracks open to my usual spots. But the bookmark is sitting in a chapter I don't remember seeing before.

"The Room Behind the Bookshelves."

"Oh, come on," I say out loud to no one.

I'm not even surprised anymore. A little offended at how on-the-nose it is, honestly, but not surprised.

I'm too tired to make it to the bed properly, so I curl up in the chair by the window—the one Larry reupholstered for me, the one that now fits like it was made for my exact body—and I start reading.

The chapter talks about magic. Not the theatrical kind. The quiet, intentional kind. It says that when you're working in hospitality, the thing that separates a space people stay in from a space people remember is whether you've hidden something worth finding.

I read the line twice.

Then I look up at the ceiling, thinking about the weird room.

Oh.

The book is still open in my lap when I grab my phone, not thinking my actions through.

It rings twice.

"It's midnight, Mazey."

"I know what the weird room is."

A beat. "…Go on."

"A hidden reading nook." I'm already on my feet, pacing. "Like, you walk in and it looks like a bookshelf wall, but one of the books—with the Reading Lane logo on the spine—you tug it, and the latch pops, and the whole thing swings open and inside is just—" I press my free hand to my chest. "Cozy. Safe. Unexpected. Like finding a world only you knew existed."

Silence.

"Jonathan?"

"I'm putting on pants."

"You don't have pants on?" I ask. The image of Jonathan pantless is definitely not floating through my head.

"See you in a few, Mazey." The call ends, and I'm standing in the middle of the room holding my phone like it's just betrayed me.

He's coming over.

It's midnight. I called a man at midnight, and he is putting on pants to come over here.

"What did I do," I say out loud.

Wilfred lifts his head from the foot of the bed, one ear up, one ear sideways, in the particular configuration that means he's judging me but hasn't yet committed fully.

I set my phone down on the nightstand. Pick it back up. Put it in my pocket. Take it back out.

He didn't hesitate. That's the thing burrowing into my chest right now. It rang twice and he answered. And when I told him—when I word-vomited my midnight revelation at him like a complete idiot —he didn't say *can this wait* or *send me a voice memo* or any of the reasonable things a reasonable person would say to someone unreasonably calling them at midnight about a bookshelf.

He said "go on."

And then he put on pants.

I catch my reflection in the dark window, and I look exactly like someone who just called a man at midnight: hair doing something inexplicable, still in the oversized shirt I've been wearing since eight, the book tucked under my arm like a security blanket.

"Oh my god," I say quietly.

He is, at this exact moment, in his car. Driving here. Because I called him. Because I found a chapter with a bookmark I didn't place, and I got so lit up about it that my hands apparently just… dialed.

I didn't even think. That's what's getting me. There was no deliberation, no *should I*, no internal debate. My brain just went *Jonathan* like that was the only logical conclusion to the sentence.

I look at Wilfred.

Wilfred looks back at me.

His other ear goes sideways.

"Don't," I tell him.

He puts his head back down, but slowly. Pointedly. In the way that means he already knew before I did and he wants that on the record.

"Let's go." I jump up, sliding on my slippers.

Wilfred's head pops up, and he jumps off the bed. Whatever his opinions on my life choices, he is not missing an outing.

I do a lap of my suite. Pick up the throw blanket from the couch and fold it, then unfold it, then drape it over the arm in a way that looks casual rather than *I just folded and unfolded this blanket*. I stack the two mugs from this afternoon on top of each other and put them in the dirty dish bin that sits on top of the mini fridge.

"This is insane," I tell Wilfred.

He's watching me from the middle of the hall with an expression of profound patience.

The foyer is dim and smells like sawdust and fresh plaster. I find the light switch and get the one bulb that's currently functional. Exposed drywall. Painter's tape along the baseboards. The front door stands solid and original in the middle of all of it, the one thing in this room that's already itself.

I position myself in front of it. Wilfred sits beside me, tail going. We both look out the window.

"Not a word," I tell him.

His tail thumps once against the dusty floor.

I swing open the front door twenty minutes later to Jonathan dressed in gray sweatpants that outline every inch of his lower half and a Spider-Man hoodie I recognize from his college years. I made fun of that hoodie the first time I saw it. I would die before admitting I find it endearing now.

"You called?" He gives me a sleepy grin before bending down to scratch a dancing Wilfred behind the ear.

"Can you turn the weird room into a hidden reading nook?" I grab the banister, foot on the first step.

"Depends." He follows behind me. "What are we talkin'?"

"A bookshelf wall. Dark wood—walnut?—with one book that's actually a latch." I pause on the landing and turn to face him. He's two steps below me, which puts us almost eye level, which I did not think through. "You tug it, and the whole thing swings open."

He's quiet for a moment, actually considering it. "What's behind it?"

"Just a room. But small. Tucked. Like finding something that wasn't meant for everyone." I press my free hand to my chest. "Cozy. Safe. Unexpected."

Jonathan looks at me for a second too long. "Yeah," he says. "Okay."

I blink. "That's it? No interrogation?"

"I'm saving it." He nods up the stairs. "Show me the space."

At the room, I close the door between us and flatten my palms against the wood, sweeping them outward in slow, exaggerated arcs. "Tall shelves. Glossy-ish but not perfect. And instead of a doorknob"—I give an exaggerated yank at invisible air and make a *click* sound with my mouth—"a book with the Reading Lane logo. The latch pops, the door swings open, and you're greeted with an alcove of whispering words."

Jonathan leans against the wall, arms crossed, watching. He has this way of going still when he's actually paying attention, and I've never quite gotten used to it. It's inconvenient.

So is the way he looks in the middle of the night—hair messy, eyes heavy. Completely unguarded… My eyes drift to his sweatpants that leave very little to his imagination.

"So, we're making an alcove?" he says. I jerk my head up. "Is that different from a nook?"

"I will go home."

"You are home."

"I will make you go home."

He grins and reaches for his phone, opening the notes app. The sleeve of his hoodie pushes up his forearm, and I look at the doorframe instead. The doorframe is very interesting. Structurally speaking.

"Okay," he says. "Secret book nook. Bookshelf door, no handle, one special book opens it. Walnut. Glossy but not precious." He's not looking at his phone. He's looking at me. "What goes inside?"

I open my mouth. Close it. I had thought extensively about the door. The inside was, admittedly, an afterthought. "I—something that feels found. Not decorated. Like someone left it exactly right and just walked away."

He nods slowly, like that made complete sense.

"You're not going to make fun of that?"

"Why would I?" He pushes off the wall and moves into the room, hands in his pockets, actually looking around now. Running his eyes over the dimensions, the window, the corner. When he does this—the shift from easy to focused—there's no warning for it. It just happens. "It's a good idea, Mazey."

I drag my gaze to the round window. The dark yard. "It's a lot for a small space."

"It's not about size." His footfalls stop behind me. Close. I can feel the warmth of him in the gap between us. "You said it yourself."

I turn.

He's closer than I expected. His eyes drop to mine and stay there, and I have the sudden distinct sensation of being seen more clearly than I intended. I do not care for it. (I care for it enormously.)

"Cozy," he says quietly. "Safe. Finding a world only you knew existed." He pauses. "I was listening."

The words catch in my throat.

"You don't have to be nice just because I stared at your crotch," I say, because I genuinely cannot stop myself from saying everything that enters my brain. Every single time. No exceptions. It's a gift.

He exhales a sharp breath and reaches for his pen. "If I built something every time someone stared at my crotch," he mutters, scrolling through the notes on his phone, "I'd be running a side business out of my pants."

"That is wildly inappropriate."

"Is it?" He doesn't look up. The pen moves in quick, practiced strokes. After a moment, he turns the page toward me—a rough sketch, just lines, but I can already see the shelves, the door, the proportions of the small room behind it. "Something like this?"

The drawing is perfect.

In the middle of the night, this man took the random string of words I threw at him and put what was in my head onto the page, as if he read my mind.

"Yeah," I whisper, looking up at him. The sound of my heart beating is the only noise for a few beats. "Exactly like that."

He nods, tucks the pen behind his ear, and heads for the door. "Get some sleep. We've got a lot of wood to buy tomorrow."

"That sounds like the side business."

He laughs, and I listen to his footsteps go down the stairs, and then the front door, and then nothing.

Wilfred appears from somewhere and sits on my foot.

"Not a word," I tell him.

His tail thumps once.

✦.✦

Nudging the nook door open with my elbow, I balance a cardboard drink carrier of paper coffee cups in my hands. The last few days have been spent arguing with Jonathan over design and visiting three home improvement stores that somehow felt like four thousand.

Watching Jonathan comb over planks of wood for hours will do that to a person.

He'd trace the grain with his fingertip, brows furrowed, bourbon eyes zeroed in on every inch of timber like it owed him something.

In that moment, I wanted to be a plank of wood. I'm not going to elaborate on that.

"Can you get the tripod while I finish sorting the supplies?" Jonathan asks. Katie's jam-packed schedule means we're on our own for this project. I tried to recruit Elliott, but he was busy with his classes and after-school clubs.

There are no distractions that keep me from interacting with Jonathan. All day. Every day. For at least a week. And he has to teach me how to do most of it, which means that intense, focused look he gets when he explains the simplest things—why anchors are essential for the floating shelves, why the wood grain direction matters—gets directed straight at me on a loop. It's fine. Everything is fine.

Less time around him. That's the goal. The goal is going terribly.

"I brought you some coffee." I hold out a paper cup. "My dad said you always get the breakfast blend, black. So, I took some liberties."

A snort escapes him. "Oh yeah?"

"Yes. But I also didn't want you to go coffee-less in case you hated it, so I brought your boring coffee too." I thrust the second cup at him. "Take a sip first."

He does. I watch the cup hit his lips with the focused attention of an honor roll student cramming for the SATs. (I got a 4.0. This is what I do with it.)

"What is this?" he asks.

"Vanilla cortado. Equal parts espresso and steamed milk, extra vanilla." I open the Reading Lane Journal to today's schedule. "We're prepping the solid-core doors and assembling the bookshelf facade today, right?"

"Yeah." He sets the cortado down and not-so-discreetly pushes the backup coffee toward my bag. "Probably don't need this one."

"Should we paint the shelves before or after we attach them?"

"Doesn't matter." He heads into the hallway.

I follow. "Actually, I was thinking I paint while you do the interior prep, then while you're assembling the shelves, I paint the room. One day instead of two."

He stops walking and turns around slowly. "We have a plan."

"The plan has inefficiencies."

"The plan," he says in the patient tone of someone explaining something to a person they find mildly exhausting, "accounts for dry time. For sequence. For not painting yourself into a corner. Literally." He crosses his arms. "Why are you trying to compress the timeline?"

The real answer sits right behind my teeth. *Because watching you work for eight hours straight is doing uncomfortable things to my nervous system, and I need this project to be over before I say something I can't take back and ruin everything approximately fifty-three days before the most important thing I have ever done.*

"Because it's more efficient," I say.

He looks at me for a beat. Something flickers across his face that I don't love—like he heard the thing I didn't say. He uncrosses his arms. "Fine. Your rodeo."

He takes a long sip of the cortado I brought for his rude ass and lifts it toward me. "Thanks for this."

"My dad added it to the menu. It's called The Extra John-tado." I rock back on my heels. "In case you ever want to order it again without having to describe your entire personality to a barista."

The corner of his mouth moves. "I'll keep that in mind."

He marches off, and I stand there for a second, watching him go, before turning back to grab my bag.

It's fallen over. I crouch to right it, and that's when I see the book half-tucked underneath. *The Keeper's Guestbook*, the bookmark still sitting in Chapter 12 where I left it. (Of course it is. It's always exactly where it needs to be. The cottage has no sense of timing and also impeccable timing.)

I pick it up. Flip to the page.

The highlighted sentence is right where I left it too, like it's been waiting.

"There is always a middle ground, if two people choose to meet there with kindness and respect."

I stare at it.

The thing about this book—the infuriating, specific thing—is that it never says anything I don't already know. It just says it at the exact moment I've run out of excuses not to act on it. Every single time. Without fail. Like it has a calendar.

I know how to meet in the middle. I'm good at it, actually, with everyone except the one person it apparently counts for right now.

I close the book. Put it back in my bag.

Kindness and respect, I think. Fine.

I go get the paint.

I'm already in the nook, book open in my lap, when a cup appears in my face.

"Here." Jonathan doesn't make eye contact when he hands it over. "Toasted marshmallow thing. The dessert one you always get."

I look at the cup. Then up at him.

He's already turning away, scanning the room, hands going to his belt to check his tools like he didn't just walk in here with my exact coffee order from memory. Like that's nothing. Like I'm supposed to just receive that information and continue existing normally.

"If this has poison in it," I say, "Nova will murder you."

"Poison-free." He crouches to check the alignment of the bottom shelf bracket, still not looking at me. "I promise."

I take a sip.

It's perfect. It's always perfect, the toasted marshmallow thing, but somehow it's more aggravating when someone else gets it right. When someone else just *knows*. Without being asked. Without being told.

"Thanks," I say. "I think."

He nods once, like that's settled, and I look back down at my book so I don't have to figure out what my face is doing.

He brought me coffee. He just *knew*, and showed up with it, and handed it over like it was nothing, and now I'm sitting here holding it like evidence of the thing I'm not ready to name.

Stop it. It's coffee.

But it's not coffee.

"Do you have the fake book spines done?" he asks.

"Yes." I set the book aside and stand. "Nova and I finished them a few days ago. We watched rom-coms and painted. Some of them we used stickers for the lettering." I'm rambling, I can feel it, but I keep going. "They turned out really good, actually. Better than I expected."

Jonathan goes still for just a moment. Not long—just a beat. It could mean nothing—and then he picks up the drill. "Yeah?"

"Yeah."

"Good." He sets the drill down again, picks up the level instead, then sets that down too. "We need to attach the shelves and the spines today. Get the latch mounted. Should be able to finish if you want to help."

"What else would I be doing?"

"I just—" He stops. Picks up the level again. "I could stay late and do it myself if you had other things to do. I didn't want you to feel like you had to be here."

"Jonathan."

"I'm just saying you have options—"

"You suck at being nice."

He exhales. "I know." But the corner of his mouth gives him away.

He steps over the coil of extension cords into the hallway, jaw set, tools clinking at his belt, and I follow him to where the door is balanced across the sawhorses. We lift it together without discussing it, settling it into position across the makeshift workspace. His end goes down a half second after mine, like he was waiting to make sure I had it first. I notice everything. It's a problem.

"This one's the most work," he mutters, pulling out the measuring tape.

I hover near my end, watching him mark the spots. "Smart move keeping the original door."

"Solid-core." He doesn't look up. "Anything hollow and the hinges would've split it."

"Still just a disguise though."

He pauses and looks up at that briefly with an expression I can't quite read. "Yeah," he says. "Still just a disguise."

He goes back to marking. I go back to watching him and pretending I'm not.

"I want it to feel like a secret," I say, to say something, to fill the specific silence that's been building between us all morning. "When someone opens it for the first time, I want them to feel like they found something."

"It will." He sets down the measuring tape and looks up at me fully this time. There it is again—that stillness, that attention that has nowhere safe to land. "I'll make sure of it."

"Okay," I say.

"Okay." He nods at the screws. "Hand me a few of those."

I scoop up an absurd handful.

"A few," he says, and something loosens in his expression when he laughs, his palm out without looking. I drop the extras back into the toolbox one by one until he closes his hand around what's left.

The drill hums. I hold my end of the door steady. We're close enough that I can hear him breathe, close enough that when he reaches across me for the level our elbows brush and neither of us comments on it.

This is fine, I think. This is just work. I have approximately zero percent of my brain dedicated to work right now, but the intention is there.

"Next one's lower," he says.

I shift to give him room and move too fast. My hand catches the angled edge of a board stacked beside us. I feel it before I see it—the top piece lurching with a sharp wooden scrape—and then everything happens at once.

"Stop—"

The drill hits the floor. His arm comes across my waist, hard and certain, pulling me back into him, and the board smacks the ground exactly where my feet were.

We don't move.

The board settles. Dust lifts. Somewhere down the hall something drips.

His arm is still across me, hand spread just below my ribs, and I am acutely aware of every point of contact: his chest against my back, his chin near my temple, the way his grip tightened when the board hit and hasn't loosened since.

The last thing I need is an injury to set back the progress, I think, and even in my own head it sounds like a lie. A bad one. The kind I wouldn't even grade on a curve.

"You okay?" His voice is low. Close.

"I didn't see it."

"I've got you." He loosens his grip—not releasing, just loosening, giving me the option—and I make a choice I'm not going to examine right now and press back into him instead.

We stay there for just a breath. His hand below my ribs, my back against his chest, the dust still settling around us.

"You've got to watch where you plant yourself," he says quietly, and his lips are close enough to my ear that I feel the words as much as hear them.

I turn.

We are very close. I can see the sawdust caught on his cheekbone, one small pale fleck just below his eye. I reach up before I've made the conscious decision to, and brush it away with my thumb.

"You had something there," I say. "Didn't want it to get in your eye."

His gaze drops to my mouth. Darts back up.

The room is very quiet.

"Thanks," he says.

He clears his throat. Steps back. His hand leaves my ribs, and I feel the absence of it like a temperature change.

"It's almost lunch." He bends to pick up the fallen board, not looking at me, securing it against the wall with more care than it needs. "I'll go grab something. That sandwich you got yesterday—you want that one again? It was good. I mean, mine was good. Yours looked good too, I just—" He stops then sets the board down. "Yeah. I'll go get sandwiches."

He doesn't look at me when he passes.

I stand in the middle of the room and listen to his footsteps disappear.

My hand is still raised. I lower it slowly.

He stepped away. He's the one who stepped away, and then couldn't finish a sentence about a sandwich, and now I'm standing here in a half-built secret room with sawdust on my thumb and absolutely nowhere to put any of this.

So, I pick up the drill, and I go back to work.

Chapter 16

Finding Anne

Mazey (holding up a velvet-spined book): "Every room needs something to find.
A book tucked behind a cushion. A note pressed inside a lamp shade.
Something that makes a guest feel like the cottage knew they were coming."
[Nova, off-screen]: "Should I be writing this down?"
Mazey: "I'm making it up as I go."
Nova: "So, yes."

"**I** love that you have a list of penis names," I say to Sawyer. Nova and I are sitting across from her in the new robin's egg blue chairs, parked at the vintage dining table that was delivered yesterday. The table is beyond gorgeous. Its weathered oak top and spindle legs—painted the same soft blue as the chairs—rest on an oversize floral rug. The rug is slightly frayed at the corners but bursting with color. The freshly installed crown molding and soft gray paint on the walls brighten the whole room.

"Oh, but what kind of romance author would I be if I didn't?" Sawyer reads from the list on her phone as if she were a newscaster. "My favorites, even though I'm not sure when I'd ever use them, include the velveteen hammer and pink pogo stick."

"Pink pogo stick." Nova laughs, wiping a tear from her eye as she continues to work on website design. "I know these aren't in your novels."

"Could you imagine?" I swing my body to face Nova and put my hand on her cheek as if she were my lover. "*I just want your trouser trout inside me."*

Nova, of course, plays along. She leans into my palm, batting her eye lashes. *"Oh, sugar plum, I thought you'd never ask. But only if I can diddle your button."*

"Diddle your button?" Sawyer scrunches up her face. "You two should stick with reading. Definitely not writing."

It's wild that a couple months ago, I could barely talk to Sawyer. Now, we're talking about penises and decorating Reading Lane.

Our friendship has grown into a three-person group chat complaining about having nothing good for supper and wanting to run away from adult responsibilities. Next week, she and Evie officially move into their new house, which Brody helped her find. It's conveniently located right next to Elliott's house across the lake. I'm comforted knowing she'll have a familiar face if she needs something.

"I can't believe so many people have been dropping off boxes of books and stuff." I add the cat-shaped bookends one of the guys working on the porch dropped off to the *quirky shelf decorations pile,* snuggling it between a brass pumpkin teapot and a vase covered in hand painted roses.

"You can never have too many tchotchkes." Sawyer opens a box filled with class novels from a thrifting adventure Nova and I went on. "It's nice you don't have to buy everything."

"Yeah, I was freaking out when we found out that the sub-flooring in all the bathrooms needed to be replaced. I had to rearrange the budget, and sadly, the decor took the biggest hit." I take a sip of the coffee Jonathan dropped off for us this morning. It's my favorite blend with the perfect amount of toasted marshmallow syrup, filling me with warm happiness.

"Katie posted about donations on our socials for gently used books and charming decor, and the public delivered," Nova says, still laser focused on her laptop. "Mostly people from Honeyville, but we got a couple packages in the mail."

"That's so awesome." Sawyer gently sets a stack of Brontë novels next to a tower of Edger Allen Poe's work.

"Hey, how is Evie adjusting to Honeyville? Making new friends?"

I ask.

"Pretty good." Sawyer crosses to the window, peeking around the sheer curtain for a better view of Elliott and Evie painting Adirondack chairs on the beach. "Elliott has really helped. He's running a Dungeons and Dragons campaign after school that she made a friend at."

Sawyer walks back to the table and pulls out another stack of books from the box. "I'm happy that he knows the kids and can tell me if they are going to corrupt my kid. Being a parent to an almost teenager is so fucking terrifying."

"No thank you. I am happy to be Evie's aunt Nova, but I am not going to be giving her non-blood cousins." Nova has vowed to avoid birthing kids, because of her type 1 diabetes, but I've seen the longing look in her eye when she sees a pregnant mom pass by or a baby carriage at the park.

"Elliott loves kids. Just wait until he geeks out over all the gross bugs he's into." I add a rotary phone to the collection from a box Tottie dropped off labeled "Shit for Mazey."

We all laugh. Sawyer and I dig back into the boxes, debating shelf space and swapping opinions on where a ceramic owl has any business being. All the while, Nova types away, quietly keeping us all together.

"Feast your eyes on this." Nova slides her laptop towards me with a flourish.

The screen lights up with a hand-drawn illustration. A storybook-style cottage is nestled between tall evergreens, stars twinkling in the ink-dark sky above. An open book rests in the foreground, its pages curled. The words "Reading Lane" swirl across the bottom in emerald green script. My favorite color. My dream made visible.

Nova nods to the screen. "So? What do you think? Should I mock it up in other colors, or is emerald green the winner?"

"I do love the green, but…" I bite the inside of my cheek, thinking about the Reading Lane sign hanging in the front. Where would I put it? "What about lavender?"

Nova tilts her head, considering. "Lavender."

"For the sign out front. On a post, so people can see it from the road." I picture it instantly—the painted wood, the same swirling script, catching the afternoon light at the end of the gravel path. "The green is perfect for the logo, but the sign should feel like an invitation. Lavender feels like that."

Nova pulls the laptop back without a word, fingers already moving. A few clicks later she turns the screen back around. Same cottage, same swirling script, same twinkling stars—but the words "Reading Lane" bloom in soft lavender, warm and welcoming.

"Like that?" she asks.

I press my hand to my chest. "Exactly like that."

Nova pops her head up. "Mazey, be honest with me. Are you aware how awesome this is going to be? Do you believe that you are putting together something so incredible?"

Sawyer chuckles. "It is awesome. I wish there were more places with the same goals as Reading Lane. Being an author has a great community, but it's mostly solo work. And it's so hard to meet anyone. The writer weekends Nova was telling me about are going to be incredible."

"That's the goal," I say, attempting to be as confident as they sound.

Sawyer flips over the box that held the classics, breaking it down for recycling. A book tumbles onto the table.

"Oh, I missed one. Wait a second, did you say this is your favorite book?" Sawyer hands me a familiar book with rose gold embossing.

Nova jumps from her chair, catching it before it tipped over. "Is that a copy of *Anne*?"

"Yeah, but there are like a million copies of this book." Sawyer shrugs her shoulders. "It's a great novel, but—"

"Is it the one?" Nova asks, now at my side, opposite Sawyer.

I flip to the inside cover.

It is the same one. I trace my finger over the handwriting. The book Jonathan gave me at my MBA graduation.

"Aww, that's the sweetest note. I wonder who it's to." Sawyer slides my finger from the top of the note, where the recipient's name is written. "That's your name."

Mazey,
You are whimsical enough to believe there is a way, unconventional

enough to find the way, and courageous enough to make the way.
Jonathan

"I thought this was gone forever." I don't need a mirror to know the color has drained from my face. "We—Bobby and I— kept looking for it, but it never showed up."

Nova filled Sawyer in on the history of this book. How it went missing when I moved back to Honeyville after college. How Bobby and I looked for it in every nook and cranny from Honeyville to my alma mater. How I eventually made peace with the fact that it was just gone—one of those things you lose in the chaos of moving on. But here it is, sitting on a table in the middle of my dream come true, found in a box of donated books on the very day Reading Lane is starting to feel real.

I stare at his scribbles for a long time. Long enough that Sawyer quietly drifts back to the boxes, and Nova gently squeezes my shoulder before returning to her laptop.

Whimsical enough to believe there is a way.

I have whispered those words to myself more times than I could ever count. In the dark of my room the night before a meeting I wasn't sure I was ready for. In the parking lot of the bank the morning I sat across from a loan officer who looked at my business plan like it was a crayon drawing. In Nova's and my apartment when I moved back to Honeyville with nothing but a degree, a bruised ego, and the quiet, embarrassing faith that maybe I wasn't done yet.

Somehow that made the words feel more fragile. Like I had imagined them. Like maybe I had inflated the meaning, the way grief does, turning an ordinary moment into something sacred just because you can't touch it anymore. Dawson used to tell me I was the whimsy to his logic. I never believed him—being whimsical was something girls way cooler than me were. I was never playfully quaint or amusingly appealing. I was a nerd.

But then Jonathan told me I was. In his handwriting. In my favorite book.

Courageous enough to make the way.

He wrote that before I made anything. Before Reading Lane was even a flicker of something I would actually do. He wrote it standing at the edge of who I was and somehow already saw who I was going to become. I don't know how to hold that without it splitting me a little open.

I close the cover carefully and set the book flat on the table, palm resting on top of it.

I have spent a significant amount of energy, particularly in the last several months, trying to file my feelings for Jonathan into a neat and sensible category. Colleague. Friend. Complicated history. That usually works fine until a moment like this one sneaks up and makes a mess of the whole filing system.

Because the truth—the one I turn over quietly and then try to put back down—is that he has been in my corner longer than almost anyone. Not loudly or in a way that asked for anything back. Just steadily, the way good people are—leaving coffee outside the door, slipping words into the inside cover of a book, trusting that one day I would be ready to believe them.

I believed them. I just didn't always know they were still carrying me.

I pick the book back up and slide it into my bag. Is this another gift from the cottage? If it is, how is that even possible?

CHAPTER 17

Unzip Me

*@slowburnordie: the shed episode broke something in me and i'm
choosing not to examine why too closely*
*@pagesandpeonies: nova sending her in a hazmat suit is the
most chaotic act of love i've ever witnessed*
*@softcoverromantic: the shed looked great at the end. totally focused
on the shed the whole time. completely.*
*@booksbeforeboys: replying to @softcoverromantic the shed. yes.
we were all watching the shed.*

Jonathan and I stand in the doorway of the miniature version of the cottage. The early morning sunlight beams through the door. By the looks of it, the previous owners emptied the big house and crammed everything they couldn't be bothered to haul away into this twenty-by-twenty tomb of abandoned junk.

I glance over at Jonathan, pull my glove on with a snap, and nod with the best serious face I can muster in this outfit. My attempts are futile as I collapse into a fit of laughter. I am fully suited as if I'm entering a biohazard zone. Not just gloves and a mask. Oh no. I'm wearing a full-body protective suit. The kind that looks straight out of sci-fi movies when the CDC has to make an appearance.

"I feel like your outfit might be… slightly overkill," he says. I can't argue with him. I'm cosplaying as a Pixar character about to save the world.

"Nova got me this specifically for this project." I adjust the elastic around my wrists. "She said if I got bitten by, and I quote, 'one of the critters that is yet to be discovered because they live in here and only here,' and died, she'd be super mad at me. Apparently, I'm one of the few that can put Larry in his place when he gets too sassy."

He tilts his head, hand coming up to rub his jaw. "So, we're risking death to help tame an old man? I'm pretty sure your mom can handle that task."

"Do not put that image in my head!" I fling my arm in a back-handed swat across his arm, immediately regretting the action as my knuckles are met with a brick wall he calls a bicep. He chuckles.

"Well, at least you'll be safe."

My eyes trace his body—only to determine how safe he will be against an army of spiders, of course. The grey sweatpants and t-shirt that squeezes his biceps in the exact right places has no effect on me. At all. I clear my throat.

"You, on the other hand, are completely screwed."

"Just what I was hoping for today. Death by spiders." He ventures deeper into the shed.

Then I remember a little fact about Jonathan I've long forgotten, and a mischievous grin spreads across my face. He's terrified of spiders. I fight the urge to rub my hands together, evil villain style, and tuck that piece of information away for later.

"What was that about?"

"What was what?"

"You did that thing you do when you're plotting to prank some-one." He mimics my expression—the grin, the gleam in my eyes. "You know you're terrible at hiding it, right?"

"Alright. Where do you think we should start?" On the outside, I ignore his demonstration. On the inside? On the inside, my heart tightens at the fact that he knows such a small gesture of mine. *No, this is not the time, Mazey. Focus on cleaning out this hot mess of a future office.* "Oh, we need to record. Let me grab my phone."

Patting down my super suit, I realize my phone is in my legging pocket. Under the layers. From the journey to the bathroom earlier, I know that I cannot access it without assistance. Nova helped me earlier, but she's left to run errands.

"What?" Jonathan glares at me.

"My phone. It's… it's in a difficult place to get to," I admit.

He runs his hands through his hair. "And where, Mazey, would that be?"

I bite my lower lip and look up at him. "My leggings. But we can just use your phone, right?"

Jonathan holds up his phone, which is nearly dead. "It's, like, eight in the morning. How the hell do you not have any battery?"

"I fell asleep answering emails last night and forgot to plug it in." He gives me a shrug.

He fell asleep answering emails? To the point that his phone died? I study him closer—the shadows under his eyes a shade darker than last week, the way his shoulders carry a new kind of weight. When did working late go from occasional to constant?

I have two choices—grill him on the serious topic of stress or try to get the guy riled up enough to forget for a few. I choose the latter.

"What kind of psychopath doesn't plug their phone before they fall asleep at night? Do you do this regularly? Now you are going to have to unzip me and reach into my pants to get mine."

His eyebrows shoot up, a grin growing across his face. "Excuse me? You keep your phone inside of your pants?"

"Have you heard of a pocket, you idiot?" I turn my back to him, biting the inside of my cheek. "Unzip me."

"You're telling me you can't do this alone?"

"Oh, I'm sorry. You're right. Totally forgot I am a contortionist. Let me just pull my arm out of socket to do a task that you could easily do…"

Before I can turn back around, I feel his shaky hand brush my hair to the side. I reach up to help. Our fingers graze, lingering longer than necessary before I gather the bird's nest of curls in my palm. His hand settles on my shoulder with a gentle squeeze, holding me in place. I hold my breath. Maybe to keep me from spinning around and throwing myself on him. Maybe because subconsciously I think it'll help speed up the process. I have no idea.

The zipper slides down, *zzzzzip* filling the silence. Shivers race up my spine, counter to the slow drag of his knuckles.

"My phone is on the left. The pocket is on the side of my thigh." My throat feels desert dry with each word.

His hand moves from the front of my thigh to the back. Time slows down. It has to. There is no other explanation for the way the search for a freaking pocket is taking an eternity.

I gulp.

Feeling the warmth radiating from him is sending tingling shivers to my lady bits, and this is not that kind of party.

Right?

Right.

"You really don't know what pockets are, do you?"

"I've never worn leggings before, so no. I don't know how legging pockets work," he grunts.

"By the waistband." Outfit regret consumes my entire soul. I'm making Nova pay for dinner tonight for making me wear a supersuit to clean out a shed. "They are high-waisted. You are going to have to lift my shirt a bit."

"Of-fucking-course. I have to touch her more. Because that's what I need right now—a hard-on," he mutters, and I feel my cheek blaze. Does he not realize he said the quiet part out loud?

He squats down, falling forward slightly into the lowest part of my back. "You are so fucking short."

"Maybe you're just so fucking tall…" I let the words trail off. Calloused fingers graze the space above my waist but below my boob. The area that sends anticipation straight to your nipples and makes them hard enough to cut diamonds.

"Too far," I gulp. "Figure out clothing, dude."

Finally, he retrieves my phone and zips me up. I feel like I need a cigarette and a nap. And I don't even smoke.

Jonathan puts the troublesome device in my face, and I swipe it from his grasp. He squints toward the back as I get the video app ready on the tripod. "The corner?"

"The corner it is," I say and trudge in that direction.

He follows. "If I die, please make sure Elliott doesn't do anything stupid at my funeral. He said he was going to avenge me with a dramatic monologue. Or a dance party."

"Totally. I'll add that to the list. Only candlelight vigils and melo-dramatic acoustic versions of pop songs." I undo a trash bag.

"Sounds delightful," he says.

His grin dares me to keep going, "Let's just hope the spider over-lord isn't home."

"You're telling me." His eyebrows furrow.

Around hour four, I peel off the last of my cleaning armor. I feel Jonathan staring. He's cataloging every inch of me. Is he planning on retrieving me more protective gear? That way he knows what size to get me? That's a reasonable reason why he hasn't stopped looking at me. It doesn't explain why my nipples peak at just the thought of his eyes on me.

I do the only thing I can think of and call him out on it. "You okay there, Chief?"

"Yep, all good," he manages, seemingly unable to peel his eyes from my figure.

"Tell your face that." I bend over in sweat-slicked and paint-smeared leggings and an old college tee stretched thin at the collar to straighten a box tower. Stray curls have escaped the bun I resorted to a little bit ago and cling to my flushed cheeks. Giggling, I turn, sit down with my back against the wall, knees pulled up, arms resting casually on top.

"You teach at the community center, right? The ones that help teach people hobbies and certifications and stuff?" I say in a quiet voice.

"Yeah, it's my favorite part of the job," he says, folding the clothes we found into donation boxes. "I've started teaching the glass-blowing class too. The old teacher retired."

I pull a stack of old paperwork out of a box and set the straightened piles into a plastic tote.

"So, is construction your thing then? Your true passion?" I ask, continuing my task.

He closes the box I just filled with packing tape. "My passion?"

"You know, your happy place. Your obsession. The thing that makes your heart feel like you've eaten a million gummy bears but not coated in sugar. Mine is reading. The whole reason we are forced to work together." I stop and look at him. "That, and to save the Pathway Program. But you get what I mean."

"My happy place…" He pauses, considering my question. "I enjoy those things, but I'm not sure they are my passion."

"Then what is it?" My question was supposed to be simple to answer. "Earth to Jonathan. I didn't ask you to solve interstellar travel."

I throw a wadded up paper towel at him, hitting him square in the forehead.

"I haven't thought about that before," he says, tossing the paper towel back at me.

"Well, think about what makes you the happiest. Where do you go when you need clarity? Or when you are sad? Or when you're happy? The thing you think about at random times throughout the day?" I break down the empty box. "For me, escaping into someone else's world helps give my world clarity. It doesn't matter the book, I find some sort of connection to what is going on in my life. The good, the bad, and the fucked up."

"I guess that would be teaching at the community center," he says. "I really love that."

"Have you ever thought about making it more?" I ask, part curious, part loving watching him squirm at having to answer personal questions.

"I'm not sure I can do that. When my grandparents retired, I knew I had to take on the company. There was no other option."

"They forced you to become CEO?"

"No, not really. They never forced me to do anything. But I also knew that they hoped my…" He rubs his hand through his hair. "My dad would be the one to take it over. But we all know how that played out."

"I don't. Not really. Just the rumors."

"After my mom died, my dad dropped me off at my grandparents', and I never saw him again. I have no idea where he is or what he is doing," Jonathan says.

The silence that follows hits different than the comfortable kind we'd built over the last four hours. This one has weight to it.

I set down the box I'm holding and look at him fully. I knew this. I knew this, and somehow hearing him say it out loud still knocks the air clean out of me.

My brother had told me once, years ago, the way kids relay information—matter-of-fact, no real concept of the gravity of it. *Jonathan's dad left. Just dropped him off at his grandparents' and never came back.* I'd been maybe twelve at the time. Old enough to understand what that meant, young enough to not fully grasp the shape of that kind of wound. I'd filed it away somewhere and hadn't thought much about it since.

I'm thinking about it now.

"I didn't know it was after your mom," I say quietly. "I just knew the version my brother knew."

He nods.

"I was seven." He sets a folded shirt into the donation box with more care than a worn-out flannel warrants. "So the details are—they're fuzzy in the places you'd think they'd be sharpest."

Seven. Around the time he met Elliott. I do the quiet, horrible math of it. Seven years old. Still young enough to believe, on some level, that your dad is coming back. That there's a reason.

I think about seven-year-old Jonathan and feel something protective claw its way up the center of my chest. Which is insane. He is a six-foot-something solid construction CEO sitting four feet away from me. He does not need protecting.

"Your grandparents," I start carefully. "They were good? I remember Elliott saying—"

"The best." And there it is. The first time in this entire conversation his voice loses the careful, measured quality he wraps around everything. It goes warm and unguarded and completely unpolished. "Everything I know about being a decent person came from them." He pauses. "Which probably explains why the bar is so high and why I'm perpetually exhausted."

A surprised laugh escapes me before I can catch it. He glances over and his expression eases slightly.

He made a joke. File that away.

"So, when the company needed someone," he says softly, connecting the dots I'd always had but never quite lined up.

"It was never really a question." I finish his sentence.

He shrugs, but it isn't careless. It's the kind that carries the full weight of something you've already made peace with—or told yourself you have. "They never forced me. They never even asked, not directly. But I knew what they hoped my dad would—" He stops. Starts over. "I knew what was supposed to happen. And it didn't. So."

So, he stepped into the space his father hollowed out and called it a choice.

I press my lips together. *Do not say that out loud, Mazey. You are not his therapist. You are a woman sitting on the floor of a future office that currently smells like mildew and questionable life decisions.*

"That's a lot to carry," I say instead. Careful. Quiet.

He looks at me sideways. "Don't do that."

"Do what?"

"The soft voice. You're about to feel sorry for me, and I need you to not do that."

"I don't feel sorry for you," I say. "I feel sorry for seven-year-old you. Present day you is annoyingly well-adjusted, all things considered." I gesture at him—the whole of him. "Infuriatingly so, actually. It's rude."

The corner of his mouth pulls up. Just barely. Just enough.

There. Something loosens in my chest at the sight of it.

"Your brother talks too much," he says, but there's no heat behind it.

"Constantly. It's his worst quality." I reach for another box and rip off the tape. "That and his truly offensive taste in movies. But that's a separate intervention."

He huffs out something almost resembling a laugh.

I glance at him from under my lashes, just for a second. He's back to folding, shoulders marginally lower than they were sixty seconds ago. The confession has been tucked back away—not gone, just returned to wherever he keeps things that are too big to leave out in the open.

He told me anyway. That's the part I can't stop turning over. He knew I had half the story and gave me the rest of it. Voluntarily. In a dusty shed at noon on a random Tuesday.

I don't know what to do with that.

I break down the empty box in my hands, the cardboard collapsing in on itself with a flat, satisfying crunch.

Nothing, I tell myself firmly. *You do absolutely nothing with it.*

My heart, apparently, did not receive that memo.

Chapter 18

"Subject remains in the vicinity long after the task is complete. Experts believe this is intentional. Subject would disagree." - Why Won't You Kiss Me?: A Field Guide to Curious Behaviors Between Soulmates, Chapter Four: "The Lingering"

Rain drums steady against the window as I head to the kitchen to make dinner, Wilfred's paws tap-dancing behind me. I toss the latest book club pick onto the counter. It lands with a thud that echoes through the too-quiet house. I pause. It's not that quiet. The rain is right there, filling every corner of the silence like it's supposed to. Wilfred's nails click against the tile. The refrigerator hums its usual tuneless hum.

I open the refrigerator and stand there longer than I should, deciding what to have for dinner, the cold air settling around my ankles. There's that feeling—the one that makes me glance toward the hallway without meaning to.

It's probably the cottage trying to steal my toilet paper.

"Not going to happen, Daisy!" I shout to the walls. "I'm here to stay, Anne."

A chuckle comes from the pantry.

Adrenaline shoots through me and I nearly jump through the ceiling.

What the actual fuck? Is someone fucking here?

I keep my eyes on the pantry door and blindly grab the nearest weapon: wooden spatula. On raised feet, I slowly turn the nob, exposing a man crouched down in the corner with a headlamp around the crown of his head.

Without thinking, I start swinging my trusty wooden weapon. The man throws his arms up to shield himself, headlamp swinging wildly and throwing chaotic streaks of light across the pantry shelves.

"Mazey! It's me, Jonathan!" The man yells, but my spatula is already mid-arc when the man's words register.

Thud.

The headlamp swings wildly as he doubles over.

"Jonathan?"

"Ouch!" He clutches the top of his head.

"Oh my God, I'm so sorry!" I lower the spatula, heart still hammering. "What the hell are you doing hiding in my pantry in the middle of the night?"

"Middle of the night?" He straightens up, squinting against his own headlamp. "It's seven!"

"I'm so sorry!" I rush to the freezer and pull out an ice pack, wrapping it in a dish towel. I turn and run into Jonathan's bulky chest. I gulp looking up at his towering form. "Here. Put this on your head."

"Thanks." He wraps his hand around mine—his warmth a stark contrast to the ice pack—and slides it from my grasp. "I had to fix the shelf before it came crashing down."

"Oh, that makes sense. Why are you doing it now, though? Shouldn't you be at home or on a date or something?"

"I was at home, but when I realized I forgot to take care of it today. I came back to prevent a domino situation from scaring you in the middle of the night." He walks over to a stool that sits next to the kitchen island. "So much for that."

"Want a grilled cheese?" I tug down two plates from the cabinet.

"Sure. Thanks."

"Have you read any of the books on the list I texted you last week?"

"Started one, actually." He shifts the ice pack. "The one with the enemies thing."

I flip the first sandwich, butter hissing against the pan. "And?"

"It's good. I like the part where they're forced to work together and hate every second of it."

"The reluctant truce." I smile despite myself. "Classic."

"Is that bad?"

"No, it's just—" I slide his plate across the island. "It's the most reliable thing in fiction. Put two people who can't stand each other in a situation where they have no choice, and suddenly you can't put the book down."

Mine don't do the reluctant truce. I think about the worn spines on my nightstand. The stories where it's quieter than a reluctant truce. Where it's a look held a beat too long, or someone remembering exactly how the other person takes their coffee without ever being asked. The slow-build. Nothing dramatic happens, and somehow that's the whole point.

"You don't like it," Jonathan says.

"I love it," I say, and I mean it. "It's just not my favorite flavor."

He picks up the grilled cheese. "What's your favorite flavor?"

I pour two glasses of water and set one in front of him.

"The kind where they don't realize it's already happening."

I set the bread and cheese on the counter and glance over at Jonathan. He's already made himself at home on the stool, ice pack balanced on his head, and is flipping through the book club pick I tossed onto the counter earlier.

"What are you reading?"

"This week's book. I need to read it before Tottie excommunicates me."

"Both of them?"

"Yeah, there are two books." He holds a book in each hand, showing me the covers of two books. The novel on the left is the one assigned for book club, Doris's pick. No telling what sort of shifter, why-choose romance it is. There may not even be a plot. It might just be straight sex. That woman is a wild card. His right hand holds a book I've never seen before.

"Did you buy me another book?" I grab the unfamiliar paperback. "Come on, Jonathan, *Why Won't You Kiss Me?: A Field Guide to Curious Behaviors Between Soulmates.* Soulmates?"

"I didn't bring it. I haven't been to the bookstore since the challenge with Sawyer." He raises his hands in the air. "You think I'm just hiding books around this place?"

"Are you?" I lean forward.

I'm still struggling to believe that the cottage understands what is going on inside of it and is presenting me with magical books that push me in the direction I should be going. It makes more sense that Jonathan is planting them.

Is Jonathan planting them? Did he plant the first one to draw me into the cottage so I'd partner with him? I think back to the day that I found *The Story of Daisy and Jonas.* I didn't see the book until I was already drawn to the cottage, and he wasn't on board with the vlog.

"Definitely not." He laughs.

Damn, I did not crack the book mystery.

I open to a random page and read a highlighted passage.

Stand in front of them. Look them in the eye. Say the thing you've been avoiding. It might be terrifying. It might make your palms sweat, your voice crack, or your knees wobble. Don't keep walking on a tightrope above a pit of wiggling jelly.

So, just ask. Stop circling, stop hinting, stop inventing cryptic metaphors about elephants, pancakes, or magical cottages. Ask the question. Let it land. Let it be messy, awkward, and human. And then you can work on love. Take the risk.

I let the words roll through my brain for a minute as I return to assembling the grilled cheese. The amount of times I've taken a risk in the past few months is astonishing. Buying the cottage, partnering with Jonathan, not returning to a job with security and benefits—and every moment in between. The world didn't come crashing down when I took the leap—at least not yet. What's one more jump?

Jonathan is mumbling something in the background about how the pantry has been a total disaster, thing after thing breaking or coming apart. I wasn't paying close enough attention, too busy parsing through the potential impact of just asking the questions I've been pondering.

"That night. In college. Why were you such an ass?" My eyes start to dampen at the memory of being shoved to the side.

"You had been drinking…"

"Jonathan." I pin him with a glare. "We both know I wasn't drunk. I had one beer over the course of the entire night."

"Mazey, don't do this." His words echo that night.

"*Jonathan.* I finally got the courage to act on what I wanted…" I sigh at the vulnerability bursting out of my chest. "And you tossed me away. Like an old cheeseburger wrapper you found under the seat in your car."

"That's not what happened." He moves to me. Reaches out to stroke my arm. I pull away. "And you know it."

"Do I? Why do you think I've avoided you? Why do you think our friendship faded into a fury of mean-spirited insults, instead of the light-hearted teasing it once was? You hurt me. I thought we were building up to some epic brother's best friend, friends-to-lovers romance. With the angst of years of seeing you heal from losing your mother. Finding yourself." My voice raises as a stream of tears runs down my face. "Turns out, I was just the naive little sister who was allowed to tag along out of obligation."

"Mazey, it wasn't like that." His palm cradles my cheek, wiping away the tears.

I shake my head away. "I heard you tell those guys at the party that you only hung out with me because I was Elliott's little sister. That you felt sorry for me because I only had one friend. Because I'd never been on a date or been kissed."

Jonathan's face squishes together, expression slack. He has no idea what I'm talking about. Jonathan had taken me under his wing freshman year of college—showed me the best places to get cheeseburgers on campus, gave me tips to help balance the amount of work so I wouldn't get overwhelmed, laughed in the quad on our way to class. We spent so much time together, Elliott started teasing Jonathan about his intentions.

I thought the crush I had fostered for years was mutual. That we were on our way to a real relationship. My first relationship.

Then Jonathan and Elliott had a house party to celebrate first semester coming to an end. Nova and I were shocked when my brother said we could go. I'm not sure why—he always included us. Hanging out with the upperclassman gave me that feeling of being included in something elite.

About an hour into the party, I was hot and needing a break from the crowd, so I went outside. Jonathan found me on the swing that hung from the only tree in their backyard. Put his hands on my back to give me a gentle push. Tingles flew through my body the second his fingers touched me. We talked and laughed like we always did until he stopped the swing and crossed in front of me. He lowered himself to eye-level. My skin flushed as sweat poured down my back. I couldn't tell if it was from nerves or the first beer I'd ever had forty-five minutes before.

The backyard was quiet apart from the low thumping coming from the party inside. Maybe that was from inside my chest? I can't remember now. I do remember leaning forward, unable to take the silence, and wrapping my arms around his neck. Our lips were so close, the air between us was nothing but our combined breath.

Until. Until he pulled back and told me not to do this and walked inside.

I followed him, needing to know where I went wrong. What did I do? I thought it was the natural next step. A kiss of the ages. One that would be found in-between romance novels described as the best kiss ever written.

Instead, I found him talking to his friends about how sorry he felt for me. How I was a loser without any friends. That the happiest moments so far in college, in my life, were out of pity because of a tragedy that happened to me in high school—losing Dawson.

I found Nova and left.

"What was it like? Because it sure felt like I was pathetic. A loser. I spent the rest of the year with my head down, throwing myself into my classes. Nova got so concerned, she made me see the counseling center on campus."

"Because of me?" Jonathan runs his hands over his face. "Jesus, Mazey. I'm so sorry."

"Because I lost Dawson. Because I was falling for—" The words catch in my throat. I wipe a stray tear from my face. "It's fine that you didn't like me. I mean, it sucked, but did you really have to talk about me to your friends? Laugh about how I tried to kiss you?"

"Mazey," Jonathan says, stepping towards me. "I was trying to protect you."

"Oh, that's rich. *Protect* me? You said horrible things about me. Those things don't just go away, Jonathan. They stay with a girl forever. In the back of their head, haunting them."

"Those guys weren't my friends. They just showed up. I saw them after I left you, and I confronted them. I don't remember their names, but one of them made a comment about…" He trails off. Rubs the back of his neck.

"Excuse me? What was that?"

"Mazey. It wasn't very nice."

"Tell me. Now."

Jonathan huffs. "He wouldn't shut up about you. About your tits. Your hips, pulling your hair when he…"

"I get the picture." I put my hand up. I don't need a visual of what Jonathan saved me from. Of what was said about my body without my consent. Of what could have happened if he didn't step in.

"He didn't seem like he would respect any woman." His face tenses. "Respect you."

"Why did you ignore me after? Why didn't you just tell me what happened?"

"Would you have listened? You ignored my calls. My texts. Everything. At family dinners, you brushed me off. You wouldn't even hand me the rolls, and I always sat next to you."

He steps closer, eyes boring into me. "Clover."

I haven't heard the nickname in a decade.

"For the record, I wanted to kiss you," he says, words coming out more breath than sound.

"Why didn't you?" I cross my arms. "And while we're at it—why do you even call me that? You never explained it. Not once in all these years."

"I wanted our first kiss to be special. Not in the backyard after I had just shotgunned a beer with your brother." He runs a hand through his hair, jaw working like he's deciding how much to say. "And, uh—" He lets out a short breath, almost a laugh, almost not. "Your eyes. They remind me of a four leaf clover."

"My eyes." I stare at him. "You've been calling me that for years and it's because of my *eyes*."

"Because I've always felt lucky to have you in my life." He finally meets my gaze, and the sincerity there makes it very hard to stay annoyed.

I look away first. I have no clue what to say to that. To any of that.

Being rejected was terrible. What sucked most was losing my friend. I had Nova, of course, but she is a social butterfly. The life of every party, organizing cram sessions before big exams and scary movie nights. I'd participate from time to time, but I'm more of a small group kind of girl. Jonathan was the same. After that night, along with picking up the pieces of my heart, I was down one of my closest friends. I felt betrayed. Destroyed.

Wait, what did he just say?

"You wanted our first kiss to be… What are you talking about?"

"I wanted our first kiss to be just us, not at a party where anyone could interrupt it. I wanted to taste *you*, not your first beer. Unless you taste like beer, then sign me up." He gives me a sly grin. "I had it all planned out. I was going to take you to that bookstore you always talked about but were too afraid to take the city bus to. The one with the second floor. Let you walk around for however long you wanted."

I'm not sure I'm breathing. I think I might have died.

"Nook and Burrow?" I whisper.

He nods.

"Once you were done, presumably after several hours"—he winks, and I go weak in the knees—"we'd get carry-out at The Dilly Pickle."

My favorite restaurant back then. Their cheeseburgers were to die for. I ate there at least three times a week until someone recognized my delivery address and commented that I order a lot from there. Then I was too embarrassed.

"Where would we eat it?" I wanted to know the rest. *Needed* to know the rest.

His brown eyes meet mine, an invisible tightrope connecting us. He drops his head to hide his pink cheeks, hair flopping forward. "Just off the duck pond. The forgotten gazebo."

I studied at that gazebo nearly every day. On the edge of campus, away from the chaos only college could create, with a duck pond and weeping willows lining the edge.

I lunge forward, wrap my arms around his neck, and kiss him for the first time.

Kissing Jonathan Kirkwood is even more than I could have ever imagined.

He falls into me, wrapping his arms around my waist. My tongue grazes his lips, deepening the kiss until the world falls away. My fingers slide up to the back of my neck, threading into his hair. He shivers at the gentle tug, causing me to moan against his mouth.

Oh fuck. I just kissed Jonathan Kirkwood for the first time. I pull back, taking a few steps back, almost tripping. I'm sure my eyes are the size of dinner plates.

"I'm so sorry. I got caught up in the moment and I wasn't thinking straight. I'm pretty sure I'm delusional from starvation. I haven't eaten since lunch—" Jonathan closes the gap between us, wraps his arm around my waist. My mouth hangs open.

"Don't apologize."

"I just wasn't sure you wanted my mouth on your mouth…"

"Do you want that?" That rumble. God his voice does something to me. To my heart. To my lady business. To my sanity.

"I do… want that."

"Good," he whispers.

His eyes drop to my lips, and the air between us thickens. I can feel the warmth of his breath, see the slight hitch in his chest as he inhales. The hand at my waist tightens, fingers splaying across the small of my back, pulling me incrementally closer. His other hand comes up slowly—giving me every chance to pull away—and cups my jaw, thumb brushing across my cheekbone.

"Then stop apologizing," he murmurs, his lips hovering just barely above mine, "and let me show you how I would have kissed you for the first time."

His mouth finds mine, softer than before but somehow more intentional. Like he's savoring every second. This kiss is different from the first—less frantic, more deliberate. He takes his time, learning the shape of my lips, the taste of me. When I sigh into him, he deepens the kiss, and suddenly I'm not sure where I end and he begins.

When we finally come up for air, Jonathan's grinning against my mouth.

"I really should go before you pass out from starvation and I have to explain to the paramedics why I kissed you instead of feeding you."

I laugh, swatting his chest. "You're ridiculous."

"And you're oxygen-deprived and running on fumes." He steps back, but catches my hand. "Eat something. Text me when you do so I know you didn't die."

"So romantic." I roll my eyes. "What about your sandwich?"

"You eat it." He brings my hand to his lips, pressing a kiss to my knuckles. "If I stay here any longer, I won't leave at all."

"Would that be so bad?" I give him a wicked smile.

"Goodnight, Clover."

"Night, Jonathan.

He lingers at the door, looking back at me one more time before he leaves, and I can still feel the ghost of his smile on my lips.

Chapter 19

Porn, in Slow Motion

"They'd worked side by side for two years without saying the thing. There are people like that. The feelings just accumulate quietly, like dust on a shelf you keep meaning to clean." - Six Gummy Bears

"**S**o." Nova settles across from me on the living room floor, a stack of paperbacks between us. "What did you have to tell us?"

"Is it about Jonathan?" Sawyer drops down beside her, completing our little triangle.

"Keep your voice down." I glance over my shoulder. "The whole book club doesn't need to—"

"The hell we don't." Tottie doesn't even look up from the folding chair she's claimed beside Verne.

"Is he courting you?" Verne practically sings it, drawing out every syllable.

"Nobody is courting anybody." I grab the nearest box of books and busy myself hauling it toward the empty shelves. Anything to avoid their faces. "But something did happen last night."

The room goes quiet in that particular way it does when everyone is pretending not to listen.

I hadn't planned on telling the whole book club. I've been on the fence about telling Nova and Sawyer. The truth is, I still don't know what to do about it—and saying it out loud would make it real.

Nova arches a brow.

"We are working together." My fingers drift to my lips before I can stop them.

"And…" Tottie leans forward, practically vibrating.

"And he kissed me." The heat crawls up my neck before the words are even out. The entire book club stares. I tear open the nearest box and start pulling out books like I'm defusing a bomb.

"Focus, people." I set a stack on the shelf with more force than necessary. "Four empty shelves, fifteen boxes. Nobody's leaving until these are sorted."

Doris fans herself with a cardboard flap. "Lord have mercy. If that man was kissing *me*, I couldn't alphabetize my own name."

"Subgenre, author, or color?" I hold up two books and examine their spines like they're the most interesting things I've ever seen.

Nova pushes the books down. "Maze. You've been mooning over him since he offered you this place. Really since we were in high school, but I digress. Now you're telling me he *kissed* you!"

"Don't forget that we need to add the Reading Lane library cards on the inside for guests to sign." I hold up a stack of the cards that are tucked into little pockets. I demonstrate how to peel off the sticky side of one and put it on the inside cover of the book.

"Are you fucking kidding me?" A tiny voice squeaks behind my interrogation group.

All of our heads shoot in the direction of Morgan. Meek, quiet Morgan. I swear there wasn't a jaw that didn't hit the ground.

She takes a deep breath with her eyes closed. "Sorry. I just mean, can you please tell us what is going on with you two? We've been watching you guys dance around each other forever. And the past few months have been… well… It's been like watching porn in slow motion."

Sawyer locks eyes with Nova and me, and we burst out laughing.

"Okay, okay." I wipe a tear of laughter from my eye. "But there isn't much to tell. We aren't dating or anything… I don't do that. We are just—It doesn't matter."

Tottie exchanges a look with Sawyer, both of them smirking like cats who've cornered a mouse.

"I don't do dating. It only ends in disappointment, right? There is no such thing as a real life book boyfriend. It's so much better to read about that stuff. Plus, he's Elliott's best friend."

"So you're telling me you are dating books and fucking Jonathan?" Tottie pipes in.

"No! We are—He just—I don't know what's going on." My body deflates. "I like being around him."

"Well no shit, sweetie." Tottie grabs a stack of books from one of the boxes.

Morgan walks over to me and places a gentle hand on my shoulder. "Mazey, I think it's safe to assume that you know you can't be in love with novels, right? Like, romantically?"

She says this with a straight face, and I do not know if she is joking. Of course I know that I cannot be in love with a book, but I also know that if I admit the feelings bubbling under my skin for Jonathan, I'm screwed. And not in the penetrative way. In the *oh-my-god-I-love-him-so-much-and-he's-so-wonderful-until-he-does-something-outrageously-dumb* way.

"The way her face looks around Jonathan, you'd think he walked right out of a romance novel," Sawyer hollers from the other side of the room. She's already filled five shelves. "Oh, and we are doing it by sub-genre and then by author. The sub-genres are in alphabetical order."

Thank god she answered that question. There is a high chance that if I had to make one more decision today, no matter the impact, I was going to go bonkers. I'm not even sure I can decide what I want for dinner. I'll probably end up with a plate of cheese, crackers, and whatever else I can find in the kitchen.

Nova sighs, plopping down to the floor. She slides another stack over to sort. "You know, you are glowing."

Five sets of eyes nail me to the wall. "Oh my god, she is!"

I wedge *Jane Eyre* between *The Great Gatsby* and *Little Women,* but my grin refuses to go away. My cheeks hurt from trying to suppress it.

Doris smiles. "Good cock will do that to ya."

"Doris!" I blurt.

"She's not wrong," Tottie sings. "Your face is proof."

"Okay, first of all, my face is normal. Second"—I set a stack of romances down a little too hard, the spines thumping—"we've only kissed."

The room goes quiet. Three sets of eyes snap to me.

"I doubt Elliott will care if you explain how you feel about Jonathan. He's very sensitive and understanding." Sawyer leans against a half-filled shelf looking off into the distance. Is she fantasizing about my brother? Gross.

"How do you feel about him?" Verne asks. "Was kissing him everything you thought it'd be?"

The laugh escapes before I can stop it—light and a little giddy—and I press a book to my chest like that might contain whatever is happening in my ribcage. "I don't know. It was unexpected. One minute I was beating him with a spatula—"

"I'm sorry." Tottie's hand shoots up. "You were what?"

"I thought he was going to murder me. It's fine." I wave her off. "And the next minute he's telling me he's wanted to kiss me since college."

"But how did it feel?"

I pause, a book forgotten in my hands.

How did it feel? Like his hands were steadying and unraveling me at the same time. Like I'd been holding my breath for years and didn't know it until he gave me a reason to exhale. I hadn't expected softness from him—hadn't expected the way he'd slowed down, like he wanted to make sure I was still there with him. I was. I absolutely was.

"Like floating," I finally say. "Like the first six-gummy-bear read of the year."

Sawyer blinks. "Six-gummy-bear read?"

Nova tosses a paperback at my head without looking up. "It's how she rates books. You know the standard five-star scale?"

I cut her off. "It's more than five stars, and stars aren't even enough. It has to be gummy bears. They are delicious."

"A six-gummy-bear rating… It can't be beat." Doris sips her coffee from the rocking chair.

"Doris, where did you get that?" I point to the cup and the chair.

"You've got a nice crew. They helped me out when you were bickering about your enemy's penis," she says, taking a sip.

"She's only rated one book six gummy bears," Morgan says, circling back. "*Anne of Green Gables.*"

"And now Jonathan," Nova says.

"Cloud. Nine. She's officially on cloud nine," Sawyer sings.

"Uh-huh." Tottie slides a stack of thrillers into place. "You'll be doodling his last name in the margins of your fucking planner."

"Absolutely not." My voice is far too dreamy to sound convincing. I'm still replaying the way his hands gripped my waist, the way he said my name like it meant something more than just syllables.

"He's not interested like that. I'm sure he was exhausted and still in shock from being attacked by a spatula." I hug another stack of books to my chest, cheeks burning.

"Uh-huh. I said something like that about my Kathryn," Doris drawls. The room goes silent at the mention of her late wife. "Oh, stop that. She was the best thing that ever happened to me, but damn was she frustrating at first. I thought she just wanted to be friends, sending me a different signal every day. Until, one day, I kissed her. Never looked back. Best days of my life."

We stay silent as we dive back into sorting. All of us reflecting on Doris and Kathryn's love. By the time the last box is empty, the shelves are glowing with stories, spines lined like soldiers waiting for their readers.

By early evening, I step back, wiping my palms on my leggings, a breath catching in my throat. Reading Lane looks more like a retreat than ever. Alive, humming with new stories ready to be told.

And maybe it's just me being ridiculously, stupidly happy, but I swear the whole room feels warmer. Like the books know. Like they're in on my secret too.

A knock on the doorframe startles the group, and we all jump in unison.

"Hey, sorry. Damn, you guys are focused. I just wanted to let you know, I'm going to pick up some pizza and some of those nachos you like, Mazey. I figured you had to make a ton of decisions, and I wanted to help. The blondies are on the kitchen counter. Need anything else?" Jonathan stands there. Like a knight in shiny decision-making armor.

The book club starts shouting drink orders at him and questions about his intentions. I, however, am speechless, for possibly the first time in my life. I just sit there. On the floor. Surrounded by my favorite people, my favorite books, daydreaming about riding my brother's best friend.

A stray book under Doris's chair catches my eye. I crawl over and pick it up. I don't even need to check the author to know where it came from. The title says it all.

Six Gummy Bears.

I flip it over and skim the back.

It's about these six people who all work at this gummy bear factory that's about to shut down. And instead of just letting it happen, they all kind of band together to try and save it—and while all that's going on, you're following each of their perspectives, so you see all these different relationships forming and feelings developing that nobody's saying out loud. Like there's all this tension, and late nights, and people who've worked side by side for years suddenly realizing they feel something way beyond being coworkers, but everyone's too caught up in saving the factory to actually deal with it. It's one of those books where you're screaming at the characters to just say what they're feeling, but it's also really sweet because you can tell how much they all care—about the place, about the work, and about each other. And by the end, it all kind of comes to a head at once. The factory stuff and the feelings stuff, and it's just really satisfying.

But how do you get the confidence to just say what you want?

ChapteR 20

The Mr. Darcy Of It All

"**I**'m so happy you waited until I could come to family dinner to follow through on the bet," Sawyer says. "What costume did you end up going with?"

"Mr. Darcy, wet shirt edition. White linen shirt. Slightly damp. I just hope he does the imperious stare all night," I say.

Sawyer presses her palms together like a prayer answered. "This is the best thing that has ever happened to me."

"You wrote eleven books. One of them won a national award."

"And none of that compares to this moment." She loops her arm through mine as we cross the yard toward the long table, already loud with overlapping conversations and the smell of whatever Larry has been grilling. "Where is he?"

As if on cue, Jonathan steps off the back porch. The white linen shirt is open at the collar, slightly rumpled, and yes—slightly damp, though I will never in my life ask how he achieved that. He catches my eye across the yard and holds it for exactly one beat too long before his mouth curves into something that is not quite a smile.

My stomach does the thing it has been doing for three weeks.

Ever since the kiss, my stomach has apparently decided to become completely ungovernable every time the man so much as looks in my direction. Which is inconvenient because he looks in my direction constantly. He always has. I just notice it for what it is now. Or what I hope it to be.

"Oh," Sawyer says quietly beside me.

"Don't."

"I didn't say anything."

"You said 'oh.'"

"Oh is a sound, not a sentence." She steers us toward the table. "I'm a writer. I know the difference."

Nova materializes at my other elbow. "He looks—"

"Don't you start either." I pull out a chair and drop into it. "We're normal. Everything is normal."

Nova and Sawyer exchange a look over my head that I pretend not to see.

The table fills the way it always does—chaotic and warm, plates passed hand to hand, someone's elbow in someone else's space. Elliott drops into the seat across from me, Evie at his side. They are already mid-conversation with Larry about something to do with the school's winter fundraiser. Jonathan settles two seats down, close enough that I am aware of exactly where he is at all times, which is normal. Completely normal.

"So, Sawyer." Mom leans forward, delighted to have a semi-famous guest at her table and doing absolutely nothing to hide it. "How are you settling in?"

"Wonderfully." Sawyer beams. "Honeyville is everything Evie and I needed. We both love it."

"And the cottage?" Mom asks.

"Perfect." Sawyer glances at Elliott with a small smile. "I have very good neighbors."

The conversation moves the way family dinner conversation does— in six directions at once, looping back on itself, someone always talking over someone else in the most affectionate way possible. I eat my food and laugh at the right moments and do not look at Jonathan more than is reasonable for a person who is completely unaffected.

"How's the vlog doing?" Larry asks, pointing a fork at Jonathan.

"Really well, actually." Jonathan reaches for the bread basket. "The book challenge video is by far the most popular video, thanks to Miss Sawyer Storme."

"The comments are still unhinged," Nova volunteers from the end of the table. "In the best way."

"What do they say?" Mom asks.

"That Jonathan and Mazey have the slowest slow burn in the history of recorded video." Sawyer says this like she is reporting the weather.

Elliott looks up from his plate. "Seems like your viewers are confused."

"About what?" Jonathan sips his tea.

"You two." Elliott waves his fork between Jonathan and me. "There is clearly nothing going on between you guys."

The table does that thing where everyone suddenly finds their food incredibly interesting. I reach for my drink. Jonathan sets his glass down. And then, because apparently neither of us has any self-control whatsoever, we look at each other.

It lasts maybe two seconds.

It feels considerably longer.

Jonathan looks away first, toward the bread basket. I look away second, toward absolutely nothing, a fixed point somewhere near the salt shaker that I stare at with tremendous focus. My ears are warm. I do not touch them.

Across the table, Elliott watches this unfold in real time. Something shifts in his expression—not quite suspicion, not quite understanding, but somewhere uncomfortably close to both.

"They're not confused,." Nova says, and I kick her under the table. "Ow! I mean, they have chemistry. Have you seen the videos?"

"I think it's wonderful." Sawyer smiles warmly, refilling her glass. "Especially after everything. I mean, the kiss alone—"

The table goes quiet in a ripple, conversations dropping off one by one as the word "kiss" settles over everyone like a stone dropped into still water.

Sawyer's eyes go wide. Her hand stops mid-pour. "I—" She looks at me. "I am so sorry. My mouth got ahead of my brain. And I was thinking about how wonderful it was that you two finally are becoming something after all these years of yearning."

"It's fine. I promise." My voice comes out remarkably steady as I force a smile at my friend.

It is not fine, but it's also not Sawyer's fault.

Elliott sets his fork down. He does not say anything. He picks up his glass, takes a slow sip, and sets it back down with the careful precision of someone choosing not to throw it.

The quiet from him is somehow louder than anything else at the table.

"Elliott—" Jonathan starts.

"Not right now." Elliott's voice is even. He cuts into his food like the conversation is over.

There are several sides to Elliott. He can be the most sweet and compassionate person in the world. He's a high school science teacher and that takes a special kind of person.

Or a psycho.

There's also the playful Elliott—and the brother so determined to make the world better he stays after school every day, signing up to sponsor whatever club his students dream up.

But this version? This version is my least favorite. His protective side. The one that drove all night from college when I almost failed algebra junior year, standing in my doorway with his arms crossed and his jaw tight, not saying the thing he was thinking because he knew if he started he wouldn't stop.

It is the version from three years ago when I backed out of buying the Victorian on Elm Street for Reading Lane, and he drove forty minutes to sit across from me at Dad's coffee shop and just looked at me for a long moment before saying "you're doing it again."

The hardest part is that I also know the other version. The one who stood by my side with Dawson when I was being bullied on the playground, ready to protect me no matter the cost. The one who shows up every year on the anniversary of losing Dawson with bad rom-coms and a bowl of popcorn big enough for two, crying until we're both laughing.

That Elliott is in there too, somewhere behind the jaw and the careful fork.

That's what makes the quiet so much worse than yelling.

I reach for my drink. My hand is steady, which feels like a small miracle, because my chest is doing something complicated and loud, and I'm fairly certain the entire table can hear. I don't look at Jonathan. I am categorically and deliberately not looking at Jonathan, which means I am extremely aware of exactly where he is and the fact that he has also gone very still.

Bobby breaks the silence.

"Where'd you two end up going this weekend?" Bobby asks, tearing off a piece of roll. "Maze said you were out of town."

Larry and Mom exchange a glance that they clearly think is subtle.

"Savannah," Larry says.

"For?" Bobby presses.

"Antiquing." Mom smooths the front of her shirt. "There's an estate sale circuit down there that runs the first weekend of the month. Very well organized."

"You drove to Savannah for an estate sale," Elliott says.

"Three estate sales," Larry corrects.

"We made a day of it." Mom reaches for her drink. "It was perfectly reasonable."

"Did you find anything?" Sawyer asks.

Mom lights up the way she only does when she's been given permission to talk about something she was going to talk about anyway. "A writing desk. Early nineteen hundreds. Claw feet, original brass hardware, not a scratch on it." She pauses for effect. "Not a scratch."

"She saw it from across the room," Larry says. "Didn't even look at the price tag."

"I knew what it was worth."

"She walked straight to it like she had a signal." He taps his temple. "Like a homing device for old furniture."

"Some people have an eye for things," Mom says simply.

Gus points at her with his fork. "Your mother has had that eye since she was twenty-two years old. Found a Chippendale chair at a yard sale for four dollars."

"Four dollars," Bobby repeats.

"Four dollars." Gus nods, satisfied.

"The desk is beautiful," Mom continues, ignoring the sidebar. "It just needed a good home."

"She talked the seller down forty dollars," Larry adds, the unmistakable tone of a man who was impressed and hasn't quite gotten over it.

Mom waves a hand. "He was asking too much."

"She was firm." Larry looks around the table like he's sharing something remarkable. "Very firm. Didn't even blink."

"It was forty dollars, Larry."

"It was the principle." He grins at her. "I learned a lot about negotiation."

"He did not negotiate once," Mom tells Sawyer. "He stood behind me and held my purse."

The table erupts. Larry points his fork at nobody in particular. "I was providing moral support."

"He was." Mom's mouth twitches. "He was very supportive."

Gus is quiet for a moment, watching the two of them with the patient expression of a man assembling a puzzle he already knows the picture of. He cuts into his burger. "Good trip then."

"Very good trip," Larry says.

Mom unfolds her napkin with great focus. "It was a fine day."

"Did you happen to see any *Anne of Green Gables* on your adventure?"

Shit. I forgot to tell Bobby that I found it.

In my defense, I have been slightly preoccupied. Reading Lane's back bathroom is still mid-renovation. The cottage book situation has graduated from mildly unsettling to actively keeping me up at night. My savings account balance looks the way it looks, which is to say not great. And then there is the other thing. The Jonathan thing. The thing

I am not thinking about while sitting four feet away from him at a family dinner table in front of everyone I have ever loved.

"I actually found it." I draw out the words.

"It was in a box that someone donated for the cottage." The table is too distracted by Sawyer's upbeat storytelling to notice when my eyes meet Jonathan's.

"You are whimsical, unconventional, and courageous," he mouths at me.

I bite my lip and smile, turning my gaze to the pile of mac and cheese on my plate.

After dinner, when the plates are cleared and people drift toward the yard and the water, Jonathan finds me at the edge of the dock reading the required book club novel—Verne's choice. A suspense-filled page turner that ends with the narrator being the murderer. I did not see this coming from Verne, but I'm loving every minute.

"We should talk about it." He plops down beside me.

"Should we?" I keep my eyes on the pages. Talk about it? I know what he wants to talk about. I'd rather jump in the freezing water than discuss *the kiss*.

"Mazey."

"I'm not avoiding it." I am absolutely avoiding it and will be until the end of time. "I'm just engrossed in this book." Not a lie, just not a full truth either.

He sits, letting me read, which is really just me staring at the paper waiting for him to break the silence, but I'm definitely not going to do it. The water moves below us. The sun starts to hide behind the tree line, and my reading excuse files out the window with the lack of light.

"The kiss—"

Wow. Okay. He's just going for it.

"Jonathan."

Elliott's voice booms from behind us.

"I have a lot to say about the kiss. But only when you're ready to hear it." He rises, towing over me, the moonlight making him glow.

"Why do you look like that all the time?" I mutter, head tilted back as far as it will go.

The corner of his mouth lifts.

"I'm going to smooth things over with Elliott."

Good luck.

My brother is super pissed. For good reason, I think? Is it really his business who I am going around kissing? I've kissed lots of people before Jonathan laid his sweet, sweet lips on mine.

It is his business. Kind of.

What if this *will they, won't they* situation ends in a *what the fuck was I thinking* and Elliott is stuck in the middle? Because we put him in the middle, in the position to pick between his adoring little sister with a fear of taking risks and a new business that could possibly bankrupt her, and his loyal, caring best friend with an adorable crooked grin and hands that could be lethal.

Chapter 21

Going Live

> *Mazey: "Tonight we're going live for the first time. If anything goes wrong—*
> *and something will go wrong—please know we practiced."*
> *[Jonathan, organizing tools on the table]: "We did not practice."*
> *Mazey: "We did not practice."*

Katie sets up her phone on the tripod next to her laptop at the dining room table, the screen for our first live event glowing bright.

"We are absolutely sure this isn't reckless?" Jonathan braces his hands on his hips. "Is this a ploy to get me to hammer my own hand?"

"Yes, sabotaging the man currently building my dreams is obviously on my to-do list," I deadpan, then glance at Katie. "How long do we have?"

"A few minutes. Need the rules again?" She narrows her eyes at Jonathan. He nods.

"Perfect." She flips her clipboard to a pink, scribbled-over page. "One of you will be blindfolded while building this adorable desktop bookshelf. The other will be giving directions."

She gestures at the dining table, where the kit waits in neat disarray. Panels of lightweight wood are stacked, ready to slot into a two-tier shelf just wide enough for a few paperbacks or journals. Simple in theory—snap, twist, done.

"Okay, showtime!" Katie yells, despite the fact that we are the only ones in the room.

She steps in front of the camera, explaining the rules to the growing number of viewers. Comments pop across the laptop screen in a steady scroll. I press my hand to my mouth to smother a laugh.

@booknerd34: Blindfold him!
@spinesandvines: Blindfold them both!
@SawdustAndSunshine: This seems dangerous...

"See? SawdustAndSunshine agrees with me." Jonathan leans close enough that his breath skims my ear.

"You're being silly," I whisper back, but when I turn to look at him, my pulse jumps.

Since the family dinner, Jonathan and I have made out in every single room of this cottage. It's been hot, scorching, but it only leaves me hungry for more. Having him this close, breathing him in, feeling his heat radiate against... it's torture. My body is already begging, and we are barely two minutes into Katie's latest video idea.

Jonathan shoves the blindfold toward me. "Here. You're up."

"I'm not wearing that." I push his hand away. "You're the construction expert."

"Clover..." His eyes narrow. It's that CEO don't-mess-with-me look that usually gets him his way.

I counter with a sultry pout, tilting my head just enough to sell it.

"Fine." He points a warning finger at me. "But you better not get me injured."

He drops into the dining chair and lifts the mask above his head. On tiptoes, I grab it, steading myself on Jonathan's shoulder. The fabric slides through my fingers before I loop it around his head and tie it too tight, yanking the knot.

He grunts and heat pools under my ribs.

"Comfortable?" My voice drips with sugar.

"Not remotely." He smirks. "Tell me where to stick it, boss."

Katie snorts so loudly it nearly derails me. The comments explode.

@HeartEyesReader: I cannot look away...
@DustyShelves: Did he mean that how it sounded?

@DIYorDie: THIS IS BETTER THAN NETFLIX.

I clear my throat, pretending my face isn't on fire. "Okay. Piece one. The flat panel in front of you."

His hand immediately finds the wrong one.

"No, other side," I say.

He grabs another wrong one.

"Oh my god, are you doing this on purpose?"

"Wouldn't dream of it." He pats the air until his hand smacks the stack and knocks the whole kit sideways. A board slides off the table and clatters to the floor.

Katie's shoulders are shaking with suppressed laughter. The comments are flying faster now.

@BookishBandit: I'd pay to watch this train wreck in person.
@ShelfieQueen: Did he just throw it on the floor???
@SawdustAndSunshine: I TOLD YOU THIS WAS DANGEROUS.

I scramble to rescue the pieces before they scatter. "This is already a disaster."

"You're the one in charge," Jonathan reminds me, hands folded like a very unhelpful student. "Maybe you should use clearer instructions."

"Oh, I'll give you instructions," I mutter under my breath, shoving the board back onto the table.

"Promise?" he shoots back, and the grin in his voice makes Katie choke on a laugh so loud she nearly knocks over the tripod.

The camera wobbles. The shelf remains untouched. My pulse is absolutely out of control.

Katie's still snickering when I shove the first board toward Jonathan. "Okay. Flat panel, right there in front of you. Hands out."

He pats the table, knocking over the instruction sheet, my coffee mug from that morning, and almost Katie's laptop before I slam his wrist down on the correct piece.

"There. That one. Don't move," my arms out.

"You're very aggressive with your teaching style," he says, smirk audible.

The comments are instant.

@Romance4Life: The mug! Don't break her "bookmarks are for quitters" mug!
@spinesandvines: How are his arms so long? And thick? They are like a weapon.
@BookishBandit: Why is this foreplay?

I chuckle at the screen and grab the side panel, daydreaming about his thick arms wrapped around me, gripping my ass. I shake my head to bring myself back to reality.

"Okay, this one slots into the edge."

"Left or right?" he asks.

"Left."

"My left or your left," he asks.

"Umm… yours?"

He fumbles until the board seesaws. I dive to catch it, but instead, I smack the corner of the table with my hip so hard I yelp.

"Smooth," he says. "Very professional."

"You're blindfolded. You don't even know what happened!"

"Oh, I know."

The comments are unhinged.

@DustyShelves: Did he just purr that??
@DIYorDie: This is chaos, I love it.
@ShelfieQueen: If they kiss on live I will die.

I shove the side panel into his hand. "Okay, slot it in. Give it a little wiggle."

He wiggles it so violently the entire structure pops apart and collapses on the table with a loud *crack*.

Katie wheezes, clutching her clipboard. I'm too busy staring at the heap of boards to breathe.

"What was that?" I practically shout.

"You said wiggle." Jonathan shrugs, making the palms-up, innocent gesture.

"You trashed it!" I scold.

"I trashed it? I trashed a board? That makes no damn sense," he says, voice raised in a playful way.

"Of course it makes all the sense! That's what happened!" I shout back.

The livestream chat is practically screaming now.

@HeartEyesReader: I can't breathe. This is hilarious.
@BookworminHeels: #TrashMyBoard
@SawdustAndSunshine: I warned you all. D-A-N-G-E-R-O-U-S.

"Okay, new strategy." I shove his chair closer to the table and grab his hands, positioning them on the panel myself. His fingers flex against mine, and I gulp. The contact sends a stupid shiver up my spine.

"Better?" I ask, a little too breathless.

"Much." His mouth quirks into that smug grin that even the blindfold can't hide. "Though, if you wanted to hold my hand, you could've just asked."

Katie groans out loud. The comments explode into emojis.

@spinesandvines: **Fans self while clutching my pearls**
@Romance4Life: Y'ALL ARE GONNA GET THIS STREAM FLAGGED.
@DIYorDie: Someone get them a chaperone.

"Okay," I say, my voice a little strangled. "Now push the peg through—"

The peg immediately flies out of his hand, bounces off the table, and disappears under the couch.

Katie loses it, wheezing so hard she can't stand up straight. The livestream chat becomes unreadable with laughing emojis.

I bury my face in my hands. "This is my nightmare."

"This," Jonathan says, blindfold still on, "is going exactly like I thought it would."

Judging by the thousands of hearts flying up the screen, he's not wrong.

Katie's still wheezing when I crawl under the couch to retrieve the rogue peg. By the time I resurface, Jonathan's managed to knock another board to the floor.

I shove the peg into his palm. "Behave, or I'm leaving you blindfolded."

"Interesting," he murmurs, but he grips the piece.

We try again, me guiding his hands. He fumbles worse than a

drunk octopus. He shoves too hard, the peg bends sideways, and the side panel nearly snaps. I yelp, lunge forward, and end up sprawled half across his lap as I wrestle the board back into place.

Katie claps a hand over her mouth. The chat is filling up so fast it's unreadable.

"Comfortable?" Jonathan asks mildly, one large hand steadying the board and the other very much braced on my hip.

"I hate you," I mutter into his shoulder, but I'm laughing too hard to sound convincing.

@HeartEyesReader: Ahh! This is everything!
@SawdustAndSunshine: Someone PLEASE take the hammer away from them.
@Romance4Life: THE. HIP. TOUCH.

After another ten minutes of Jonathan dropping boards, pegs ricocheting across the room, me barking orders while Katie shrieks with laughter, we finally manage to get the bookshelf upright. It wobbles and leans a bit to the left, but it's done.

"There," I say, flinging my arms out to present the masterpiece. "Ta-da!"

The livestream explodes with clapping emojis and gifs.

Jonathan yanks the blindfold down and squints at the crooked shelf. "Solid. Should last about ten minutes."

Katie swoops in with her clipboard like a game show host. "And that, ladies and gentlemen, is how *not* to build a bookshelf!"

The comments roll in faster than we can read them.

@BookishBandit: BEST LIVE EVER.
@spinesandvines: Forget Netflix, I want a weekly episode of this.
@EverBrightHQ: This is the type of company we want to be a part of. Our team will be reaching out.

Jonathan leans close to the camera, sawdust in his hair, blindfold hanging around his neck, grin wicked. "Next time, she wears the mask."

I shove him out of frame, laughing so hard my stomach hurts.

Katie ends the stream before the chat combusts. The three of us double over just as the wobbly little shelf creaks.

"Sorry about the nonsense, Katie," I hear Jonathan say behind me as I inspect the last comment in the live chat.

"Honestly?" Katie says, wiping tears from her cheeks. "That was perfect. Utter disaster. Internet gold."

Jonathan smirks at me, one brow arched. "What's wrong?"

"Did you see this?" I point to the comment. "EverBright is a pretty large company. They are building new offices all over the country. I think they are a green technology business. If I remember correctly, they are pretty big deal. I used to see their name all over the news when I worked in the office."

"And they want to work with Phoenix!" Katie jumps up and down, clapping her hands. "I'm going to get working on this introduction now."

The shelf leans, groans, and collapses flat on the table.

Katie howls. I drop my face into my hands. Jonathan just sits there, stunned.

"You two have officially broken the internet," she gasps, reaching for her phone and dances out of the room. "But it's doing exactly what we needed it to do! I'm heading back to the office. Call you later, J."

I press my face into my hands, half-laughing, half-hiding. "We're never living this down. I'm sure Elliott will be calling you the second he sees it, with a threat."

Jonathan wouldn't tell me the details of the conversation he and Elliott had last month at the Mr. Darcy family dinner, but Elliott has backed off. Some. He still occasionally looks at Jonathan the way a man looks at someone who has moved the furniture in a room he's lived in his whole life—like everything is technically fine but the angles are wrong, and he hasn't decided yet whether he hates it.

Jonathan just leans back in his chair, blindfold still hanging loose around his neck. "Worth it."

He tugs the blindfold free, letting it dangle from his fingers. Daring me to grab it.

"That was a disaster," I murmur, heart still racing.

His voice dips, low and gravelly. "Disaster looks good on you."

I should roll my eyes. I should shove him away and start re-stacking boards. Instead, I'm already leaning in, caught by the glint in his eyes. His hand slides to the back of my neck, warm and sure, pulling me down until our mouths collide.

This kiss is nothing like the teasing pecks we sneaked in between rooms before. This is hungry. His tongue sweeps against mine, stealing every breath I have.

I climb into his lap without thinking, knees bracketing his thighs, my leggings covered in evidence of the day's work. His rough palms skate up under the hem of my shirt. He groans into my mouth when my hips rock forward, grinding down against the solid length pressing through his jeans.

"Clover." His warning is shredded with want, his hands flexing at my waist, holding himself back. "What if someone walks in?"

I nip his bottom lip, tugging it between my teeth before checking the time on my phone.

"It's lunchtime, and thanks to your need to take care of your employees, everyone is enjoying time away from the worksite, at the diner, eating on your dime." I whisper against his mouth.

That's all it takes. He drags me closer, one hand sliding up my spine, the other cupping my ass as if to prove exactly how not fragile I am. My head tips back with a gasp as his mouth moves to my throat, heat flooding every nerve when he sucks gently at the skin there, teasing, claiming.

The broken bookshelf lies in ruins beside us, but his fingers tangle in my hair, his teeth graze my pulse, and suddenly I couldn't care less about splintered boards. My body arches into his, and when his hand slips under the waistband of my leggings, pausing for confirmation. I throw my hands on his shoulders to steady myself.

"Jonathan." I look him straight in the eye, all playfulness gone. "Touch. Me. Now."

"Bossy." He slides his hand down my panties, reaching my core. A finger dips into my wetness, curled to perfection. I buck in response.

"It was so hard not throwing you down on this table and making you scream my name," he hums against my neck.

A broad thumb roams over my clit, and another finger joins the first. He matches the lazy rhythm of my hips. I'd die happy being this man's hand puppet.

He leans forward and nips my hard peak through my shirt.

"Jonathan." I whip my shirt off, exposing him to a lace bralette.

"Fuck, Clover," he pulls back to examine my cleavage, fingers pausing inside me. "You are beautiful. Every part of you."

With that, my bra is gone, and his mouth is on my right nipple. I'm grinding on one of his hands while the other one works my left nipple.

His fucking hands.

His fucking mouth.

The trifecta of excellence.

"Clover."

That name. Damn, that name makes me grip his body builder biceps for dear life.

"I've wanted to know how you feel for so long. I've thought about the expression on your face right before you…"

"Right before I what?" I beg him to finish the sentence. I need him to finish the sentence. I want to know every little thought he has ever had. Especially if it is about what he thinks about me, since I am—apparently—terrible at reading the room, so to speak.

His pace shifts from teasing to relentless, his thumb circling just right while his fingers drive me higher. My breath stutters, and I clutch at his shoulders, desperate.

"Jonathan." My voice is high and airy.

"Right before you let yourself…" The words are drawn out, each sound its own word.

God, I should feel guilty. But I just want to know what the end of this sentence is. I want to shatter all over him. I want to bury myself in his arms and never move again.

I should be thinking about the retreat, the unfinished inventory, the twelve unread emails rotting in my inbox. I should be thinking about my brother—his best friend, practically family, a man who used to ruffle my hair and steal pizza off my plate like I was twelve years old.

I am not twelve years old.

I am very, very aware of that right now, straddling a man whose hands should be registered as weapons, in the dining room of the building I've mortgaged my entire future on, having what might genuinely be the best orgasm of my adult life.

There should be a list. A pros and cons list. A sensible, color-coded spreadsheet with tabs.

Instead, I'm grinning against his chest like an idiot, still trembling, and thinking—with complete, mortifying sincerity—that I would like him to do that again. Immediately. On every surface of this building. Starting with the table he apparently had to resist throwing me onto.

The table I still have to eat breakfast at.

The table that seats twelve.

I am so screwed. And somehow, shamelessly, all I can think is I can't wait to come all over this man's hand.

"You are so fucking sexy, Mazey," Jonathan growls into the nape of my neck.

I still my hips, grab his cheeks between both hands, and force him to look at me. He did not resist; he seemingly cannot take his chocolate eyes off a topless me.

"Fucking tell me," I blurt. I'm so close to tumbling over the edge, to coming all over this man's hand.

He gives me a grin I have never seen him give anyone before. It's wicked and sexy and accompanied by a shift in speed from his thumb. And it's mine.

"Come for me." He growls against my throat.

It's enough to push me over the finish line.

Something in his mix of reverence and roughness snaps my control. My words dissolve into a broken cry as my orgasm crashes through me, shuddering from my core all the way out. I grind against his hand shamelessly, moaning his name until I collapse against his chest, trembling and grinning through the aftershocks.

My eyes go wide when he frees his hand and licks each finger, tasting me.

"That's just the appetizer, Clover." A laugh breaks from my throat, and I give him a playful push. He pulls me closer and wraps his arms around me.

"Oh yeah?"

"Yeah." He nuzzles into me, kissing my collarbone.

I have never felt sexier than I do at this moment. Straddling my brother's best friend. In my future retreat's dining room. Forgetting all the responsibilities I have.

Chapter 22

Message in a Bottle

Mazey (at the market, holding up a small paper bag): "Someone just handed me a bag of gummy bears and said Reading Lane inspired them to finally start their own thing."
[She looks directly at the camera for a moment.]
Mazey: "I'm not crying. It's allergies. We're in a field."

The delightful-yet-mysterious *Gummy Bear* novel sits on my night stand next to the once-lost *Anne*. Every time I think I've figured out the rules of the cottage, they change. A never-ending board game with an over imaginative four year old.

I thought that once I finished the instructions, metaphorically (kind of), that it would be out with the old, in with the new. A fresh mission. The latest task to fix my life. But then the missing book showed up out of nowhere (okay, from a literal box of books, so there's a chance it wasn't the cottage at all. But how the fuck else would it get in there? It should have been compost on the side of I-95 by now). And the freaking *Gummy Bear* book is still in my possession.

This is the longest I've had a cottage book. I've read it approximately a zillion times. The cottage should really become a published author. Like, in the real world. Somehow, all six characters have their own point of view chapters, and it's not confusing or annoying to keep track of everyone's history or names.

I'm terrible with names in books. Especially if I have to say them out loud. A fantasy novel with names a mile long and letters that you never hear? Don't ask me to say them out loud. I will butcher the beautiful pronunciation. Nynaeve—is it "Nigh-NEEVE"? "Ny-NAY-veh"? Nova has informed me it's actually ny-NEEV.

Fortunately, all the names in the gummy bear book are one syllable—fool proof. We've only been formally introduced for about a half a year now, but the cottage knows me so well.

In the story, the floor supervisor wants to protect her team from the factory closing. So, naturally, I investigate the rules of having employees, something I do not currently have to worry about as I have no employees—unless you count Nova, but she sort of hired herself, and I'm not paying her. I have a spreadsheet covering the dos and don'ts of having a staff, fair wages, and the right time to hire.

The new hire is trying to find her place among the chaos of a closing factory—searching for belonging inside something that's already been handed a death sentence. Which, honestly, good for her. But I don't need to learn that lesson right now. I'm not looking for somewhere to belong—I'm building the somewhere. The spreadsheets, the rules, the figuring it out—that's not me trying to fit inside someone else's structure. That's me making my own. So, while I genuinely root for her (she's very likeable, the cottage did a good job), her chapter isn't mine. Not this time.

And the book is still here.

A couple of the other employees are navigating life with children working a job she is dramatically overqualified for, but can't afford to leave because of the killer benefits and retirement, both things that I am nowhere close to experiencing.

The last two metaphorical gummy bears—the union rep, Scarlet, and the owner's kid, Marco—have a secret crush on each other.

Scarlet has accepted a new job in the wake of the factory closing. She's planning to move across the country for new opportunities by chapter twenty, but she is met with a life shattering epiphany. About half way through, she tells Marco that, after all these years, she is in love with him.

In the second half they create plans to save the factory with the other four people, with several failed attempts, until they finally save it. The big question is—will Scarlet stay for Marco? Or will he leave behind his family's legacy and follow her across the country, leaving the only job he's ever known (and, admittedly, isn't in love with).

He leaves with her, his family doesn't hate him, and he ends up teaching figure drawing down the street from their walk-up in New York. They are annoyingly happy with their new life. Oh, and the single mom gets the job she should have running the place.

"This is about the stupid conversation I don't want to have with him, isn't it?" I shout at the ceiling.

Wilfred, who is asleep at my feet, legs in the air, exposing everything his mama gave him, opens his eyes. I see the annoyance on his face, and I stick out my tongue at the fur ball that doesn't have to worry about being overly attracted to someone he should not be.

The thing is packed with character arc after story arc, so I'm sure I missed something.

I swipe the offending paperback from the table, only for it to fall to the ground with a smug thud.

"Ugh." I grumble to the ceiling. Wilfred *pffs* at me. I roll to the side of the bed, lean over the edge. One leg is up in the air while my hand searches for the book. Teetering on the edge of the bed, my fingers graze a thick rectangle.

"What the fuck?" I whisper, pulling myself onto the bed with the grace of a newborn giraffe attempting to roller skate.

It's a brochure for the pop-up market that will be downtown this weekend. Earlier this week I tried to convince Nova and Sawyer to go, but they both have adult responsibilities preventing them from going on a shopping spree that should wrap up making this place look less like a dude's rented apartment and more like your grandma's cozy, safe home.

Going alone sounds terrible, so I tossed the pamphlet in the trash on Monday.

My phone dings.

Katie: We need a new vlog post. Similar to the one you guys did at the bookshop. Any ideas?

Instinct has me ignoring the text, and I toss my phone on the pillow next to me. I'm not sure why she'd ask me for ideas. I'm barely able to keep my own socials afloat. I typically just scrolled through everyone else's feed, admiring the creativity in their posts.

I pick up the brochure and look through it again. Damn, this market looks perfect to get some of the things we need.

"What if it was for the vlog? I could force Jonathan into going with me. He even has that big-ass truck," I say to the sleeping dog now laying on his side, in the exact position he'd be in if he were standing. He gives zero shits about the situation.

I snap a picture of the market and add it to the message.

Mazey: What about this?

Katie: This is perfect!! I'll get Jonathan on board. Thank you!

"I see what you're doing. I just don't understand how the fuck you are doing it!" I shout, again, to the ceiling.

"Do you know what we are looking for?" Jonathan grumbles, parking the truck in the makeshift lot in the empty field near the square.

Jonathan—I know from the years of him sleeping over with Elliott and the past few months of seeing him at the butt-crack of dawn (my favorite time of day— is usually irrepressible in the morning.

"I have a list." I pull out the folded paper from my bag and shove it at him. "What's your problem, grump-butt?"

"Grump-butt?" He raises an eyebrow, turns off the truck. "Sorry. Stressed about work and everything. I really need this vlog to take off."

"I thought you were getting good traction with EverBright showing interest and everything? Katie said you've gotten a bunch of new customers after the live vlog."

The live vlog.

Sweet lord baby Jesus, why did I mention the live vlog? When I tied up my green Converse this morning, I vowed to pretend the kiss didn't happen. To forget the delicious way Jonathan knew my body without having ever explored it before. How he coaxed me into soaking his hand by telling me how he has wanted to know what I look like when I *come.*

I pretend I didn't bring it up—skate right over it.

"Did you see that we finally got the entire Mary Shelley shelf filled?"

"I did." He grins. I assume he knows I'm avoiding the whole we-kissed-and-you-made-me-come-like-no-one-else-ever-has situation. Let's not forget it was in the dining room of the retreat we are building. He just sips of the coffee I brought him—The Extra John-tado. "Let's have a look at the list," he says.

He examines the yellow paper with light blue lines as if he will never see it again and is expected to purchase everything on it from memory. I fold and unfold the canvas totes I plan on filling to the brim.

"Want to make this a competition?" I fill the silence because if I start the conversation, it can't become one I don't want to have.

"And how would we do that?" His head raises slowly, an evil villain formulating a plan with his trusty apprentice.

Dammit, how did I forget he loves to compete?

"We both search for the best bookshelf decor." I make up the rules to the game that doesn't exist but that I obviously have to beat him at. "And we'll have Katie post a picture and let the viewers decide," I say, making up the rules as I talk.

"You'll lose. You good with that?" He smirks at me, hand on his seat belt waiting for the green flag to wave.

"Says the guy who had to dress up for family dinner in a damp shirt. In December."

"And who is the winner of every game of Uno we've ever played?" He slap-grasps the steering wheel, pride in his eye.

"Uno, the game of luck. No strategy, just pulling a card from a deck and hoping for the best." I roll my head to him on the back of the seat. He rolls his head to me and somehow scoots closer.

This close, I can see the exact place where his jaw meets his ear and the way his lashes are slightly too long for someone who has no business being this distracting at eight in the morning, and my brain does the thing it has been doing since the dining room: it stops being a brain and becomes a single, useless, humming note—because he smells like the coffee I brought him and something underneath that is just *him*. His eyes drop to my mouth for half a second, maybe less.

I lean in first.

I will think about that later—probably forever. The fact that it was me. That after all the almost-moments and the careful not-looking and the canvas totes clutched in my lap like a shield, it was me who closed the distance. And Jonathan, to his credit, doesn't make me close all of it. He meets me halfway, the way he always does, the way I am only now understanding is just who he is. Then his hand comes up to my jaw like he has been thinking about exactly where to put it, and the coffee and the cold morning air and the rows of vendor tables outside cease to exist entirely.

After several minutes, he pulls back slowly, forehead dropping to rest against mine. We stay like that for a moment, just breathing, the truck quiet around us. Then he shifts just enough that I can see his face, and he gives me the grin. Not the one I've always known—the easy, familiar one he gives everybody. This is the other one. The one I didn't know existed until I started bossing him around in the early mornings at the cottage. It's the one that only showed up after I said something ridiculous or refused to let him win gracefully. This version is different. Wicked, but lighter. Playful in a way that makes it hard to be a serious person. It doesn't have the weight the other smiles carry. It's just—bright. Uncomplicated. Like something in him has put something down.

"Are you ready to get your ass kicked?"

I couldn't help myself. I love poking the fight-to-the-death-over-a-made-up-game beast.

"Oh, it's on." He hops out of the truck and takes off. I follow, stumbling over the uneven ground. Colorful tents, flapping in the breeze, line the street. Each one is bursting with handmade candles, vintage bookends, jars of local honey, and enough whimsical signage to make a Pinterest board weep.

Jonathan glances over his shoulder at me, already several steps ahead. He shoved his sleeves up to his elbows, his thick forearms on display, and swings one of the canvas totes, which I insisted we bring, over his shoulder.

I'm distracted by the number of things I *need* in my life. Vintage rugs? I must have them. Handmade candles? Essential. A decorative bowl that serves no purpose but looks impossibly aesthetic? Into the tote it goes.

"Would you slow down?" I huff, my phone camera is on him. "This is a market, not a marathon. You're supposed to browse, not bulldoze."

"There is a lot of shit on that list, Clover!" he mutters, but his pace slows.

I slow to a walk, scanning every booth for something to destroy whatever Jonathan finds. My eyes snag on a pair of bookends tucked near the back. Frogs playing tiny violins. One even has a tambourine. I pick them up, grinning before I even realize it. Totally absurd. Definitely mine. But not for the competition.

A few steps away from those, a mason jar sits near the front of the table, its lid painted gold and glued shut like it's guarding a secret. Inside, a tiny wooden bookshelf leans against a faux brick wall, lined with handmade books no bigger than my pinky nail. There's even a paper coffee cup on the floor and a cat curled in the corner. It's sleeping beside a rug the size of a postage stamp. Someone even hung fairy lights—*actual* fairy lights. Like a strand of lights shaped like fairies. I grab the jar too, but I'm sure I can find something even better to kick Jonathan's ass with.

Then I spot it.

Tucked between a tray of beaded rings and a basket of felt stars, a tiny glass bottle catches my eye. There's a scroll curled up inside, sealed with a dab of deep red wax. The tag beside says "Message in a Bottle. Write Your Own Love Story" in handwritten, looping letters. My fingers hover over it, already itching for a pen.

Cash hits the table, and I collect my treasures, plus some wooden spoons that have funny faces burned into them, and toss them my tote.

Jonathan is a few booths over, something behind his back. His smug expression is enough to send me into fight-or-flight mode.

"What did you find?" I demand, stepping closer.

A butterfly garden forms in my stomach at his grin. "Wouldn't you like to know, Clover?"

Oh, this man is insufferable. And somehow even more endearing with that look etched across his face.

"Fine," I say, lifting my bottle, trophy-size, a crooked grin plastered on my face. "Let the viewers decide. But just so you know, I'm about to crush you."

"We'll see," he drawls, nudging my shoulder with an expression that makes my knees weak.

With a flourish, he presents a weathered wooden shadow box with chipped cream paint along the frame. Someone must have rescued it from a forgotten attic or storage shed. Inside, neat rows display vintage typewriter keys, each round letter worn smooth with time. Together, they spell out "my favorite genre is happily ever after."

Faded, yellowed book pages line the background, and a delicate pressed flower—lavender or baby's breath—sits in the corner. Artwork made for anyone whose soul lives between the pages of a well-worn romance novel.

"How? Where did you even—?" The words tangle in my throat, useless against the lump rising in my chest. It's beautiful. I brush my fingers over the frame. "The quote… It's perfect. I love it. So much."

"It reminded me of you," he grunts. "You're always talking about happily ever afters or whatever."

"You may have a chance to win," I say, nudging him. "We better send Katie a picture of these. She said she could set up a poll or some-thing. Let the world decide our bookshelf décor fate."

"You go first. I want to see what we are working with," Jonathan says, holding up his phone.

"Got it," I nod. I hoist the bottle over my head, my mouth agape in exaggerated shock. Then I kick it up a notch, striking a series of truly ridiculous poses. One hand on my hip, the other dramatically clutching the bottle.

Jonathan stumbles over, eyes glassy and shoulders shaking, still trying to catch his breath. He reveals his piece like he's just won an art competition, then flips the phone into selfie-mode with a grin that's all mischief and pride.

"Round two," he says, stepping beside me. "Let's make some magic."

"You better commit, Kirkwood," I tease.

After a series of pictures together, my favorite being the one where we are both cradling our prizes to our cheeks while making a duck face, we walk again through the booths. The energy is pure happiness.

"We should probably find the stuff for the cabinets. I bet they are a hot commodity." He quips after a couple minutes.

We zigzag between booths, ducking at swinging tote bags and side-stepping a toddler mid-tantrum in a tutu and cowboy boots. My own canvas bag sags with finds ranging from tiny honeybee spoons to a floral tea towel stitched with the words *Plot Twist*. At one booth, I run my fingers over a stack of dreamy, crinkled linen napkins dyed in soft ombré pinks. A few steps later, the warm scent of vanilla and something citrusy wraps around me. I bought one of the *Everything's Peachy* candles on display, and the one next to it called *Once Upon a Frappuccino*.

I turn to point something out to Jonathan, except he isn't there. One second he was beside me making a snarky comment about a crocheted octopus tea cozy, and the next he is gone.

I scan the crowd with a spin. Not him. Not him. Definitely not the guy in the *Hot Dads Do It Better* T-shirt.

A familiar silhouette finally appears, tucked behind a couple arguing over enamelware. He is at a booth decked out in warm woods and copper tones. Cutting boards engraved with herbs, timers shaped as pears, and rolling pins embossed with daisies are scattered across the tables.

"You will never believe what I found," I say, pulling out the set of book salt and pepper shakers.

"I remember my mom telling me about a bowl like this. My dad looked everywhere for it when they first got married." He holds a white glass mixing bowl with a line of olive-green florals cascading through the middle. I put my arm around his waist in a sideways hug. His body stiffens at my touch. He looks down at me as I keep my eyes on his damp ones, waiting for his next words, and he relaxes. "She loved green. That's your favorite color too, right? He searched everywhere for a mixing bowl that was the exact right size for her pancake recipe. One with green flowers on it to match the apron she always wore when she made his favorite mashed potatoes."

A tear slides down his cheek. "I guess they had garlic and bacon in them."

"I bet they were incredible," I say as quietly as possible.

"They were. Grams would make me them whenever I didn't feel good. I think she was bringing a piece of my mom to me." He breathes out a soft chuckle. "You know, it's so weird to be in this place, where I lived a life thinking my dad was a villain. But it's possible something else happened. My mom was wonderful. She couldn't love someone so horrible, right?"

"I never met him, but you're part of him and you aren't horrible." I smile at him, but his eyes are at the market over my head.

"Hey, check it out." He points to a kiosk. "It's a knob paradise."

"You go ahead, I want to check something out first." He nods and takes off in his standard speed walk to the table.

When he is gone, I flag down the older woman who is collecting money for the table. "I'll take this bowl, please. Can you wrap it so no one can see what's inside?"

"Of course, dear." She says, and she gets to work wrapping up the bowl.

I walk up to a dumbfounded Jonathan, scanning the boxes upon boxes of cabinet pulls scattered across four tables.

"This is… a lot," I mutter, staring at the selection.

"You love it," he whispers back. I look at him and his grin is priceless. "You bought it, didn't you?"

"There was no other option."

"Katie texted. She let me know that I won." Jonathan's eyes sparkling before he digs through a bowl of mismatched drawer pulls.

Chapter 23

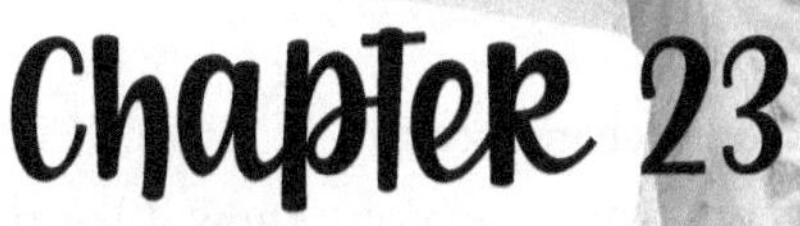

Pick Up Gummy Bears

Mazey (quietly, sitting on the sunroom couch): "I've been reading a lot about in-betweens lately. The chapters where nothing is resolved yet and you're not sure if the story knows where it's going either."
[She closes the book in her lap.]
Mazey: "I think I'm in one of those chapters."

Over the past few weeks, the "what are we" and the "what's going to happen next" between Jonathan and me have consumed my thoughts. I blame my nosey book club for planting the thought in my head that day almost two months ago.

There have been glimpses of his feelings—a kiss here, a make-out session there.

The problem with glimpses is that they're just that. Glimpses. A window you pass by too fast to know if what you saw inside was real or just the light playing tricks.

I've become an archaeologist of small moments. The way he texted back immediately that one time, and then went quiet for three days. The kiss that felt like a statement, and the morning after that felt like a question mark.

The cottage would know what to do with him. Probably assign him a one-syllable name and give him a whole novel about how wonderful he is.

The honest thing—the thing I don't really say out loud—is that the uncertainty isn't just about him. It's about whether I'm someone who gets to have the thing. Not in a self-pity way—or maybe a little in a self-pity way. More like, I've been in the in-between for long enough that I have to figure it out. I need answers. I need to know if he wants to risk everything to try this.

But I also need him to make the first move because I'm all out of bravery for taking risks.

Scarlet waited until chapter twenty to say the thing. I'm somewhere around chapter eleven, and I still don't know if I'm the one who needs to say it or if I'm just waiting to find out if I'm even in his book at all.

I toss a velvet pillow on the midnight-blue couch in the sunroom. My stomach flitters knowing that Jonathan will be here any minute. He's going to be so excited. Katie was going over some of the logistics of this week's shoots when Everbright, the company that commented on the live vlog wanting to partner with Phoenix, called to let Katie know that a courier should be at the Phoenix offices tomorrow with the paperwork to make it official. I asked if I could tell him.

Jewel tones gleam softly under the warm lighting, casting shadows all around, like twilight has settled in for good. The deep, moody walls cradle rose gold frames holding windows to other worlds: fairies lounging in moonlit gardens, mermaids sprawled on ocean-washed shores, griffins and pegasi soaring over distant castles. Everything about the room whispers *fantasy*. Like a portal you might accidentally fall through if you let your guard down.

Snacks are on the vintage-inspired coffee table, perfectly positioned before the mounted TV above the fireplace, which is currently paused on the menu for season three of *MacGyver*—the 1985 version, not the reboot. Finding it wasn't easy since no streaming service wants to acknowledge its greatness, but the library came through. If tonight goes well, I'll order the entire collection and give it the shrine it deserves.

The doorbell rings as I switch on the dragon lamps. Wilfred's tail starts wagging, and he lets out a little bark of excitement.

"Hi." My voice is an octave higher than normal. "Welcome to the cottage."

For some godforsaken reason, I do that strange little bow thing cartoon characters do when they open a door, like I'm some butler welcoming him into a fancy mansion instead of my home.

So much for not being weird.

Jonathan steps inside. His dark eyes sweep over me, lingering just long enough to make my stomach flip. "Well, hello."

"Hi." I put my arms around his neck, pulling him down for a kiss. Electricity shoots through me. "I have some good news."

"Oh yeah? What's that?"

I don't answer. Instead, I guide him to the couch with a hand on his back, and he sinks into the overstuffed cushions like his body finally got permission to relax. He blinks up at me, bemused. I grab the softest blanket in sight and drape it over him with the solemn care of someone tucking in a cherished heirloom. His brows draw together in quiet confusion, but there's a smile tugging at the corner of his mouth, like he's not sure what's happening—only that he doesn't want it to stop.

"Is this… a ritual?" he asks, voice low and amused as he situates the blanket.

"Nope," I murmur, already fluffing a pillow behind his head.

"Are you going to strip for me? Is that the good news?" His eyes twinkle. He runs his hands up and down his thighs.

"I'd probably injure myself if I attempted that." I shake my butt, attempting to look like a professional dancer. Judging by the grin on Jonathan's face, he doesn't mind that it looks more like I was trying to get my underwear out of my crack without anyone noticing.

Preparing myself with a deep breath, I stand in front of him. I keep tugging at my shirt sleeves, searching for something to do with them. I close my eyes and let the words fall from me.

"Okay. So… Everbright is sending over the official paperwork to Phoenix tomorrow."

Jonathan's eyes hit his hairline. His mouth opens, then closes, then opens again.

"Really? I thought that they were just commenting for the algorithm." He scrunches up his face. "I mean, Katie jumped on the opportunity to organize the introduction. We had some conversations with them, but nothing was solid."

"Having Katie spearhead the company is paying off." I plop down next to him.

"Yeah, I guess so." His face falls, and he stares off into the distance before shaking it off and painting on a—to my Jonathan-trained eye—fake smile. "That's great. I'll go over it with Katie tomorrow, but based on the few conversations we had, it sounds like this is the opportunity we were hoping for with the vlog."

"You seem upset."

"I'm fine. This is great. It should save the Pathways Program and Phoenix."

I don't buy it. Something else is going on. I thought we were past this. Hiding stuff. When he came clean about why he was a jerk behind my back in college, I assumed we could talk about anything moving forward. He was a dumbass for that—so many better ways to handle that. But we were young and dumb. He probably thought it was the smartest way to get those creeps away from me.

We're in our thirties now, way past hiding things for the sake of the other. Is it better to protect each other by not being open and honest, or to be there for each other when the shitty stuff happens?

Am I any better though? I want to give us a try. Like a real try. Like, be exclusive and stuff. God, I sound like a twelve year old. Part of me is still afraid that I'm too much of a mess. Maybe not a total mess, but I'm like, eighty-five percent mess, fifteen percent girl who somehow has a master's degree. I fake most of my confidence, I pretend to have my shit together, and I am constantly worried that someone is going to figure out I have no clue what I'm doing. Now would be a great time for the cottage to give me a book on how to navigate my feelings about Jonathan.

He's perfect at everything. Wait—is he, or is it that I've had heart-shaped glasses on all these years, skewing my opinion of him? He was terrible at the LIVE vlog challenge—taking direction was not his forte. And the amount of times he second-guessed himself during the book challenge was ridiculous. He could have picked up literally any book—there is a reader for each one—as long as it wasn't a duplicate. But he kept picking them up and putting them back as if he were shopping for himself. It was adorable how much consideration he put into that challenge.

"I'm starving. Should we eat while we watch?" He glances at the TV, still paused on the menu. "Season three of *MacGyver*? Good choice, by the way. It's my favorite."

I know it's his favorite. He only talked about it for the past week, craving comfort TV.

"Food during the show, duh." I hit play on the remote before reaching into a bowl of plain potato chips.

"I don't think you understand," Jonathan says during the opening sequence.

My eyes narrow. "What don't I understand, exactly?"

"That this is the best TV show in existence. Nothing tops watching a man defuse a nuclear warhead with a paperclip and a shoelace."

I snort. "Please. Half of his solutions wouldn't pass a high school science class."

"Blasphemy." He clutches his chest. "You dare speak against Saint MacGyver in his holy mullet?"

I bite the inside of my cheek. "He's basically a Boy Scout with better hair. You know what would've happened in real life? He'd trip over his own gadgets, and… boom." I mime an explosion with my hands.

"Bite your tongue." He tries not to laugh. "MacGyver could get us out of literally any situation."

"Any situation?" I arch an eyebrow. "What if we were trapped in this cottage with only… hmm… a stapler, a ball of yarn, and three stale Oreos?"

"He'd build a helicopter," he blurts around a pizza roll.

I lose the battle, dissolving into laughter. "A helicopter? Out of Oreos?"

"Double-stuffed Oreos," he clarifies, deadpan.

I wipe my eyes, shaking my head. "You're ridiculous."

He grins, reaching for me, and I don't resist as he pulls me against his side. We're still shaking with laughter, our bodies pressed together on the couch. And when I finally catch my breath, I realize I've tucked myself perfectly into the curve of his shoulder. His arm settles around me like it belongs there, warm and solid, and I let myself sink deeper into him, my cheek resting against his chest as the last of our giggles fade into comfortable silence.

"And yet," he points out, "you are curled up next to me."

My cheeks flush, and I tip my chin defiantly. No way I'm admitting that I wanted to see him smile. To do something he loves with him. "Jonathan?"

"Yeah?" His voice is soft, like a hug floating around me.

"I want to always be curled up to you." I'm the kind of tired that makes me forget there are consequences for the words that come out of mouths. His response matters, but it doesn't matter, if that makes any sense. It matters that he knows that I mean it. I always want to be curled up next to him.

I practically feel the *Gummy Bear* book vanish into thin air with my confession.

He pulls me closer, kisses the top of my head. I swoon when I hear his deep inhale.

"That's the only thing I've ever wanted."

"Jonathan?"

"Yes, Mazey."

"Thanks for letting me use you for your warmth."

He barks out a laugh, and I smirk victoriously. I'm not cold, but the heat radiating off him fills a gap in my body temperature that I wasn't aware needed filling. My eyelids fall, lashes meeting lashes. I force them open, blinking against the exhaustion. Between our filming schedule, figuring out how to start a business, and the millions of decisions I've had to make in the past few weeks, I'm wiped. I sink lower into Jonathan, giving into the darkness behind my lids.

"Careful," he murmurs, tugging the blanket over my shoulders. "You keep dissing MacGyver, he's not going to save you from falling asleep right here."

"Good. Then he can build me a pillow out of Oreos." My voice is muffled into his chest and my eyes flutter closed. I'll worry about doing something so routine, so intimate, with my brother's best friend later. Right now, the only thing my body is focused on is how comfortable this man is and how I feel more relaxed than I have in weeks.

Sometime later, I jolt awake, forgetting where I am and who I'm tucked into. A motionless sweep of the room tells me I'm in the back living room, an old tv show on.

It comes back to me when my gaze reaches Jonathan's hand curled under my shirt, tickling my skin. Dammit, I ruined the celebratory *MacGyver* night.

Complicating my next move, I spot Jonathan's phone falling out of his free hand. His thumb is still on the screen, lighting it up. Being the curious person that I am, my eyes flick back to the glowing screen, scanning faster than I should.

"Brainstorm vlog themes. Order more nails for the shed roof. Schedule another check-in with Dr. Kim."

My throat tightens. The list isn't just work. It's everything. Every part of him, laid out in bullet points. Like he has to carry the entire universe in his Notes app. And tucked right in the middle, like a throw-away line, is "pick up gummy bears."

My chest squeezes so tight I almost laugh. Almost cry. I don't know—both?

"Spying, are we?" His voice rumbles low, and I snap my head up like a kid caught with her hand in the cookie jar. His eyes are half-lidded, sleep-heavy, but there's no missing the glint of amusement there.

Scrambling to cover, I throw my arms up and stretch. "Man, that was a good nap."

He huffs, grabbing my arms back into his nook. "Uh huh."

I grin, but the weight in my chest won't let me brush it off. He's exhausted. Always working, always planning, always taking care of someone. Including me.

Tracing the edge of his knuckles, I say, "So, what now?"

He doesn't answer right away. Just studies me, like he's trying to decide if I mean it. Then his hand under my shirt flexes. "I can think of several things, but I need to head out. Early morning."

Disappointment floods me, but I nod in understanding. "Same. Katie has us doing something ridiculous tomorrow, I'm sure."

Laughing he stands, turning to me. "Thank you for tonight. I really needed it."

"Of course. Anytime." My smile is fake, but he doesn't seem to notice. "See you tomorrow."

I watch him walk out the door before scooping up a sleeping Wilfred to head to my own bed.

Chapter 24

Permits and Paperwork

*"Asking for help isn't the hard part. The hard part is admitting
the couch was never yours to carry alone in the first place."
- Stop Carrying the Couch Alone, You Weirdo*

"You really didn't have to do this. I would have gotten around to
it… at some point." I pace in the shed after a very impromptu
lunch with Nova, which is now obvious Jonathan orchestrated.

Last week, the crew finished painting the walls a retro sunflower
yellow, which brightened the future Reading Lane headquarters for
everything behind-the-scenes at Reading Lane. Other than the old
desk that came with the place, the room was a blank slate. After Jonathan taught me how to strip and repaint the antique desk with a bold,
moody teal, I'd shut the door and forgot it existed.

Along the back wall, white filing cabinets stand in a neat row,
freshly unboxed and perfectly aligned. On top, there's a growing city of
paper sorters, stacking trays, and upright organizers. Some are already
filled with printer paper and card stock, others still empty but full of
purpose. The printer, unopened, sits beside them.

My desk looks different, too. Across the surface is a spread of file
folders in soft blush and mint shades, not haphazard but placed with

intention. Next to a book-shaped pen cup are several packs of the high-lighters and pens that I convinced Jonathan were elite when we went journal shopping. He's even moved the stuff I was working on at the dining table, keeping everything in the unruly-but-intentional piles I sorted everything into.

Most of the items he got were from my "list of things to get" I was keeping on the fridge. But the small desk lamp in the shape of a Shih Tzu puppy is something I didn't know I needed in my life. He must have added it, thinking I'd prefer it to the overhead lighting most days. Or that I'd love the quirkiness of it. Both are accurate.

"Clover, this is when you say 'thank you' and move on." He opens packages of dry-erase markers from the mountain of sacks I assume hold even more office supplies.

"Thank you," I murmur, my voice catching just a little.

The dining table, still covered in color-coded sticky notes and half-labeled folders, feels miles away now. He noticed. Even when I tried to pretend I had it all under control, he noticed.

"Especially for hanging the white board. It was awkward writing on it leaning against the dining room wall. And you didn't even smudge my list. Very impressive." Failing to fall into the urge, I plop down onto the chair, scooting up to the desk.

"It's no big deal." He nods at my desk. "Don't you have a list of crap to do?"

The planner that holds the ever-growing task list for the opening holds my focus. My thoughts fire like popcorn in a hot pan, filling the white space with color. My eyes skim the list, and somehow it feels longer than it did a minute ago. Bullet points blur together, each one heavier than the last. I tap my pen against the margin, trying to find a starting point, but all I can think is *where the hell do I even begin?*

"What's next, Clover?" Jonathan's voice startles me out of my trance. Strong arms wrap around me from behind. My lids close, and I inhale his scent. The racing horse in my chest slows to a prance.

"Figuring out how to do all this." I flail my arms in front of me.

"We'll get it taken care of. Don't worry." He kisses my cheek before walking over to the stack of artwork that we got from the pop-up market.

"Easier said than done, my dude," I mutter, rolling my eyes at the back of his annoyingly broad shoulders. He's never had to wrestle with doubt. Things seem to fall into place for him.

The thought sours in my chest, sharp and uninvited.

I shove it away.

He's not perfect. I know that now. I have seen it in the quiet moments, the cracks he doesn't hide when it's just us. That's what I find most intriguing. He never asks me to be perfect, either. He doesn't deserve to carry my insecurities, too. He isn't... We are just... messing around.

I go back to the list, trying to pick a line up of things to accomplish.

"How about here?" He lifts a picture of a floating library in the sky being held up by balloons.

His words are barely audible to me.

The opening is only 53 days away.

"Yeah, sure, whatever is fine." I wave my hand in a whatever works motion as I examine the tasks I scheduled myself for today.

Fuck. How did I forget that?

The planner glares up at me from my desk. Damn, my own aggressive handwriting is judging me. The appointment to pick up my permit has been sitting there for weeks, and yet I have exactly ten minutes to get downtown and make it happen.

Peeking over at Jonathan to see if he's paying attention, I realize he is busy hanging another painting. I shove my planner and whatever else goes with it into my bag, snatch my keys, and whirl toward the door. Only to crash straight into Jonathan's chest.

"Oof." I stagger back, rubbing my nose. "Damn, do you have to be built like... like... that?"

"You weren't complaining last night," He gives me a saucy wink and steadies my shoulder. "Where are you running off to?"

"I'm not running anywhere." I pat my stomach. "Just going to run errands and to get food. I'm starving."

"I'm hungry too. Let me finish this and I'll go with you." Jonathan finishes hammering in a nail. "Or leave me a honey-do list. I can do that too."

Honey-do list? The thought of getting twice the amount of work done in half the time is tempting. Or Jonathan driving me to the permit office while I shuffle through the paperwork on the way. He could even provide back up when I plead my case.

Shaking my head, I charge to the door. There's no way I can let him help. Not when I've fought to prove that I can handle all of this. It'll prove that I can't do this. If I can't get a stupid permit on time, everyone will realize I'm not meant to be opening Reading Lane.

"Oh no, that's okay. I can bring something back for you. How about that burger and sweet potato thing you got last week?"

He pauses, and his gaze flicks to the whiteboard. Then to the half-empty coffee cup on the table.

"What's next on your list? I can hang these later. Let me help," he says, giving me a knowing look.

"Nothing big. I got it, really." I sidestep towards the door, tripping on something. I look down to see a book titled, *Stop Carrying the Couch Alone, You Weirdo.* No author. I kick it to the side and mutter, "I do not have time for your nonsense right now, cottage. I have to get to the permit office."

"What was that?" Jonathan asks over his shoulder.

"Nothing. I'll meet you at home later—I mean the cottage. I will meet you at the *cottage.* Later. With food."

I swing the door open and flash him my best definitely-not-panicking smile. "See you later!"

"I'm here to help. All you have to do is say the word!" he hollers at me as I shut the door.

I won't be saying the word. Instead, I will get this permit. Hopefully.

If I don't get there in time, I don't know what will be worse… the permit delay or the look on Jonathan's face when he realizes I was never as put-together as I let him believe.

✦·✦

I pull into Honeyville's combination Town Hall, County Clerk's Office, Building Department, Economic Development Office, and, on the weekends, Bingo Hall, with three minutes to spare.

Digging through my purse for my phone, which will not stop buzzing, I attempt to rush out of my car, only to be pull backed into my seat because I forgot to take off my fucking seat belt. Once I finally free myself, I run to the door. The fucking thing doesn't open, but I do run right into the glass door. The impact rattles my skull, and my phone slips from my grip. My nose stings. I blink up at the door.

CLOSED.

The bold red sign mocks me from the other side of the glass.

"DAMMIT!"

"Mazey?"

My insides lurch with fresh annoyance.

I spin around, already half-prepared to glare at the person, but it's Doris. Her eyes are twinkling with barely contained laughter.

"Well, sugar," she drawls, reaching up to tap the "CLOSED" sign. "That's quite the entrance."

"Need to get a permit filed," I grumble, wiping my now probably broken nose. "I didn't see the sign."

"Ain't that obvious, dear." She holds out her fragile hand to help me up. I brush it aside, standing on my own. "Just finished setting up bingo for tonight."

"Oh. Yeah. That's tonight. I probably won't be able to make it. I have—"

"A lot to do?" she finishes. "I know, I know. Not a problem. I'd bribe the permit lady, but last time I tried she threatened to call the sheriff. Suppose not everyone is interested in alien porn."

"Thanks anyways, Doris." I brush off my ass.

"Wasn't today the last day to get that permit filed to avoid that giant fine? You couldn't stop talking about it last week at book club." She wanders over to the bench just left of the door and pats for me to sit.

"Yeah. I totally forgot about it." And now I'm going to have to pay some outrageous amount to keep the grand opening on track. I can't remember the exact number, insisting that I didn't need to commit it to memory since there was no way in hell that I was going to miss the deadline. I do remember Nova and I being outraged on its behalf. It was some insane number that felt unreasonable.

"Happens to the best of us." Doris digs around her handbag and pulls out a package of chocolates. "Here, have one. That fella from the craft store—the handsome one that took me flamenco dancing—keeps buying me them. They are delicious, but the poor man is too old for me."

I select a cube that I hope is filled with caramel and not some cherry nonsense. "Isn't he like seventy-five or something?"

"Seventy-three. I'm more of a mid-sixties kind of gal."

I chuckle. Doris gives no shits and seems to have time for anyone that needs a chocolate on a bench. I'd love to have a version of her attitude towards life. Carefree. Never worried about the consequences of her actions. Meanwhile, I'm on pins and needles thinking about getting the budget corrected for the giant mistake that could have easily been avoided.

Organizing that gorgeous office Jonathan finished for me sounds nice right about now. Something to get my mind off of the mess of today. That man is really handsome, but he has no sense of the proper location for office supplies.

The long middle drawer was chaos when I peeked in it. Paperclips in the same bin as staples—gross. I have a whole system; he has absolutely no respect for the system. He just shows up and sets up an entire office and hangs a whiteboard and adds a Shih Tzu lamp and notices things I never asked him to notice, with zero regard for what that does to a person who was perfectly fine not being noticed.

Chapter 25

Happy Birthday, Mazey Lane

*"We pay a price for everything we get or take in this world; and although
ambitions are well worth having, they are not to be cheaply won,
but exact their dues of work and self-denial, anxiety and discouragement."*
- Anne of Green Gables, L.M. Montgomery

"Happy birthday! How are you feeling, Bug?" Mom calls from the kitchen counter, far too chipper for how early it is on a Sunday. She insisted on having the first family dinner at Reading Lane on my birthday. We call it family dinner, but really that means eating all day and hanging out together with whoever wants to come. It's an open invitation. If you're smart, you show up first thing in the morning to get first dibs on the smorgasbord of breakfast pastries.

"I'm okay. I'm just trying not to think about turning the big three-one today." My hand migrates to a croissant from the mountain of baked goods she either made all weekend or picked up from Something Sweet on her way over. "These are good. Yours or Mel's?"

"Those are Larry's," she drawls. Pink crosses her cheeks.

"Larry? Nova's dad, Larry?" I ask, nearly falling off my stool at the island. "It's nine in the morning. Is he here?"

"No…" she starts, but her sentence gets steamrolled by Nova storming into the kitchen, a wicked grin stretched across her face, hands on her hips.

"Judith. Bea. Lane." Nova turns to me. "Happy birthday, babe." Then she turns her attention right back to my mom.

"Nova, I do not have time for your shenanigans right now."

"Oh, but you have time for my dad's shenanigans?" Nova's grin only widens as she interrogates my mom. I grab another pastry as I settle in, equally invested in the drama and satisfying my growling stomach.

We've known they've been sneaking around since we were working on the fantasy living room. They got into the cutest paint fight, emerald green smeared across their faces. Then it got awkward when Jonathan pointed out the sapphire handprint on my mom's ass. They've done a piss-poor job hiding their flirtation. Or the fact that their cars always end up at each other's houses.

We love it. We're rooting for them. But it's also way too much fun to mess with them.

"Nova! Whatever are you talking about?" my very guilty-looking mother says as she turns her attention back to the omelets on the griddle.

Nova strides forward in full mock horror, winks at me, and launches into round two.

"Well," she says dramatically, "I stopped by my dad's this morning to pick up his old ass, and he was still in bed. Which is weird. So naturally, I assumed something terrible had happened. When I woke him up with a cup of water to the face, he said—get this—he had a lady over."

She huffs and stares at the ceiling like she's praying for strength, though her mouth twitches with suppressed laughter.

"Oh? A lady? That's nice…" My mom smiles, like she's remembering her night with the motorcycle-less motorcycle enthusiast.

"Was it Sheryl?" Elliott walks in the room holding a plate of fruit. Sawyer and Evie are behind him, skipping no beats to join in on the fun.

"You guys ride together?" I wave my pointer finger between them.

"It made sense to ride together. Since we're neighbors and all," Sawyer says with a nervous laugh.

"She's been gunning to be Larry's old lady for years. Every time she takes his order at the diner, she gives him those eyes," I say, grinning as I toss a wink at Nova while Mom keeps her back to us.

Nova whispers in my ear. "Umm, we need to revisit the whole Sawyer and Elliott thing, right?"

"Oh, for sure." I nod.

"Sheryl?" A gruff voice booms from the doorway.

Nova spins around. We both freeze, and she rushes over and practically hides behind me like I'm her human shield. I casually hand her a jelly-filled donut for her trust.

"Dad!"

"Thanks," she says, accepting it. "Carb count?"

Larry steps further into the kitchen, pausing with his classic dad expression—half warning, half amusement. It's clear he knows she needs to put in her bolus dose in the insulin pump clipped at her hip… but he also knows she's not getting out of this conversation. He glances at me and grins, annoyance with his daughter written all over his face. "Happy birthday, Miss Maze."

"Thanks, Lare," I say. Turning to Nova, I gesture to the chart. "On the fridge."

It's the same one we update before every family meal. A grid of dishes, ingredients, and carb counts scribbled in color-coded ink. After Nova's diagnosis, Larry had grabbed a Sharpie and said, "We're making this easy. No math at the table." And just like that, it became a ritual. No questions, no spotlight, just the numbers, always there.

Her eyes scan the chart. I walk over and point. "That one's raspberry."

Nova nods, already calculating her bolus and tapping it into her pump with practiced ease. I notice that she's taking longer than usual. A quick peek at her pump tells me that she is hitting buttons in the settings menu, but changing nothing.

"I know you're done with your bolus, Nova," he says, crossing his arms. "You ready for your lecture?"

I can't help the snort that escapes me.

"Now, girls." He leans over the counter and somehow looks both of us in the eyes at the same damn time. "I am in love with Judith. She is my old lady. I'm going to need you two to get on board because I don't plan on her going anywhere soon. Or, well, anytime ever. Is that clear? That means stop giving her a hard time."

"In love? With Me?" My mom slowly turns to Larry, who is wearing worn jeans, a grey Harley Davidson shirt tucked in—belly rolling over—and a leather vest. He is truly the opposite of my mom, but also the perfect fit.

He examines her up and down like she's the most incredible thing he's ever seen.

"How did she not know?" Nova whispers beside me, her eyes locked on them just like mine. "It's so obvious. Did she think he goes around mowing everyone's lawns and giving them rides to work when their car breaks down?"

"Or what about that time you guys stayed with us for a week in middle school," I wheeze. "My mom swore she heard someone trying to break in? He slept on the couch every night… only to find out it was a family of raccoons raiding the garbage." I hide my chuckle behind my hand.

Nova snorts softly. "I think they've been in love for like… fifteen years."

"Did they finally figure it out?" Bobby says, presenting me with a beautiful present wrapped in sparkly purple paper and a giant silver bow.

"They did," Elliott says.

Happiness radiates off the couple in question. They are squeezed in the corner of the counter, laughing and waiting for the waffle maker's light to go off. I can't help but smile. My mom deserves to be that happy all the time.

A giddiness rushes through me and I remember the present. I reach for it. "Can I open it?"

"I'd be offended if you didn't," Bobby says, wrapping his arm around my dad's waist and pulling closer.

I tear through the paper. There's nothing better than opening a gift from someone who loves you. Except maybe giving one in return. A gift means they thought of you while wandering through a store, or spent the time to make something with their own hands. It's their interpretation of who you are, wrapped up and handed back to you. And when you find the perfect gift for someone you love… there's nothing better.

It's a set of personalized library stamps. One reads, "From the Library of Mazey Lane" with a little gummy bear perched on a stack of books. The other says, "Reading Lane's Library" stamped beneath the logo Nova designed. Tucked alongside them is a giant set of library cards with colorful pocket inserts. Those are personalized with the Reading Lane logo too, in an array of bright colors.

Tears line my lashes. "Thank you so much. It's perfect."

"It's from all of us," my dad says.

"Don't worry though, there are more presents." My mom grins.

Ever since the accident, my birthday has been bittersweet. It feels wrong to make a wish when the person who should blow out the candles beside me isn't here to steal the first slice. Wrong to celebrate a day that marked my beginning… and his end. I swallow back the "why not me" and the "he should be here." But the thoughts always find their way up, sour in my throat.

Especially when everyone's looking at me like I'm supposed to beam with joy. *Yay! I've made it through another year.* Like survival is a party trick. I haven't forgotten that Dawson isn't sitting in the chair beside me, eating cake with ghost hands.

I didn't choose to survive the accident. Didn't pick my life over his. I was on the opposite side of the car. The side that took the least amount of impact. It was just luck. Good or bad is yet to be determined.

The rest of my patchwork family trickles in, including the book club and some of the crew, and we settle at the giant table outside between the weeping willows near the lake. My mom bribed the crew to build a duplicate table to the one at her house with free coffee from Gus's. I'm not sure dad knows yet. According to her, it's a small price to pay to foster a sense of community for guests. I have to admit, she's totally right.

Bobby sticks the candles into the vanilla cake that is shaped like a giant gummy bear. Grams starts humming some off-key rendition of "Happy Birthday," moving her arms like she is a conductor, encouraging everyone to join in.

I sit there with a smile stitched in place as everyone sings. When they reach the "Happy birthday to…" part, the group says both Dawson and Mazey—like they do every year. My mom sits beside me, her hand steady on my back. Her voice falters on the last note, but she doesn't stop. Just grabs my hand and squeezes.

The song ends. The candles flicker. Everyone's eyes are on me.

"I feel like this wish is high-stakes," I mutter, loud enough to earn a few chuckles.

"Don't overthink it," Larry calls, spraying whipped cream directly into his mouth.

"Easy for you to say. You're not being peer-pressured by fire and frosting." The crowd chuckles.

I close my eyes, the darkness behind my lids filling with fragments of the past months. The clatter of hammers in half-finished rooms, paint-smeared hands gripping coffee cups, receipts and spreadsheets scattered across my desk. Laughter spilling from people who were strangers not long ago but now save me seats at crowded tables. For a breath, it all flickers like a reel of proof that I've built something genuine.

But even as the images glow bright, I feel the shadows pressing in—the rooms still unfinished, the questions still unanswered, the huge part of me still unconvinced.

I wish I could stop pretending I belong here.

The candles go out. Everyone claps. And just like that, the moment passes. Jonathan slides into the empty chair next to me, scooting it so close sunlight can't shine through. His knee bumps mine under the table.

"You did it," he whispers.

"Barely." I lean in, humor in my hushed voice. "That wish was a lot of pressure. The cake was almost collateral damage."

He smiles, just for me, and his fingers brush against mine. When I don't pull away, his hand curls around mine, tucking them under the tablecloth, out of sight. "Still proud of you."

My mom appears beside me with a glass of lemonade mixed with tea, condensation already beading down the sides. I pull my hand from Jonathan's and slap it onto the table.

"We got your favorite," she says gently, setting it down in front of me like an offering.

"Thanks, Mom." I lift the cup my lips, the familiar tart-sweetness anchoring me for a second.

She lingers, a complicated mixture of sadness and joy landscaping her face. A representation of the complicated feelings that my birthday represents. With a soft breath, she reaches up and tucks a strand of hair behind my ear, the same way she used to when I was little and trying to hold in tears. "He'd be so proud of you, you know."

"I hope so," I manage, my voice smaller than it was a second ago.

The day turns into evening. People scrape plates clean. Laughter ebbs and flows. The fire pit crackles as the sun sinks behind the trees. When the last bit of light fades from the sky and the air turns cooler, my parents pack up leftovers for every single person that attended, a true testament to their caring hearts. Mom is carefully scooping the world's most controversial potato salad into containers when Jonathan leans close again, lips brushing just beneath my ear.

"That stuff is the worst," he mutters.

I whip my head toward him. "I know, right? She ignores my cries to not make it. It's like spooning vinegar into regret."

He chuckles and hits me with one of his, in my opinion, world famous grins. "Wanna disappear for a bit?"

I glance toward the edge of the yard, where the trees lead down to the dock. "What's the plan? Romantic forest walk or dramatic birthday kidnapping?"

"Little of both?" He stands.

I bite my lip, looking up at his outreached hand. "But only if there's cake involved."

"Deal."

We sneak off with all the subtlety of teenagers ditching a family reunion, a giant plate of cake in hand. Wilfred trails behind, sniffing the air. The sky's gone dusky, the lake catching the last hints of gold, and everything smells like smoke, grass, and sugar.

We settle on the dock, feet dangling into the water, the cake between us. The quiet settles around us, thick and gentle. It's the kind of quiet that's both overwhelming and comforting at once. I feel it in my bones. In my breath. For the first time all day, I let myself exhale without guilt.

It's still there, of course. That familiar weight, the echo of what's missing. But it's quieter. Manageable. Held back by warm hands and steady voices and people who refuse to let me carry it all alone.

Jonathan's phone makes the familiar ping of a new email. With a heavy sigh, he pulls it out, his brow furrowing as he reads the message. His fingers hover over the screen for a moment before he starts typing, his face crumpled in concentration.

"I hate my job," he says, shoving the device back into his pocket.

"No shit," I say. We don't look at each other. We just sit, facing the lake. "What would you do if you could do anything?"

"Teach. Blow-glass. Be happy," he says without a second thought.

"Then do it." The words slip out as if getting fired from my job was easy. I pause for a second. Walking away from the corporate grind wasn't hard.

"Yeah, that's a choice." He chuckles.

"There's always a choice. Losing my job was so scary… then opening this place… but also… maybe the easiest." I shrug. "I couldn't stay somewhere that stole my joy. And, well, the whole treating employees terribly thing didn't help either."

He runs his fingers through his hair. "I'm failing Phoenix. I'm the reason we're in this financial mess."

"Don't be so dramatic. It's not all on you. Don't you have a finance team?" I turn to him. The moonlight bounces off the water, leaving a sparkling trail. "Let's play what if."

"You just made that up, didn't you?" He laughs.

I nod. "What if you could follow your dreams? Tell me what that looks like."

I lean in, my elbows on my knees. The cake sits untouched between us. Every time he pauses, I give him a small nod of encouragement. He describes a glass-blowing studio downtown with tables set up for sketching designs and workbenches lined with all the tools waiting to create.

He tells me about how he'd teach more courses for the Phoenix Pathway Program in the evenings, more opportunities for students to learn and grow.

We linger under the stars long after the music fades, the hush of night wrapping around us like a blanket. Laughter and shouted good-byes echo from the driveway as the last guests trickle out, car doors slamming, tires crunching over gravel. Still, we stay snuggled in close as words flow easily. I'm inside the fantasy with him.

He trails off, watching the fireflies over the water. His hand inches closer to mine until his pinkie finger locks with mine, the way a promise is sealed. We sit with it for a moment—his dream hanging in the air between us, unhurried, like it has nowhere to be.

Something shifts in my chest. Quiet and certain, the way things settle after a long time of being unsettled.

I built a soundproof nook for the person who needs to disappear. A wide path for the person who is afraid the terrain won't hold them. A big table with conversation cards for the person who booked a solo retreat and is secretly hoping to meet someone.

I built all of that because I knew those people. Because I *am* those people.

Maybe that's what belonging looks like. Not the absence of grief, or doubt, or the wish that the chair beside you wasn't empty. Maybe it's just—this. Cake on a dock. Someone's dream spilling out under the stars. The weight is still there, but it's held differently.

I reach over and finally pick up my fork.

"Happy birthday, Dawson," I say quietly, to the water, to the sky, to wherever he is.

Then I take a bite of cake.

Chapter 26

Prove It

"He wasn't new to her life. That was the thing that undid her. He had been there the whole time, in the background of every chapter, and she had somehow convinced herself a person that familiar couldn't also be the person. And then one Tuesday, for no particular reason, she looked at him and understood that she had been wrong about that for years." - The Long Way Home, Sawyer Storme

I've been alone at the cottage with Jonathan a million times over the past few months, but tonight, sitting under the stars on the quiet dock, it's different. The endless questions that have lingered in my mind about what that kiss meant in the kitchen the night I found out that I wasn't just his best friend's annoying little sister have dissolved into the starry sky. I know what Jonathan is to me. Maybe that's all that matters.

"Jonathan?" I pretzel my legs and face him.

"Yes, Clover." He positions himself to mirror me, our knees touching.

I tug at the sleeve of my sweatshirt until large hands still them.

A braveness takes over, one I wasn't aware existed inside me. Or maybe it was dormant until I decided to buy a cottage and partner with the guy I've crushed on for over a decade.

"You know what I want for my birthday?"

Jonathan looks over, the corner of his mouth lifting. "What's that?"

I turn toward him on the dock, knees brushing. "You."

The word hangs in the air. Somehow, we are as close as two people can get without climbing on each other. I've never stared into someone's eyes like this before. I'm overwhelmed and calm at the same time. Pressure to be perfect, to never fail, seems like a foreign thought because the way he's looking at me feels like everything I touch will turn to gold.

In every romance novel I've ever read, someone always says something like *his gaze bores into my soul.* I always thought it was just poetic license. A pretty thing writers say.

It's not. The first person who wrote it was telling the truth.

Those chocolate eyes are giving me a piece of Jonathan. I see our past—kids chasing each other across the playground playing tag, pushing each other into the lake on hot summer days. I see the present—building a dream side-by-side, navigating through the ups and down of a renovation and internet fame. And I see, the most terrifyingly exciting part, a future. Our future. It's not crystal clear, for good reason. I'm not a fortune teller by any means—I'll leave that to Nova. But Jonathan and I are together, and that's all I need.

"Me?" Jonathan finally asks, his voice just above a whisper.

"Yes. You."

For a heartbeat, he just stares at me, like he's memorizing this moment. Then his hand slides to the back of my neck, fingers threading into my hair, and he pulls me to him.

My body arches toward his, heat pooling low in my stomach. His mouth moves along my jaw, the base of my neck, and I gasp, clinging to him for a moment before I pull back.

"We should go inside." I stand, holding my hand to him.

He looks up at me, mischief dancing all over his face in the moonlight. His hand grasps mine as he stands. "We should."

He scoops me into his arms. His skin is warm against mine. His hands settle under my thighs, lifting me effortlessly.

"What the hell, Kirkwood?" I squeeze his neck for dear life, instinctively coiling my legs around him like a boa constrictor.

He laughs into my hair, arms tightening like the threat means nothing to him.

"I'm going to break your arms," I say.

"I've thought about this too long to care about my damn arms." His darkened eyes sear through me. "Is your apartment okay? We could go back to my place. Fuck, I'll get us a penthouse in Charleston. Anywhere I can take my time with you."

I couldn't want him more.

The thing about Jonathan—he's more. He's more perfect. More kind. More caring. He's more everything—good and bad—in all the ways that compliment my less. He falls into me, wrapping his arms around my waist. My tongue grazes his lips, deepening the kiss until the world falls away. My fingers slide up to the back of my neck, threading into his hair. He shivers at the gentle tug, and I moan against his mouth.

I swallow hard. Jonathan has thought about me. Not just thought about me, but *thought* about me. His face—okay, his body—has been on a loop since I figured out how to masturbate in the eighth grade. When does someone start getting themselves off? Maybe I was a late bloomer? I was for basically everything else.

Did Jonathan think about me his first time like I thought of him? Holy shit. The guy I've been swooning over since middle school is ready to carry me up two flights of stairs to fuck me.

We stop more than once to make out. On the porch swing—me straddling him, swaying with every movement. He kisses down my neck. Nips through my t-shirt around my nipples. In the foyer, knocking a canvas painting of cats playing poker, which Elliott found at a second-hand store, off the wall.

Eventually, we make it up the thousands of stairs. I run my fingers through his beard. God, it's just as soft as I daydreamed about. So fucking soft. My stomach flutters. I don't know what's going on. Is this real life? I pinch myself.

"What are you doing?" Jonathan dips down for me to open the door to my apartment. "Did you just pinch yourself?"

"Maybe… This doesn't seem real. This feels too good to be true." I feel my cheeks heat.

"It's real, Clover." He sets me on the bed. Stands in front of me.

"Prove it." I smirk at him and grab the hem of his shirt, pulling him down. I lay back, bringing him with me. He catches himself, bracketing me with his thick arms.

"Oh, I'm going to prove it to you." He crashes into me, lips pressed against mine. He tastes so good. Feels so good. Warmth radiates off him, creating a warm cocoon between us.

"Can I take this off?" I bite my lip as I tug on his shirt. I've seen this man topless on more than one occasion—swimming in the lake, that time my dads convinced him to weed their entire herb garden in the dead of summer. Hell, last week when he was working on the porch. This though. This is different. I get to touch him. Feel him. Trace the lines of his arm muscles if I want.

He whips the shirt over his head, a silent answer. His body is magnificent. Not overly sculpted, but it's clear he's strong. The kind of strength that comes from working, building. Not from a gym. I doubt he's ever paid for a gym membership.

"Your turn." He kisses me. "If you want, I mean. No pressure."

I nod, and he helps me wiggle out of my shirt and sports bra, pulling them over my head. Jonathan shakes his head, dark locks tumbling into his face. "Sweet Jesus."

His mouth is on my neck, moves down until my nipple is in his mouth. He twirls his tongue around it in alternating patterns. Slow, slow, fast, slow, slow, fast. My fingers run through his hair, pulling him closer.

His touch pulls a sound from me that I don't recognize as my own, something soft and undone. Jonathan stills instantly, lifting his head, eyes searching my face like he's memorizing it.

His weight settles between my thighs, solid and grounding, and for a moment we just breathe—my hands on his back, his face tucked into my neck like he belongs there. He kisses along my jaw, my collarbone, lingering as if he's savoring every inch he's waited years to touch.

"I'm going to take these off," he murmurs, fingers hooking into the waistband of my leggings. He pauses, eyes flicking up to mine, giving me the space to decide.

"Yes," I say immediately, lifting my hips to help him. There's no hesitation in me.

He slides them down my legs slowly, deliberately, like this is something to be appreciated, not rushed through. His hands follow the movement, warm and sure, until he tosses them aside and looks at me like I'm something unreal.

"God," he exhales, shaking his head again. "You're—"

"Jonathan, I need you to take your pants off."

Relief loosens his shoulders, and he presses his forehead to mine, laughing through a breath. "Oh, of course."

He stands, slips off his pants. I sit up on my elbows, taking him in. Every inch of his thick… body. He wraps his hand around his cock, pulls on it a couple of times. The sight of him does absolutely nothing to calm me down.

"I need to taste you." he says quietly.

I spread my legs, an invitation. "Then do it."

He drops to his knees and slides me across the bed so my ass is on the edge, kissing my thighs. Working his way to my center. The novel I was reading the day that I found the cottage pops into my head for some reason. The hero, licking the heroine's clit like his life depended on it. Like it was the best thing he'd ever done. At the time, I thought that was made up. There's no way a person in the real world would enjoy running their tongue all over my soaked slit, but—fuck. Jonathan is acting like my wetness is his last meal and he couldn't be happier.

He adds two digits, and my entire body quivers. My back arches, and a moan falls from my mouth.

"You are beautiful."

Something in my chest cracks open at that. All the years of wanting, of watching from a distance, of telling myself he was a dream I'd outgrown—it all dissolves into this one truth: he's here, choosing me, and I'm choosing him right back.

He climbs up my body, grazing my skin the entire way.

He hovers over me for a breath, eyes locked on mine, like he's grounding himself before crossing the final inch. His hand slides down my side, thumb tracing slow, absent-minded circles against my skin, and the tenderness of it nearly undoes me.

"Mazey," he says, my name rough on his tongue. Not a question.

A promise.

"I'm here." I pull him closer, my forehead tipping to his. "There are condoms in the nightstand."

That's all he needs. He opens the top drawer, pulls out the foil packages, rolls on the condom.

The way he comes to me is careful, deliberate—like he's listening with his whole body, adjusting to every breath, every shift. It isn't frantic. It's deep and consuming, the kind of closeness that makes everything else disappear. I cling to him, my legs tightening instinctively, my hands pressing into his back like I need the proof of him there.

He moves with me. Not rushing, not holding back either. Every kiss feels anchored, intentional, as if he's trying to say things his mouth can't quite manage. My name slips from his lips again and again, soft and wrecked, like he's been waiting years to say it this way.

I lose myself in the rhythm of us—heat building, breath stuttering, the room filled with quiet sounds we don't try to stop. My world narrows to the scrape of his beard against my skin, the weight of him, the way his hand finds mine and laces our fingers together like he doesn't want there to be any confusion about this being shared.

When it crests, it's not explosive. It's overwhelming. A full-body surrender. I break beneath it, my head tipping back, his name falling from my mouth as he follows me, burying his face in my neck like he needs to hold on.

After, he stays exactly where he is, chest pressed to mine, breath slowly evening out. His thumb keeps moving, tracing idle lines on my arm, grounding us both until the room comes back into focus.

He lifts his head just enough to look at me, his expression open and unguarded. He brushes a kiss across my mouth, soft, lingering, nothing like before.

"Hi," he murmurs.

I laugh quietly, still a little breathless. "Hi."

He gathers me closer, like this is where I belong. I don't argue with the thought.

Instead, I fall asleep in his arms—again.

Chapter 27

What the Hell Am I Doing?

[Camera tilts up slowly to a whiteboard covered in half-legible scrawls.
In the corner, a sun with the number thirteen inside it, drawn in red marker.]
Mazey (off-camera, to Wilfred): "Don't look at me like that."
[Wilfred looks at her exactly like that.]

"**U**gh, why are my hands so freaking sweaty," I say to the fuzzy companion sitting at my feet, staring at the array of colors looming on the whiteboard. I wipe my hands down the side of my jeans and squint, stepping forward. Does that say "find new coffee distributor" or "decorate coffee bar"? Who knows. I've been scribbling crap down between rolling around naked with Jonathan and squeezing in planning sessions with Nova for the opening.

Now, I can't make heads or tails of my scrawls. Except for the most daunting item, bright red—jumping out at me in my nightmares—the countdown to the big day. A thirteen inside of a sun glares down at me from the right-hand corner of the board, thanks to Katie.

Wilfred paws at my leg, letting out a tiny rumble.

"I know, Buddy." I slide down the wall, my fuzzy companion stumbling into my lap. He's snoring before my hand hits his ear for a scratch. Poor guy, he followed my pacing until two o'clock in the morning, listening to my ramblings.

There are plenty of people who have volunteered to help give this list a dramatic reduction, but I can't bring myself to take anyone up on the offer. The combination of avoiding burdening my loved ones and the need to do everything by myself is thick.

"Well, Willy." I sigh, running my fingers through his plush "Where do we start? Groomer appointment, probably. You're looking a little… *ruff*. Oh man, that was terrible."

Ping. My phone flashes a notification for a vlog comment.

I've been avoiding them. Ever since we gave the den its dramatic facelift, the feedback's been… less than kind. Since when did "community engagement" turn into a free-for-all on my mental stability?

Yes, I had a rough week. Okay, maybe two. But are strangers with usernames like @ReadOrDie69 qualified to assess my mental health and business acumen based on one vlog where I cried into a box of cookies?

If I'm being honest, I get it. I mean, I'm questioning myself too.

Oh, and I still haven't received shipping confirmation for the books I ordered for the swag bags. Even with Nova's crafting magic, there's no way to conjure the paperbacks out of thin air.

The event is meant to be dreamy with music and dancing. Fairy lights strung between the trees. People escaping into reading nooks with romance novels tucked under their arms. Guests crafting in the garage-turned-art studio. A community celebrating a shared passion.

Exactly what I want Reading Lane to be.

If I can pull it off.

If I don't screw it up.

Ping.

"Where is the stupid thing?" I ask no one in particular, searching under piles of papers and books for my phone. "I do not have time for this today."

I uncover another author-less book. *Every Terrible Idea I've Ever Had and How It Wasn't The End of the World.* I toss it to the side.

Ping. "Where is my freaking phone?"

I shovel a stack of papers off my desk. "There you are. Guess talking to myself is helping."

A flood of notifications fill the screen.

I move through a handful of texts. Updates from Mom about snacks, a reminder from Elliott to take my vitamins (rude), and Jonathan asking if I slept last night. The answer is no, but I lie and say I did.

I pull up my email.

Subject: Update On Your Order
From: Bulk Books (admin@bulkbooks.com)

Hi Mazey,
Since we did not hear back with confirmation about your order for Reading Lane's grand opening, we are closing the request as the shipping window for such a large order has closed.
If you need assistance in the future, please consider using us.

Wishing you the Best,
-The Bulk Books Team

My head falls into the tornado of papers. I close my eyes and let the phone tumble out of my grasp. Fighting off the rising tide of *I fucking screwed up again*.

I forgot to confirm the book order.

How am I supposed to prove I deserve to be in this position? That the risk I took was worth it? I am failing Dawson.

I look at the mile-long list of things to do on the white board across from me.

"Guess I should get to work on the landscaping. Want to help, pup?" I pat Wilfred's head. He groans then flops over.

✦˙✦

I hold pink dahlias in front of the shed, deciding between them or the purple ones. All the siding for the exterior of the shed, garage, and cottage wrapped up yesterday. Jonathan suggested a beautiful sea green, a refresh of the original sage with a slight twist. It suits the place—a mix of modern and the twenties.

"What do you think, Wilfred?" Wilfred smells each plant. Then proceeds to chuff on each one. I giggle. "Both it is."

"The place looks incredible," a familiar voice says behind me. A voice I haven't heard in six months. "The entire office has been buzzing about the transformation. I'm told that you are the brains behind it. And the success of the overall plan—including the timeline and the budget."

I turn slowly to see my old boss, Margot, standing in front of me in a tan pantsuit. Her feathered hair blows in the wind. I realize I haven't thought about my life before Reading Lane for weeks—months, even. Am I responsible for the timeline and budget success for this renovation? I did create the original project plan as part of the business proposal I gave to Jonathan before buying the place. Updated it along the way. Made sure that we cut what we don't need and selected comparable, more affordable options when possible. But that's what a business owner does, right? And I haven't done it alone. Jonathan has helped along the way, guiding me with realistic expectations and logical thinking.

"Hi, Margot. What are you doing here?" My job at Pixel Perfection was remote, but there were several of us that lived in close proximity to the headquarters. Margot and I were two of those people. We were never close enough to grab dinner after work or meet up for a movie or anything like that. But we'd see each other on occasion at the mall the next town over, greeting each other with a quick wave.

"I've heard a lot about this place." She lifts her chin, examining the property. The lake's breeze flows around her. "Thought I'd check it out for myself."

"Oh, yeah. The vlog. Lots of followers." I stand, awkwardly slide my hands into the pockets of my overalls. "Want to come inside? I think there's some of my mom's fresh squeezed lemonade in the fridge."

"That's okay." She waves my offer off. "I do have something I need to discuss with you, Mazey."

"I sent back all my equipment. I swear." There is a really good chance I'm going to puke all over this lady's patent leather heels.

She chuckles. "No, no. Nothing like that. I want to talk to you about an opportunity."

"An opportunity? You fired me, remember? I fell asleep during a company-wide meeting." What kind of opportunity is there for someone who loses a job like that? She was right when she fired me. I wasn't living up to my potential. The safe route wasn't the best route for me. I can see that clearly since jumping into the so-called fire.

For the first time since I hit the job market, I've felt fulfilled in my career. It's just starting out, but I've loved every minute of it. From designing the suites, to planning out special event weekends, to creating the menu. Sure, there are parts that I haven't loved—the uncertainty that I'll have success running such a specific style bed-and-breakfast, resort-style getaway is always at the front of my mind.

"Pixel Perfection is launching a new software. It's specific to this type of place." She gestures to the cottage. "Luxury getaways. Mom-and-pop style retreats."

"We already are using a software. I'm not sure I can manage to make this switch this close to the opening." I ramble, thinking of any excuse to get away from the sales pitch she's clearly trying to give me. Right? She's trying to get me to use the software featuring it on the vlog. Smart move.

"Yes, that would be nice if you could. I'd give you a hell of a deal." I knew it. "But that's not what I'm getting at."

"It's not?"

"I want you to be on the team. The pay is high since you'll be part of the design team, not a project manager. You'd be part of the task force that will brainstorm features this software needs. Since you've been in it first hand, your expertise will be most valuable."

"Reading Lane hasn't even opened yet. I haven't run it," I argue.

"True, but you have built it from the ground up. We'd want you to work with whoever you decide should run it once you leave to continue to get ideas. There'd be some travel to other potential new customers as well." She pulls out a thick, black folder from the briefcase slung over her shoulder. "Look these over. I'll touch base after the weekend if you have any questions."

All I can do is stand there. Stunned, holding the paperwork with an offer I never saw coming.

"And Mazey, that job"—she points to my hands—"is secure. I included the reports to back it. This place, as lovely as it is, is a shot in the dark."

Instinct kicks in, and I give her a pageant wave goodbye, and then she's gone.

Chapter 28

Mazey's Choice

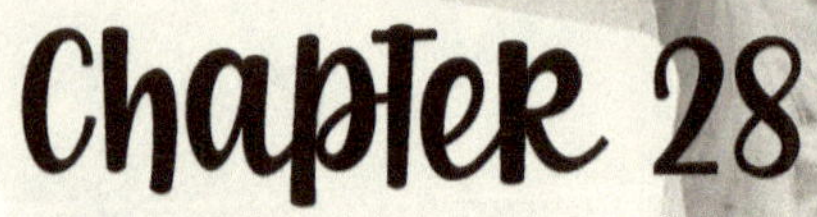

"**D**id you want that yarn organizer on the wall or in a cabinet?" Jonathan walks up the path from the garage, his gaze sliding to the little red convertible disappearing into the distance. "Who was that?"

"My old boss," I mutter, handing him the folder. "She wants to hire me back."

He opens it, scanning each page. His eyes go big. "That's a lot of money. And it's guaranteed for—" He looks up at me. "Five years. Damn. What did you say when you turned her down?"

"I didn't turn her down." I reach for the folder. "I didn't give her an answer."

Jonathan closes it slowly, watching me. "Okay." A beat. "Do you want to go back?"

"It's a lot to think about."

"Mazey." His voice is careful now, like he's already felt the thing I haven't said yet.

I turn toward the cottage, needing to move, needing to not be looked at right now. Every major slip—the permits, the book order, the budget bleed—it all happened after Jonathan and I started whatever this was—is. Was. I genuinely do not know the correct tense and that is also a problem.I've tried to separate the two things. I can't. They're tangled up in each other, and something has to give, and I know which thing I'm capable of letting go of, even if knowing that makes me want to sit down on the ground.

"Jonathan." I stop walking but keep my back to him. "I think we need to talk."

"Then turn around." His footsteps close the distance between us, unhurried. "Whatever it is, look at me when you say it."

I turn around.

Well, that was a mistake.

His expression is open in a way it almost never is—no armor, no careful distance—and it makes what I'm about to do so much harder. I have catalogued approximately one million versions of his face at this point. This one is the worst one.

"I need to step back from—" I press my lips together, squeeze my eyes shut for half a second. "—us."

The silence that follows is enormous.

"What?" It comes out quiet. Not angry. Confused and soft in a way that splits me open.

"I'm losing focus. The book order. The late permit fine. Everything that's fallen through the cracks since you and I started—" I gesture vaguely between us because I still, after all this time, do not have a word for what we are. "I can't afford to keep dropping things. There's too much at stake."

"You think that's because of me?" He takes a step closer, and I take a step back. His jaw tightens. He notices. "Mazey, I'm not the reason you're overwhelmed. You let yourself drown before I ever kissed you. Long before we…"

"I know that." My voice cracks at the edges. "I know it's not your fault. That's not what I'm saying."

"Then what are you saying?"

"I'm saying that when I'm with you, I can't think straight. And right now I need to think straight. I need to be able to look at a to-do list and see a to-do list, and right now when I look at it I just think about—" I stop. "It doesn't matter what I think about."

"It matters to me."

I think about you. I think about being wrapped up in your arms, kissing your adorable face, touching your adorable beard. I think about the conversations I can't wait to have about the logistics of your favorite show and about how you can bake anything perfectly even though baking is the most difficult task known to man. That's the problem.

I don't say any of that though. Instead, I say nothing. Because my heart is breaking and my insides are crumbling and I hate this decision I'm making but I also can't not make it.

Because Dawson.

I can't be so careless about Dawson's dream.

Something moves across his face—something quick and barely contained. He turns away, runs a hand through his hair, and when he looks back at me, there's a careful blankness I recognize. He's putting the walls up. I've watched him take them down, brick by brick, over the past however many months. Watching them go back up is its own kind of grief that I do not have time to be having right now.

"So that's it." Not a question.

"It's not it. It's just—a pause. Until after the opening. Until I get my feet under me."

"Mazey." He says my name like it costs him something. "You know that's not how this works, right? You can't just pause something and expect it to be the same when you come back."

I do know that. I know it so well I can't look him in the eye when I say, "I have to try."

He's quiet for a long moment. A bird calls from somewhere across the lake. The breeze moves through the grass between us. I adjust my simple, black-framed glasses and focus on a specific blade so I don't have to focus on his face.

"Let me help you." His voice drops, stripped down to something raw. "I'm not a distraction, Clover. I'm right here. I will show up every single day and help you carry this thing."

My throat tightens so fast it hurts.

"That's the problem," I whisper. "You already do. And when you do, I forget to look at my to-do list and I forget to check my emails and I forget everything except—" I stop. Swallow. "I can't afford to forget right now."

"You can't afford to let someone love you, you mean."

The word lands like something dropped from a great height. I don't answer. I can't. He searches my face for a long moment, and then he exhales slowly. Nods once. A small, terrible nod, like he's accepting a verdict he already knew was coming.

"Okay." He picks up his jacket from the porch railing. "Okay, Mazey."

"Jonathan—"

"No." He shakes his head, gentle but final. "Don't apologize. Just—don't."

I watch him walk down the path. I watch him get in his truck. I stand there until I can't hear the engine anymore, and then I walk into the shed and I sit down on the floor with my back against the wall and both hands pressed over my mouth like I can hold it in by force.

The shed still smells like sawdust and wood stain and the coffee he brought over three weeks ago when we worked in here until midnight. The Shih Tzu lamp is on. I don't remember turning it on. Everything in this place has him in it—the whiteboard, the teal desk, the pens he moved without disrupting my piles because he already knew the system.

I built this with him.

And I just told him to leave.

I pull my knees to my chest and cry—the ugly, silent kind.

Chapter 29

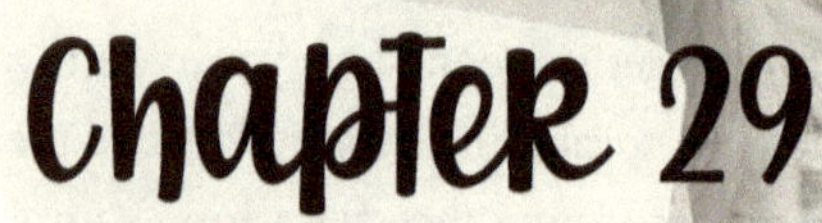

Bee Hive: Take Two

*"Don't confuse working on yourself with punishing yourself.
There's a difference." - Doris*

A week passes the way weeks do when you're trying not to think about something—fast and blurry and exhausting, with a dull ache running underneath all of it that you keep mistaking for productivity.

And I am very productive.

I painted another coat of sealer on the welcome sign. I reorganized the linen closet… twice. I mapped out every single item on the grand opening checklist and then color-coded it by urgency, category, and whether or not I can delegate it, which took four hours and accomplished absolutely nothing except keeping my hands busy.

Wilfred follows me from room to room with the specific energy of a dog who knows something is wrong and has decided his job is to be a warm, snoring shadow until it gets better.

I don't cry after that first night on the shed floor. I'm not sure if that's growth or just the numbness that sets in when you make the choice yourself and you can't even be properly angry about it.

Jonathan's truck doesn't come down the lane. I don't expect it to. I told him I need space, and he's giving it to me, because of course he is. Because that's exactly who he is, and somehow that makes everything harder instead of easier.

Katie has Nova and Sawyer step in for the vlog, claiming to the internet that Jonathan is sick. Because that's what he tells her. That he's sick. I don't know whether to be grateful or gutted that he makes it easy on me like that. Probably both. Probably I'll be both about most things involving Jonathan for a while.

I make the mistake of reading the vlog comments.

I know better. I genuinely know better. And yet.

I open my phone and scroll, sitting cross-legged on the bathroom floor at seven in the morning because that's apparently who I am now.

@romancereadergirl: ok but has anyone else noticed the vibes are different lately?? like something feels off
@cottagecoreobsessed: replying to @romancereadergirl RIGHT like where is the banter. mazey seems tired.
@bookishbabe22: replying to @romancereadergirl she's been doing everything herself this week. i miss them together on camera 💀
@hopelessromantic_irl: idk i just have a feeling. the way he looked at her in that last video... and now he's suddenly gone for a week? i ship them SO hard and i am nervous
@bookishbabe22: replying to @hopelessromantic_irl don't do this to me i cannot handle a reading lane breakup arc
@thereadingnook: replying to @hopelessromantic_irl STOP IT. they're endgame. they have to be endgame.

I close the app.

They're not wrong, the commenters. They're watching a forty-second clip and clocking something I've apparently been wearing on my face for a week. I'm not sure whether to be impressed by them or horrified by myself.

The internet decides we're a love story before I even admit it to myself, and now I'm the one who ended it, and they don't know yet, and eventually they will, and I have absolutely no idea what I'm going to say when that moment comes.

Nothing is always an option.

I set my phone face-down on the bathroom tile. Wilfred pushes the door open with his nose, takes one look at me on the floor, and sits down directly on my feet.

"Yeah," I tell him. "Me too."

Nova is patient with me in the way only Nova can be—present without pushing, showing up with coffee, and not asking questions I'm not ready to answer. But last night, she sat on the edge of my bed and said, very gently, "The book club is doing dollar drop night tomorrow. You're coming."

I say I have things to do.

She says, "Mazey."

"Fine."

✦

The Bee Hive looks exactly the same as it does every Thursday. Same low lighting, same sticky menus. Doris is already waiting in the corner booth like she's been there since last week and simply never left. I slide into the booth across from her, and she doesn't look up from her knitting.

I'm right back where I was seven months ago—same bar, same dollar drop night, same lemon drop special on the chalkboard.

Except this time I don't have a book from the cottage. After I brushed off the last one, *Stop Carrying the Couch Alone, You Weirdo*, all the books disappeared.

Even the cottage seems disappointed. I really hope it doesn't give up on me entirely. The magic of that place is the whole reason I finally decided to follow my dreams. To take the risk.

Unlike the last time I sat in this booth, I know I can do it. The cottage, the opening, the whole impossible thing—I believe in it. It's not the pity party I threw myself then. At least, not when it comes to my career.

But when it comes to Jonathan, that's a completely different story. I'm in love with him. I said it; I'm in love with that bearded, steady, infuriating man. And have been ever since I can remember. And I'm the one who ended it. For the right reasons… I think.

"Another round!" Sawyer and Nova arrive with hands full of lemon drops, carefully setting them on the table, sliding one in front of each of us.

"This isn't necessary. I have so much to do at the cottage. The grand opening is three weeks out."

"Don't worry, Mazey. We've got this." Verne pats Kai's leg.

Verne and his new partner, Kai, are exactly as adorable together as I hoped they'd be. Kai—the icy blond bombshell the whole club has been begging to meet—was worth every bit of the wait.

"God, you two are the epitome of adorable," I say to them, genuinely.

"It's hopeful," Nova says dreamily. "Like things happen when you are absolutely not prepared… or when you are on the verge of giving up completely.

Nova's serial dating isn't going well, but she isn't giving up. She says it the way she says most things—like it's simple. Like it's just a fact sitting on the table next to the lemon drops.

Hopeful.

I turn the word over in my mouth. I want to borrow it, try it on, see if it fits someone who made the right choice for all the right reasons and still feels like she left something vital on the floor of a shed.

Kai reaches over and tucks a strand of hair behind Verne's ear without thinking, the way people do when touching someone has become as natural as breathing, and I look away before the ache in my chest becomes something I have to explain.

I'm happy for them. I am. I'm happy for them, and I'm gutted for myself, and apparently those two things can exist in the same booth on a Thursday, taking up equal space, neither one canceling the other out. I pick up my lemon drop.

"I'm still worried about the books," I say, because I am, and because it's easier than the other thing. "I drop the ball on confirming the order and the permit fine wipes the budget."

Sawyer straightens, raises her chin. "Don't worry about that, darlin'. I'll put a call into my agent—ARCs, signed copies, maybe even some author friends at the opening if we time it right." She waves her hand like this is nothing. "I've never once used my connections for anything. My agent is going to be thrilled I'm finally asking."

"Sawyer." My throat does the thing.

"I've been dying to use my *connections*," she says, shimmying her shoulders. "You're giving me an excuse." She squeezes my hand across the table. "We've got you."

I swear, in a past life, Sawyer is a saint. I see her when she thinks no one is watching—throwing an extra twenty on the table after pancakes, watering the flowers at my dad's coffee shop when the leaves start to fade.

"Where's Evie tonight?" I ask. "This was last minute. We could've met at the cottage."

"Elliott has her!" Tottie hoots, slamming her empty glass on the table.

"Is that true?" I ask.

From what I can tell, Elliott and Sawyer spend a lot of time together—movie nights with Evie, grocery runs, Elliott driving her home from school three times a week so Sawyer can write. I can't help but hope something is brewing there. They both deserve it.

"It's true." Sawyer's cheeks go pink. "He helps her with her homework. She likes him."

"So are you two—" Nova makes a gesture with her fingers. I push her hands down before she can finish it.

"Just friends," Sawyer says quickly. "Though I haven't seen him as much lately." Her voice slows just slightly. "Jonathan's been coming over a lot." She catches herself. "I'm sorry, Mazey. I didn't mean to bring him up."

My heart skips and then speeds up. I take a sip of my lemon drop and wait for it to settle.

"It's fine," I say. "I'm the one who ended things. I don't get to be weird about his name." I pause. "I never even told Elliott, by the way. Well, not officially. Jonathan kind of did, I think."

"He knows," Sawyer says. "Jonathan talked to him—the Mr. Darcy day. He wanted to make sure Elliott knew how he felt about you. Didn't want anything standing in the way."

I sit with that for a moment.

He cleared the path before I even knew there was one to clear.

"Sounds like him," I say quietly.

Nobody fills the silence. They let it be what it is.

"So." Doris doesn't look up from her knitting—tonight it appears to be socks with a giant dildo worked into the pattern. "What actually happened? The real version."

"Just wasn't the right time. Too many things falling through the cracks." It's the answer I rehearsed. Clean and reasonable.

"Mm." She turns her needles. "That's the version you tell people at the grocery store."

I press my lips together.

"You ran," Morgan says, appearing from nowhere and dropping into the empty chair. "Brody's at Jonathan's right now with a giant tube of edible cookie dough. They are watching *Ten Things I Hate About You.*"

"What a problematic movie," I say. "I love the 2000s of it so much, though."

We all nod, nostalgic smiles plastered to our faces.

"Poor guy." Tottie gives me a pointed look over her glass.

The image of it lands somewhere soft—Jonathan on his couch, Brody beside him, the two of them eating cookie dough out of a tub because of me. I press my lips together and look down at the table.

"I didn't run. I paused." I say it steadily. "I ended it for the right reasons. I need to work on myself."

Doris finally looks up. Unhurried. A little merciless. Completely kind.

"It's been a week," she says. "Have you stopped dropping things? You know, has kickin' him to the curb helped?"

I open my mouth. Close it.

The color-coded spreadsheet floats through my mind. The linen closet. The welcome sign I repainted, not because it needed it but because I needed something to do with my hands at eleven o'clock at night.

"No," I admit.

"No," she agrees gently. "Because it was never about dropping things." She picks her knitting back up. "Don't confuse working on yourself with punishing yourself. There's a difference."

I don't have an answer for that. I just sit with it.

Tottie raises her glass, grinning. "To working on ourselves."

My book club family—and Kai—cheers to that.

Chapter 30

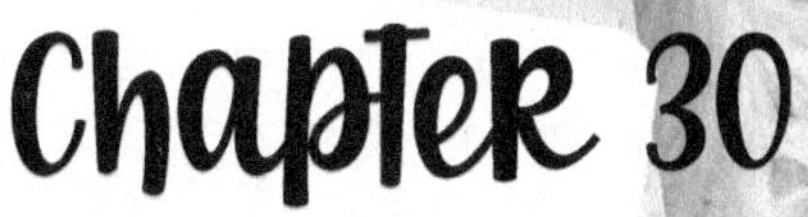

The Elliott Conversation

"There's such a lot of different Annes in me. I sometimes think that is why I'm such a troublesome person. If I was just the one Anne it would be ever so much more comfortable, but then it wouldn't be half so interesting."
- Anne of Green Gables, L.M. Montgomery

Nova made pasta from scratch tonight, which she does approximately once a year and only when she's in a specific mood that I've never been able to predict or replicate. We ate at her kitchen table with the events calendar spread between us and argued about whether a cocktail hour counts as an event or just a vibe. (It's a vibe. She disagrees. We tabled it.)

It was a good evening. The ordinary kind, where nothing significant happens and you don't realize until you're driving home that you needed exactly that.

Elliott is already on my porch when I get home.

He's sitting on the top step with his elbows on his knees and a paper coffee cup in each hand, and he looks exactly the way he did in high school when he'd wait outside my room after a bad day—not knocking, not forcing his way in.

Just. There.

I stop at the bottom of the steps. Wilfred pushes past me and head-butts Elliott's shin with zero hesitation. Wilfred has never once in his life waited to see how a situation was going to go.

"Hey, bud." Elliott hands me one of the cups to scratch him behind the ears. He doesn't look up at me right away.

"How long have you been sitting here?" I climb the steps and take the cup. It's warm. Whatever blend Dad made today, it smells like brown sugar and something floral. I sit down beside him and we both look out at the lake for a minute.

The sun is getting low. The water's gone that particular shade of gold that only happens in late afternoon, right before the light gives up entirely.

"About twenty minutes."

"Weirdo."

We sit with that for a while. It's a comfortable quiet that only exists with people you've known long enough to have run out of things to perform for. Elliott and I used to have this in abundance. Somewhere in the last few years it got harder to find, buried under the distance we both pretend isn't there and never directly discuss because that is appar-ently what we do.

"So." He draws out the *oh* sound. "How are things?"

"Things are good." I pause. "And bad. And everything in between."

He nods. Doesn't push. That's a new development—this version of Elliott who can sit in a moment without immediately trying to fix or redirect or make a joke to cover the gap. I wonder when that happened. I wonder how many other things have changed in him that I missed because I wasn't paying close enough attention.

"How are you doing?" I ask, because I mean it. Because I haven't asked enough lately and I know it.

"According to Sawyer—"

"According to Sawyer?" I turn to look at him.

He grins, but it's the slightly sheepish kind. "According to Sawyer, I've been a bit of an asshole."

"You don't say."

"She suggested I might be a bit"—he tilts his head, choosing the word carefully—"over… protective."

I don't say anything. I let that sit between us the way he let my *good and bad and everything in between* sit, because he deserves the same courtesy.

He turns the cup in his hands. Picks at the cardboard sleeve. "It's not—I know I've been hard on Jonathan. And on you, about Jonathan. And probably about other things that were never actually about the things I said they were about."

"Elliott."

"I'm getting there." He exhales. "I know that's not an excuse. But losing him—Dawson—and almost losing you. I know it was so long ago, but it feels like it was this morning that I got the phone call that my little brother was gone forever."

The phone call that his little brother was gone forever.

I know that phone call. The one that made losing my twin real. I sat on the floor of a hospital hallway and waited for Elliott while everyone else did the things that had to be done, and when he got there we didn't say anything for a long time. We just sat on the floor together. I don't think we've talked about that since.

"And since then, I have felt the need to make sure you don't get hurt." Elliott looks at me. "You've had so much hurt. So much. You deserve so much more." He shakes his head, turning the cup in his hands. "I thought Jonathan was—I didn't realize he was—" He stops. Makes a face like he's searching for the right word and landing somewhere he didn't expect. "You never told me he gave you the collywobbles."

I almost do a spit take.

"The *what?*"

"You know." I absolutely do not. "The collywobbles."

We laugh. Then he asks the questions I knew he was going to ask.

"What happened between you two? I mean besides my—" he thinks for a beat. "What did Sawyer call it?"

"Jerk-ness."

"My jerk-ness." He nods solemnly. "Besides that. What happened? I figured after he dressed up as a sexy, wet hero from one of your books—"

"Mr. Darcy." I snort a surprised laugh.

"Yeah, Mr. Darcy… whatever that means." Elliott was not into romance like Dawson and I are… like Dawson *was* and I am. He's more of a graphic novel kind of guy. "I just thought after our conversation that I was going to have to get over it."

"The conversation that you made him have with you?" I push. I am still wondering everything that was said that day between those two.

"Yeah. That one. I handled it badly. But not just the dinner—all of it. I could see something was happening between you two for months, and instead of talking to you about it like an adult, I just… went stiff every time his name came up. Made it weird."

"It was a little weird," I admit.

"A lot weird." He sets his cup down. "And at the Mr. Darcy dinner, when Sawyer said—" He exhales. "When I found out about the kiss, I didn't handle it right. I took Jonathan outside after, and I said some things I'm not proud of."

My stomach tightens. "What things?"

He rubs the back of his neck. "I told him that if he hurt you, he'd lose me—and that if this was just him finally taking what he wanted without thinking about the fallout, I needed him to walk away now."

I stare at the lake. "Elliott. He's not that kind of guy."

"I know."

"That's not—you can't say that to someone."

"I know," he says again, and this time his voice is smaller. "He didn't back down, for what it's worth. He looked at me and said that the only person he'd ever hurt by walking away was you. That he'd spent years trying to do the right thing by both of us, and he was done apologizing for caring about you." He pauses. "Then he said… that he loved you. That he'd been in love with you since before either of you knew what to do about it. And that he wasn't asking my permission."

I have to breathe through that for a second.

He said he loved me. To Elliott. Months ago, before the nook, before the cortado, before the sawdust on his cheekbone and the sandwich he couldn't finish a sentence about. Before I told him to leave. He said it to my brother, in what I can only imagine was the most Elliott conversation in the history of Elliott conversations. And he didn't tell me. He just kept showing up. Kept moving my piles without touching the order of them. Kept learning my coffee order and fixing my shed and saying *I've got you* like it was the simplest, most obvious thing in the world.

I have been so busy being afraid of dropping Dawson's dream that I didn't notice I was the one doing the dropping.

"Mazey." Elliott's voice is careful.

"I need a second," I say.

He gives me one. That's the new Elliott thing again—the sitting in it. I'm going to need to thank Sawyer for that at some point.

The water has gone from gold to pink to the deep, flat blue that means the day is almost done. Wilfred hasn't moved from across our laps. I put my hand on his back and feel him breathe.

He said he loved me.

And then I told him to leave.

"Alright. Time to tell me what happened." He claps his hands together. "I really will kick his ass if he hurt you."

I tell Elliott everything. That I kept screwing things up with Reading Lane. Dropping the ball on really important stuff. The permit I missed and had to pay a stupid big fine for. The book order I never confirmed. The budget bleed I didn't catch until it was already a problem. And how every single one of those things happened after Jonathan, and how I couldn't separate the two in my head no matter how hard I tried, and how I convinced myself that the responsible thing—the right thing—was to put the retreat first and deal with the rest later.

How if I failed Reading Lane, I would let Dawson down. I'd let myself down.

"Mazey, do you want it? The retreat? The cottage? Jonathan?"

Do I want it? Do I... want it?

I've been so busy treating Reading Lane like a debt I owe Dawson that I forgot it's also mine. That wanting it for myself isn't a betrayal of him. It's not choosing me over him. It's not forgetting him or replacing him or moving on in the way people say *moving on* when what they mean is *moving away.*

Dawson would be so annoyed at me right now. He would make the face—the specific one, the one with the eyebrow—and say something like *Maze, I left you the entire plan we made for a bookish retreat—the place that we wished we could go to to nerd out about all the novels we loved, and now you're worried that you'll disappoint me? Are you kidding me? Reading Lane is not supposed to be a guilt trip. It's the opposite, you idiot.* And then he'd steal whatever I was eating and change the subject because that was always how he said the hard thing without making it hard.

He didn't leave me a dream to carry like a weight. He left me one to live in. And somewhere between the permits and the paint colors and the midnight phone calls about hidden reading nooks, I've been doing exactly that—living in it—and punishing myself for enjoying it too much.

Two things can be true at once.

I can want Reading Lane for me. I love falling into a world that is so far from my current one that I forget dragons aren't flying through the air. I love yapping on and on about how the best friends finally figured out they are perfect for each other and end up banging all over the kitchen counter.

Over the last seven months, I've also learned that I love this part—the figuring out who might book a room and what they need before they even know they need it.

I can also want Reading Lane for Dawson.

Those were never in competition. I just convinced myself they were because grief needed somewhere to put the guilt, and apparently I volunteered.

And I want Jonathan.

So much.

I want Jonathan the way you want something you didn't see coming. Not the wanting that shows up loud and obvious and announces itself at the door. The quiet kind. The kind that's already made itself at home before you noticed it was there. I want the coffee he brings without being asked and the way he goes still when he's actually listening and the sketch he made at midnight on his notes app because I called him and he answered on the second ring and said *go on* like it was the only reasonable response. How he treats his employees, defending them and creating opportunities for them to soar.

Taking a risk on his best friend's little sister to save the program he loves so much.

All because he believes in people. He believes in people even when every reason not to has been thrown at him.

I want all three things. That's the problem. I convinced myself I had to choose, and instead of choosing, I just—dropped the hardest one and called it responsibility.

"Yeah," I say finally. "I want all of it."

Elliott looks at me for a long moment. "Then why are you sitting on a porch with me?"

Chapter 31

I Know What I Need To Do

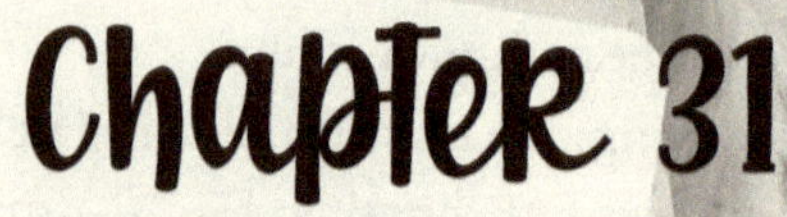

"Dear old world, you are very lovely, and I am glad to be alive in you."
- Anne of Green Gables, L.M. Montgomery

"I'll order the Thai food, you start looking up therapists for us." Elliott highlights the first and third items on the brand new to-do list. We are sitting at the dining table with the events calendar, a legal pad, and the particular energy of two people who have just cried on a porch and decided to do something about it.

"Us?" I look up from my laptop.

"Us." He doesn't elaborate. He doesn't need to. We sat on that floor together once already. We can sit in a waiting room together too.

I find three therapists within twenty miles who take our insurance and have availability before the Thai food arrives. Elliott picks the one whose website has the least stock photos of people staring thoughtfully out of windows. It feels like a reasonable metric.

"Okay." I pull the legal pad toward me. "Grand opening. We are definitely going to need to ask for some help from… Well, everyone."

"I'm certain that won't be a problem."

We go through the list methodically, the way we used to do homework at the same kitchen table when we were teenagers—heads down, dividing and conquering, occasionally stealing each other's dumplings. The guest rooms need staging. The flower beds along the front path need planting. I have a whole vision for this. Elliott has strong opinions about peonies that I never knew about and honestly respect, and he says Evie and him can do it, no problem. Apparently she loves gardening. The Reading Lane social accounts need a proper launch post, not just the placeholder content Nova and I threw up in February.

And the whole thing needs to be a literary dress-up party.

Just like Daisy and Savvy did when they ran this place.

"Wait, explain this one again." Elliott points at the item with his chopsticks.

"Grand opening party. Guests come dressed as their favorite literary character." I steal another dumpling. "Or a character from whatever book they're currently reading. Or a vibe. The vibe is also acceptable."

"What's the vibe?"

"Bookish. Romantic. Hell, whatever they want." I grab my phone and text Nova and Sawyer my revelation for the grand opening. "Think less Halloween, more—you show up as Elizabeth Bennet because you've been her your whole life and you finally have somewhere to be her."

Elliott thinks about this. "I'm coming as Atticus Finch."

"You absolutely are not." I laugh. Elliott hates *To Kill a Mocking-bird*. It was a required reading in high school. He complained the entire time, saying there is no way that Scout is really an adult in a kid's body and that Boo was really just an introvert.

"Fine. The guy from *The Martian* or *Green Goblin* since Jonathan will probably be Mr. Darcy again."

God, I hope so.

"That's more you." I write "literary costume party—finalize details and figure out costumes on such short notice" on the list and circle it twice. My phone chirps.

"Nova is already making a mood board. It's very detailed. I'm a little scared of it."

He nods, satisfied, and reaches for the pad. "Okay. What else?"

We go through the rest of it—buying extra linens, staging, the final walkthrough checklist, the catering order for opening weekend. It feels manageable in a way it hasn't in weeks, possibly because I'm not trying to carry it alone in a shed at midnight, possibly because Elliott is surprisingly good at this when he's not being overprotective, possibly both.

Then he points at me with his chopsticks.

"Now that's settled. Time to tackle the big one."

As if making a plan to fix the grand opening I've derailed, and scheduling therapy to learn coping skills for managing life and work and happiness and sadness and everything in between, isn't big stuff.

"Jonathan." He looks at me, waiting for me to argue.

"Jonathan," I agree.

We sit with it for a second.

"You need to do one of those grand gestures." He waves the chopstick around, and I fear for my life. He's got the same energy as Wilfred, who is currently begging for Pad Thai on seated hind legs.

"Grand gesture." I pluck the chopsticks from his grasp. "Good thinking." I hesitate. "But what if he doesn't want one... What if he doesn't want me? I mean he could have done a grand gesture and he didn't."

"You told him to leave you alone. He will never go against what you want. Ever. That's just not him."

I know this. If you tell him to make sure to call you every third Tuesday of the month at exactly 4:03 p.m. eastern standard time, he will. You could set your watch to it.

But if you tell him never to call you, then he'll wait until 4:04 p.m. eastern standard time, even if he was on fire and needed a glass of water.

"He loves you. He's loved you for almost as long as he's been my best friend." He scoops the last of the noodles up, totally using the chopsticks as a shovel instead of how they are supposed to be used. "So, what kind of grand gesture?"

"I have no idea. I've read so many grand gestures, but none of them seem like the right one."

He pulls the legal pad back. "I feel like you're a specific kind of grand-gesture person, and we should figure out what that is before we commit to anything else. You'll end up doing one of those weird things you do when you're nervous."

I raise my brow at him. "You know, like bow or curtsy. Or pretend you are a knight."

"She told you?" I thought Sawyer and I were past that moment. I haven't bowed to her in months.

Elliott laughs. "You know who would be excellent at this?"

"Brody and Morgan?"

"Brody and Morgan."

"Fucking finally!" Morgan, the normally very demure individual, shouts the second she opens the door, storming to the living room and plopping onto the couch. "Jonathan has been on our couch every day since, eating all the edible cookie dough and watching rom-coms. I love the dude, but damn. I need some alone time with this one." She throws her thumb over her shoulder at Brody.

"She's a little on edge. Almost the end of the school year, and her classroom is basically a zoo," he explains.

"I heard that," Elliott agrees, parking on the arm of a chair that sits kitty corner from the couch.

Morgan kicks her sandals off and tucks her feet under her with the ease of someone who has been coming to this cottage long enough to stop asking permission. "Okay. Grand gesture. What are we working with?"

"She needs to get Jonathan back," Elliott says.

"Obviously." Morgan looks at me. "What has she tried so far?"

"Nothing." I pace the floor. Pacing will help me think of a way to unscrew what I've screwed up with Jonathan.

"Good. Clean slate." She pulls her knees to her chest.

Brody, who has been suspiciously quiet for approximately forty-five seconds, looks up from his phone with the expression of a man who has just had what he considers to be a very good idea. "Skywriting. There's a guy in Charleston that does it—"

"No," the three of us say simultaneously.

"It's romantic—"

"It's cool, but it's too much." Morgan leans forward, hand on chin, deep in thought.

"Flash mob?" Brody says earnestly.

"Brody. Have you met Jonathan?" I ask. "I've never seen him interested in dancing a day in his life. He'd be worried if everyone was hydrated enough and if they were wearing the proper shoes to actually pay attention."

"You are the sweetest human ever, but you suck at grand gestures." Morgan takes his phone out of his hand and wraps her arms around his bulky shoulders.

"Say that to the Morgan of six years ago." Brody laughs, making both of them bounce. He looks at Elliott and me. "She loved the classroom supply surprises and the flowers."

"That's because you took the time to get to know her," I say.

Wait a minute. I know Jonathan.

"I know what I need to do."

✦˙✛

VLOG ENTRY

[Camera opens in Mazey's favorite corner of Reading Lane—the future main lounge, where sunlight filters through oversized windows. Wilfred snores on a rug in the background. Unpacked boxes are stacked behind her, and a steaming mug sits at her elbow with a whiteboard titled "LAST CHAPTER (!!!)" with chaos scribbled beneath it.]

Mazey (sitting cross-legged on the floor, eyes tired but honest): "Hey, friends. So… the Grand Opening of Reading Lane is almost here."

[She does jazz hands. A little halfhearted this time. She notices. She laughs at herself.]

Mazey: "We're in the final chapter. Which is—yeah. A lot."

[She exhales, tucks a piece of hair behind her ear, looks at the camera like she's been working up to this.]

Mazey: "Before we get into rugs—we have thirteen. That is not a joke, and I will explain later—I need to talk about something. Something I've been sitting with for a while."

[She picks up her mug. Puts it back down without drinking from it.]

Mazey: "You guys have noticed Jonathan isn't in the vlogs this week. Katie covered for us. He said he was sick, which was—kind. That's very him."

[She pauses. Looks down.]

Mazey: "He's not sick. I asked him to step back. From the project. From… us."

[Wilfred shifts in the background. The room gets quiet in a specific way.]

Mazey: "And I want to be honest about why, because you've watched this whole thing and you deserve the real version. Not the grocery store version."

[Small, rueful smile at that.]

Mazey: "I convinced myself it was about focus. That every time I dropped the ball—the permit fine, the book order, the budget stuff—it was because of him. Because of us. That I couldn't think straight when he was around, and I needed to be able to think straight."

[She shakes her head slowly.]

Mazey: "But here's the thing I didn't say out loud until about three days ago, sitting on a porch with my brother eating Thai food: I was dropping things long before Jonathan. I have always been someone who drops things when the stakes feel too high. That's not new. That's anxiety. That's imposter syndrome. That's me, standing in the middle of something I love and waiting for the moment I ruin it."

[She looks up.]

Mazey: "Jonathan wasn't the reason I was overwhelmed. He was actually the reason I kept going. And I told him to leave."

[Beat.]

Mazey: "I think… I think I convinced myself that if I let someone love me while I was in the middle of something this important, I'd jinx it. Like I didn't get to have both. Like I had to earn the good stuff by suffering through the hard stuff alone first."

[She laughs quietly, but it doesn't quite reach her eyes.]

Mazey: "Spoiler: that's not how it works. Apparently."

[She pulls her sleeves down over her hands. A fidget she probably doesn't notice she does.]

Mazey: "He said something to me before he left. He said—" [she stops, steadies herself] "—he said I couldn't afford to let someone love me. And I didn't answer. Because he was right, and I knew it, and I still let him walk to his truck anyway."

[Long pause. Wilfred snores. She glances at him with a look that is pure gratitude for the interruption.]

Mazey: "So. That's where we are. Grand Opening in three weeks. Thirteen rugs. And me, trying to figure out how to be brave about the thing that scares me most."

[She looks directly into the camera. Steady now.]

Mazey: "It's not the retreat. It never was."

[Soft smile. Real one.]

Mazey: "Thanks for being here. For watching all of this—the good vlogs and the ones where I clearly haven't slept. I'll keep being honest. Even when it's messy. Especially when it's messy."

[Wilfred lets out a tremendous snore. Mazey looks over her shoulder.]

Mazey: "…Also, his name is Wilfred and he has been emotionally supportive through all of this, and I think he deserves a mention."

[Fade out with soft music and a graphic that reads: "#ReadingLaneRetreat—almost there ♥" with a doodle of Wilfred asleep on a pile of rugs.]

Comments

@thereadingnook: she said "it's not the retreat. it never was." and i had to put my phone down. MAZEY.

@RomComsAndCoffee: The grocery store version vs the real version. I felt that in my chest. Thank you for giving us the real version.

@hopelessromantic_irl: okay but "he was the reason I kept going and I told him to leave" is the most painful thing she has ever said and I need to lie down

@bookishbabe22: replying to @hopelessromantic_irl SHE KNOWS. SHE KNOWS WHAT SHE DID. this is the arc. THIS IS THE ARC.
@cottagecoreobsessed: wilfred getting his flowers at the end is the only thing holding me together right now
@PracticalRealist44: Still not sure why any of this belongs in a renovation vlog.
@LyraRae: 🔥 replying to @PracticalRealist44 because she's a human being and not a floor plan, my friend. scroll tenderly.
@BookishSoul_89: "I didn't get to have both." Mazey I am sending you so much love. You get to have both. You always did. 🤍

ChapTer 32

Happily Ever Chapter

*"Taking a risk wasn't the reckless thing she conditioned herself to fear.
It was an act of hope." - Happily Ever Chapter*

The knock comes so hard it rattles the frame.

I'm already on my feet before I'm fully awake, Wilfred scrambling off the couch in front of me, nails clicking on the floor. As soon as the rain started, I lost the battle against dreamland and fell asleep on the couch with a half-read manuscript on my chest and the lamp still on.

I'm disoriented, stumbling towards the door.

I stop, Wilfred circling back, realizing I'm not close enough behind him.

Who the fuck is knocking at my at door in the middle of a thunderstorm? This has the making of a horror flick.

Do I open the door, potentially getting slaughtered by an axe-wielding serial killer? Or do I grab my phone and Willy and coward in the bathroom until the police get here to save me?

Knock. Knock. Knock.

"Mazey."

My whole body goes still.

I know that voice in every register. Calm and measured across a job site. Low and careful when he's choosing words. Warm in the dark when it's just us. This isn't any of those. This is something stripped of all the care.

This voice is urgent, the need to be heard pulsing through my name.

"Jonathan?" I need confirmation.

"Yes, Mazey, it's me. Open up. I need to… I need to talk to you."

I race toward the door, but I stop.

On the entry table—where only a marble-based lamp sits—is a book. Sitting in the circle of soft light like it's been waiting for this very moment. The exact moment I need help getting over the edge of fear and into *my* life. Giving me permission to use my courage to jump into the unknown.

Happily Ever Chapter.

"Mazey?"

"One second, Jonathan. I need just one more second."

"I'm not going anywhere."

A rush of air makes my curls flutter. It feels like an eternity since the cottage provided me with guidance.

The cottage has been quiet since I ignored it (for the second time) right before… right before I told Jonathan to leave. I thought it was mad at me, angry that I brushed off its offer of guidance.

But maybe after that, it decided it was my turn to figure out my shit. That it had done everything it could and the rest was mine to carry. I used to think that felt like abandonment. Now I think it was just the cottage stepping back and letting me find out what I was made of without a hand at my back.

Turns out I needed to fall apart a little first. Needed the shed floor and the lemon drops and Doris's merciless kindness and Elliott on my porch with two cups of coffee, finally learning to sit in the hard thing instead of flinching away from it. The void wasn't punishment. It was space—room enough to grow into someone who could actually receive what this place, and that man on the other side of my door, have been trying to give me all along.

I hold the book in my hands, turning to a dog-eared page.

Really? The cottage dog-eared the page? There it is, the payback for ignoring two books I was gifted.

She'd spent so long treating her heart like something fragile, something best kept wrapped in warnings and what-ifs. As if love were a cliff edge instead of a horizon.

"Mazey." His voice through the door is quieter now. Not less urgent, just lower. Like he's run out of loud. "Please."

Taking a risk, she decided, wasn't the reckless thing she'd been taught to fear. It was an act of hope.

I slam the book shut and open the door.

Jonathan is soaked. He didn't wear a jacket. His hair is plastered down, flannel dark with rain, and he's breathing like he ran the whole way here and didn't notice. He looks at me the same way he looked at me the day I turned around—open, unguarded, all the careful distance gone—except this time there's something else underneath it. Something fraying at the edges.

Neither of us says anything for a moment. Wilfred pushes past my legs and headbutts Jonathan's knee, unimpressed by the drama of it, and Jonathan reaches down without looking and scratches his ear on instinct. That small automatic thing—*I've got you, even when I'm falling apart*—breaks something loose in my chest.

"I saw the video," he says.

"You did?"

"I—" He stops. Exhales through his nose. Runs a hand through his wet hair, which does nothing. "I didn't have a plan. I just—I couldn't stay on that couch."

"You drove over in the rain without a plan."

"Yeah." A beat. "I do dumb things when I'm—yeah."

Something in me wants to laugh and cry at the same time, but I can't afford either right now so I just say, "Come inside. You're soaking my porch."

He steps in. I close the door behind him. The lamp catches the rain on his shoulders, his jaw, his eyelashes, and I think: *I did this. I sent him away and he still showed up in the rain without a plan and I did this.*

"I'm sorry," I say. It comes out smaller than I mean it to. "I was so convinced I had to choose—that wanting everything meant I'd lose everything. And I picked the thing I thought I could control and I—" My voice snags. "You're the one I dropped and called it responsibility."

He's looking at me. Not moving. Not reaching for me yet. Just—listening. The way he always listens, that particular stillness, like whatever I'm saying is the only thing happening in the world right now.

"I know I can't just say that and have it be okay," I say. "I know that's not how it works. But I need you to know that I wasn't protecting Reading Lane when I sent you away. I was protecting myself from something I didn't think I deserved." I press my lips together. "And I'm done doing that."

The quiet that follows lasts long enough that I almost fill it. Almost.

Then he crosses the room in two strides and cups my face in both hands, and I don't have time to finish the breath I'm taking before his mouth is on mine.

It's not careful. It's not the first-time tentativeness or the slow-build of before. It's the kiss of someone who drove over in the rain without a plan, who's been holding something in for weeks, who is done being patient. I grab the front of his wet flannel with both hands and kiss him back just as hard. Somewhere behind us, Wilfred makes an offended noise and retreats to his bed.

When we finally break apart, we're both breathing unsteadily and his forehead is against mine and his hands are still on my face like he's not ready to let go of the geometry of us yet.

"I've been in love with you," he says, rough and quiet, "for so long, I can't remember what it felt like before."

"I know." My voice is wrecked. Hearing him say the words is so much different than just having the knowledge. It's real. "Elliott told me. About the Mr. Darcy dinner. What you said to him."

Something moves across his face. "I meant all of it."

"I know that too." I tilt my head up and kiss the corner of his mouth, his jaw, the hinge of it where I can feel the tension he's been carrying. "I'm in love with you. I should've said it the first time. I'm saying it now."

He exhales like he's been waiting for it. Like he knew, but knowing and hearing are different things, and he needed to hear it.

We end up on the couch eventually, his arm around me, my legs across his lap, both of us quiet in the way that happens after something important gets said and the air hasn't quite settled back to normal yet. The rain taps against the windows. The lamp is still on. Wilfred has forgiven us and draped himself across our feet.

"Your shirt is still wet," I say.

"Is it bothering you?"

"Kind of." I sit up. He looks at me. I reach for the top button of his flannel.

"Mazey." A warning. A question. A low warm note that I feel in my sternum.

"Jonathan." I hold his gaze and undo the next one.

He lets me. He watches me with that specific attention. It's not passive and not patient exactly. It's present, and it makes me feel seen down to the bones. When I push the flannel off his shoulders, he catches my hands and holds them for a moment.

"You sure?" he asks.

"I've been sure for months," I say. "I just kept getting in my own way."

He pulls me in slowly, one hand at the back of my neck, and this time the kiss is different again—unhurried, deliberate, like we've finally got the time. Like neither of us is going anywhere. I sink into it, into him, into the warmth of his chest under my palms and the way he makes a low sound when I run my fingers up the back of his neck.

We move together without hurry. Every touch deliberate, every pause held just long enough to breathe each other in. When he lays me back and looks at me—really looks, like he has nowhere else in the world to be—I stop holding anything back.

It is tender and true and nothing like I feared and everything I wanted. After, we stay tangled together while the rain slows outside. Wilfred snores, and the lamp throws its warm circle across the floor.

His thumb traces slow circles on my shoulder.

"The opening's in less than two weeks," I say eventually.

"I know."

"There's still a lot to do."

"I know that too." I can hear the smile in it. "We'll figure it out."

We. Just like that. Like it was always going to be we.

I close my eyes. Outside, the rain softens to almost nothing. The cottage settles around us, quiet and certain, and I think about the book on the entry table—the dog-eared page I didn't put there, the lamp I didn't turn on, the way this place has always seemed to know what I needed before I did.

Maybe happily ever after wasn't a destination at all.

Maybe it was this. Right here. Choosing to turn the page anyway.

Chapter 33

It's Not Nothing

@thereadingnook: the way i am STRESS EATING watching this countdown. we are so close.
@hopelessromantic_irl: i have taken three personal days off work for the grand opening weekend and i regret nothing
@bookishbabe22: the fact that reading lane is actually happening. ACTUALLY HAPPENING. i remember when this was just a cottage and a dream.
@cottagecoreobsessed: i need everyone to be okay. that's all i'm saying. i need everyone to be okay.

The fire has been going for an hour and nobody wants to leave.

That's the thing I notice first—that nobody is checking their phone or making noises about early mornings. Sawyer is deep in conversation with Nova about signing schedules, Elliott is stealing marshmallows directly from the bag like a feral child, and Jonathan is just… here. Solid and warm beside me, close enough that our shoulders touch every time either of us breathes.

I have a list in my lap. I've had it in my lap for forty minutes.

"Okay," I finally say, sheepish. "I need to go through it."

"Obviously," Brody says, not looking up from his s'more construction. "We've been waiting."

"You could've said something," I say.

"And miss watching you try not to ask? Never."

Jonathan reaches over and taps the list in my lap once, like a quiet go ahead.

"All right." I take a breath. "Social media. Katie—you still good on the posts and responding to comments?"

"I've got it," Katie says. "Scheduled through next week and monitoring everything."

"Perfect. Books. Sawyer, you're managing The Story Porch and coordinating with your author friends for the signings?"

"Handled. And I may have roped in one more author today. So, we have four, including me. They are staying at the inn and with me." Sawyer gives a thumbs up as she stares at her phone screen. "Verne wanted me to tell you that if you send him one more fucking text message, he'll come over and destroy your books."

"I just had a few follow-up questions—"

She looks at me over the top of her phone.

"Fine." I stand to look around for my dads. "Catering. Gus' Cafe and The Diner are set, right? Where are Gus and Bobby?"

"Right here! I tested recipes yesterday. They are exactly what this party needs," Bobby says, tugging his cardigan close to his body as if he got a cold chill. "I've never seen such a twist on comfort food. That diner has a way of turning something ordinary and adding some class."

Bobby claps his hands together, then turns as if he just remembered the best thing since sliced bread. "Wait until you try Gus' literary-themed drinks. My favorite is The Plot Thickens. It's thick and rich with all the caramel mocha."

Dad gives a triumphant grin. "Yeah. We tested the coffee syrups this morning. The entire house smelled incredible all morning."

There is some laughter around the fire.

"Entertainment," I continue. "We've got book signings and book bingo. Shoot, I could really use another person to call numbers... I could—"

"We'll do it!" Sawyer practically shouts as she raises her hand. "Me and Evie... We are happy to do it. It's after the signings, and Nova's helping coordinate that." She looks over at Elliott. He smiles at her.

I look at my brother, slightly annoyed. "You have lined up that high school band, right?"

Elliott nods. "They're good. Think Florence and the Machine vibes, but with fewer instruments and a lot more teen angst."

Everything is falling into place after I finally admitted I don't have to do this by myself. Each text I sent out asking for help in the final stretch before the big opening was met with eager acceptance and excitement.

The book club is working on the decorations and plans to meet early for the final setup—fluffing pillows and all. Nova confirmed the inn has five overflow rooms reserved, and Larry assured everyone that only minor construction touch-ups remain.

After a long conversation with Nova, we decide to hire someone to manage our finances. As much as I like to make sure I am in control of the budget, the stress of making sure we aren't in the red is too much.

Silas started last week and has already been killing it with the budget. Within days, he put together a detailed three-year growth plan that left me both impressed and slightly dizzy. According to him, Reading Lane could easily sustain three employees within the next few years, and—if we reinvest smartly—expand to include two additional cabins and even a small beach house. He rattled off numbers and projections with the same ease I use when rattling off my favorite romance tropes. And for once, I don't feel the weight of the finances pressing down on me. Instead, I feel… hopeful.

I sit back down next to Jonathan, the firelight casting a warm glow across his face. He turns to me with that steady gaze of his, and he leans in close, his voice hushed and tender. "You've got this," he murmurs into my ear, the promise wrapping around me. Then he presses a soft kiss to the side of my head, lingering just long enough to make my breath catch.

I wrap my arms around his bicep, anchoring myself to him, and rest my head against his shoulder. His flannel is soft, worn in like only a favorite shirt can be, and the heat of his body seeps through the fabric, grounding me. I close my eyes for a moment, letting myself sink into the safety of him.

"I really do," I whisper, more to him than anyone else. More to myself, maybe.

I open my eyes and look around the fire.

Katie scrolls through scheduled posts with one hand while holding a beer with the other. Sawyer laughs at something Nova said, her whole face in it. Elliott, still stealing marshmallows, catches my eye and raises one at me like a toast. Bobby and Dad argue cheerfully about the correct ratio of caramel to espresso in The Plot Thickens. Larry puts an arm around my mom, both of them not paying attention to anyone but each other.

All these people showed up. They keep showing up. And they didn't wait to be asked twice.

I built something worth showing up for.

Around us, the fire crackles and sparks, embers dancing up into the star-scattered sky. Laughter floats through the cool night air, mixing with the shuffle of cards and the rustle of snack bags being passed around. The smell of toasted marshmallows, campfire smoke, and someone's spicy chili clings to everything. We stay out later than we probably should, pulled in by the easy rhythm of friends and the soft hum of anticipation for what the next few days might hold.

Time blurs, marked only by the shift of constellations above and the emptying plates around us. But I don't mind. Not with Jonathan beside me, his presence a quiet reassurance in the flickering dark.

The next day, everyone pitches in for the final setup. Guests are arriving in the morning—*actual paying guests*—and every corner of Reading Lane and the Inn has to feel like magic.

I stand by the edge of the lawn, clipboard in hand, directing Nova and Elliott to adjust the twinkle lights strung through the trees above the temporary wood dance floor. The lights drooped overnight, but it's nothing a couple zip ties and a ladder can't fix. For once, my heart isn't trying to punch its way out of my ribcage. We are doing this. *I* am doing this.

I adjust my glasses and glance down at my checklist. Only seventeen items left. That is practically a miracle.

"Where did all of this come from?" I stop in front of a clothing rack that definitely was not here yesterday, stuffed with capes and waistcoats and at least three different crowns and what appears to be a full

Mr. Darcy situation in the corner.

Kai appears beside me, thoroughly unbothered. "Verne."

"Verne did this?"

"He's been collecting from the theater department at the high school, the vintage shop on Fourth, and approximately every person in town who owns anything that could pass as literary for the last two weeks." Kai smiles the smile of someone deeply in love with a person who does things like this. "He didn't want anyone to feel left out."

I look at the rack for a long moment.

"I need to hug him."

"He's by the book wall," Kai says. "He's been waiting."

I find Verne exactly where Kai said he'd be, straightening a row of spines that didn't need straightening. I hug him from behind and he laughs, surprised, patting my arms with both hands.

"It's perfect," I tell him.

"It's nothing." He waves his hand.

"It's not nothing. It's everything."

I'm still smiling when Jonathan falls into step beside me, nodding toward the dance floor. "We should consider making that permanent. What do you think, Clover?"

The nickname still does something to me. Probably always will.

He looks unfairly good for someone who's been hauling crates of candles and signage since sunrise—sleeves rolled, shirt smudged with a streak of paint from the porch post we fixed earlier.

I raise my eyebrow at him. "*We?*"

He grins. "Yeah. We are a *we*, aren't we?"

Before I can respond, he scoops me up into his arms. I yelp, giggling, as my clipboard slips from my fingers and lands in the grass.

"Always," I say, arms winding around his neck.

He sets me down gently and kisses me. Not a showy kiss, more of a habit kiss. The kind of kiss that is guaranteed to greet you every morning, tuck you in every night, and every opportunity in between. The idea of *us* as something consistent makes my chest bloom with something terrifying and thrilling and beautiful.

"Boss," Katie calls out, jogging across the lawn. Her braid bounces against her back, face tight with worry. "There's a bit of a problem."

Panic sparks in my stomach, just for a second. I brace for the mental spiral—this is the part in the story where I usually lose it. Where I doubt everything.

But instead of freezing, I square my shoulders. "What's going on?"

Katie glances between us, fiddling with the edge of her pink flannel sleeve. "So, I've been pushing social media pretty hard the last few days, right? Well, apparently a few influencers didn't get formal invites. They're upset and posting about it. It's small for now, but I'm worried it might catch fire."

The smile fades from my face for a breath. I see it in Jonathan's eyes—his reflex to protect me, to jump in and fix it before I unravel. But I'm not unraveling. Not this time.

I exhale and look just past Katie's shoulder at the seating chart pinned to the chalkboard wall. A dozen threads click into place in my brain. I shift my stance, tuck a pen behind my ear, and bend to grab my clipboard.

"Would Jonathan and I filming an open invite on our socials help?" I ask the expert. She's the one that has gotten us to the blue checkmark club after all.

"Totally. Make it personal. And apologize—with feeling." She pins Jonathan with a look that could cut a diamond. "Explain that you didn't realize how many people would want to attend… That's the truth, right?"

"I'm still wrapping my head around the fact that anyone wants to be here," I say, honestly.

Katie smiles. "Nova can reach out to the ones who've posted already and apologize. It was a mistake, and we own it. Everyone is welcome."

I scribble quickly. "We'll offer shuttle service from the inn in the next town—ask Larry if he can drive. If they can't make it on short notice, we'll give them a discount for a future booking and send them a swag bag."

"Great idea," Katie says. "I'll grab Nova and be back in ten to record?"

I nod, already sketching out bullet points for the video script. "Perfect."

She darts off, calling for Nova as she disappears behind the hedge.

I feel arms wrap around me from behind. Jonathan presses a kiss to the side of my head. "You're incredible, Clover. How are you really feeling?"

I lean into him for a second, letting the question settle.

"Like puking… but only a little." I laugh softly. "But also really, really good."

He smiles into my hair. I turn and kiss him, quick and light, before heading toward the porch.

He follows, of course. He always follows now.

"Plus," I add over my shoulder, "I'm fantastic at solving problems when I'm not worrying what everyone else thinks."

His laugh warms my spine.

Chapter 34

[Camera opens on Reading Lane's front path. The flower beds are freshly planted, peonies visible along the edges. Mazey is crouched in the dirt, glasses slightly askew, pointing at something off camera. Jonathan stands behind her with his arms crossed, looking at whatever she's pointing at with the expression of a man being asked to have an opinion about flowers.]

Mazey: "Elliott planted these. He has very strong feelings about peonies apparently."

Jonathan: "Everyone has strong feelings about something."

Mazey (looking up at him): "What are your strong feelings about?"

[He looks directly at the camera. Says nothing. Just smiles.]

[Cut.]

Caption: t-minus two days. we're almost there.

I bump my shoulder into Jonathan as we walk down Main Street, our laughter echoing softly under the warm glow of the street lamps. Honeyville's got that late-night quiet that I love. Empty sidewalks, glowing windows, the smell of sugar and something fried lingering in the air.

"You are unhinged," I say, shaking my head, grinning. "Not only did you act like you've never seen a rom-com before—you threw popcorn at the screen."

"I had a valid reason." It's forced calm in his voice. "That was the worst third-act breakup I've ever seen. Absolute trash. I stand by every kernel I launched."

I lift a brow at him, unconvinced. "Valid? You hit a teenager in the head."

"She was on her phone the entire time," he mutters. "I'm not saying I'm proud of it, but I'm also not saying I regret it."

I snort. "Okay, vigilante."

He glances at me, fighting back a grin.

"Look," he says, gesturing with his drink. "I like rom-coms. I do. The falling in love part? That's the good stuff. The glances, the hand brushes, the near-kisses that get interrupted by a dog or a rogue snowball or someone's very poorly timed epiphany? Beautiful. But the third-act breakup? It's always the same. One bad conversation and suddenly they forget everything they just learned about each other."

I hum, not buying it.

"I mean, seriously," he goes on. "They spend the whole movie learning how to be vulnerable. Actually letting someone in, and then one misunderstanding happens and boom. Radio silence. No one talks. They just crumble like wet drywall."

"You're really heated about this," I say, unable to hide my smile. "You've got a whole thesis on communication failures in rom-coms."

"I do." His voice grows. "It drives me insane. You can fall in love with someone and still have hard conversations. That's the point."

He takes a long sip from my cup and stares at nothing in particular, jaw tight. It is adorable to see him so worked up about a movie. Maybe that hits a little close to home, the agony of a loved one leaving. His mom didn't wake up and decide to leave, but her death created a gap in his heart all the same.

"You okay there, bud?" I tease. "Need a hug? Closure? An alternate ending?"

He side-eyes me. "I need people to stop writing characters who give up."

That stops me. "Hey, Kirkwood. Look at me."

"Yeah." He exhales as he turns his body to face me.

"You know you're stuck with me for the long term, right?" I say, wrapping my arms around his waist. "Unless you do something really stupid."

"What would qualify as really stupid?" The corner of his mouth ticks up, and he pulls me in closer to him, making us chest to chest.

His warmth is intoxicating, taking my mind to an activity that involves less clothing. I refocus. "Well, not stocking your gummy bear supply. Or continuing a book that you don't love but feel obligated to finish."

"That's a weird one. Why wouldn't I finish it?" He tilts his head.

"Why would you continue to do something you don't love?" I question.

He kisses me like we've done it a hundred times, and still somehow I'm in awe that I get to have his lips on mine. When he finally pulls back, breath warm against my skin, he murmurs, "You never stop inspiring me."

I tickle his ribs, cracking up at his childish giggles. The look in his eye tells me he is not going to let me get away with that. I take off running. "I'll beat you to Gus's!" I holler over my shoulder.

His footfalls grow louder behind me. Seconds later, his bulky arms wrap around my waist, lifting me up. Kicking my feet in faux protest, I release a squeal. Kisses pepper my hair as he sets me back onto the ground.

"You should have known I'd catch you," he says and lets out a heavy breath.

"Yeah, yeah. I am in desperate need of coffee…" I trail off when I catch Jonathan's expression. He is staring at the old art studio tucked right between the diner and Gus's. The place has been vacant for years since the artist that used to own it was discovered and moved to Chicago. She comes back every so often to teach a class here or display her work during tourist season.

Something is different today though. There is a for sale sign in the window. I know exactly what Jonathan is thinking. It would be perfect for the Pathways Program. Jonathan has been wanting to move out of the community center and into a dedicated space. With the partnership with EverBright, it's not outside of the realm of possibility.

He's got that expression—the same one he has when he's working through something. The serious concentration of a man redesigning the space in his head. I pull out my phone and dial Brody's number.

He answers on the second ring.

"Hi Brody," my voice causes Jonathan to whip his head to me. "You know anything about the old art studio next to Gus'?"

"The one with the haunted shelves?" he responds.

Jonathan mouths, "what are you doing?" at me. I give him the one minute gesture.

"That's the one. I was walking to Dad's shop and saw a for sale sign in the window. Is it available?"

He whistles low. "Let me check."

A pause. Some typing.

Then he says, "You're in luck. It is. The owner is ready to retire and move to Cabo. Doesn't want to make the trip back enough to make the cost of owning it worth it. But she wants it in good hands, of course."

"Can you get us a walk through?" I ask.

He laughs. "Us?"

"Jonathan and me. I think Jonathan has a worthy cause," I say.

"Of course. The owner is in town for Reading Lane's opening. Would tomorrow at nine work? I know you guys are busy finishing set up. Morgan's so excited you asked her to help. She had me help her with the book wall last night. It looks incredible."

"That's perfect." I grin at Jonathan. "She's doing a great job. She's incredible at party planning. I might have to hire her when I have big events."

"I'm sure she'd love that," he says. "I'll see you in the morning, Mazey."

"Thanks, Brody." I hand up the phone and turn to Jonathan. "Want to see your possible dream tomorrow?"

He lifts me into a hug. "Absolutely."

I kiss his dumb grin. "How are you planning on balancing all of this?"

"I have been talking to Katie. She wants to continue doing the extra work she's picked up since my focus has been on the vlog project." He beams. "I didn't think I would take her up on it, but I think I'll talk to her about it more."

"She's gonna love being the boss all the time," I chuckle.

Jonathan intertwines our hands, and we scroll to the cafe. I take in a deep breath as I listen to Jonathan explode with the ideas he has for the studio. It's clear this has been something that has been on the forefront of his mind for a long time. I'm just happy he finally gets to join me out of the make-believe and into the made-reality.

Chapter 35

Grand Opening

"Found exactly what I didn't know I was looking for. Will be back. Took the book from the nook. Sorry. Not sorry." - Reading Lane Guest Book, First Entry

My brown lace-up boots squeak on the hardwood when I turn the corner of the second floor as I do the final check before guests start to arrive for the grand opening of Reading Lane. With a deep inhale, I pause the way one does before opening a gift you're almost too scared to touch.

Nova braided my hair into two thick braids (thank you clip-in extensions for making my hair long enough to braid) and tied the ends with golden ribbon, just like Anne's. I adjust the soft golden dress Mom spent three evenings hunched over the sewing machine to finish in time—puffed sleeves and all.

The guest rooms glow. Sheets are crisp, pillows are without a wrinkle in sight, mugs (with the Reading Lane logo plastered across the side) gleam beside compact coffee makers. In the bathrooms, a basket of travel-sized soaps and lotions sits perfectly centered—lavender, eucalyptus, mint—arranged like someone actually thought about what a person needs to relax and unwind. Because Larry did. Larry went above and beyond staging each of the suites.

I walk down the stairs and my heart skips. Of course, I saw the setup last night, but sleep (especially when you are so exhausted you can't see straight and any horizontal surface looks like the perfect place to crash) has a way of resetting your ability to be floored by things.

The cottage hits different now. Chalkboard signs with Nova's hand-drawn notes welcome guests to the grand opening. Easels in every room display our favorite books for every kind of mood. Fresh flowers on nearly every surface, sitting beside cake stands topped with cupcakes and cookies. I have already eaten two of them and arranged the remaining to eliminate the evidence.

The best part is the back living room, the room where Jonathan and I snuggled in close and first confessed our true feelings for each other. Verne and Kai have converted it into a pseudo-dressing room lined with racks of costumes from a variety of books. There are even some costumes that lean into literary puns, like the couple costume that Verne and Kai are wearing—Plot (Verne: a simple dress shirt and khaki pant situation with a tie) and Twist (Kai, dressed in a show girl costume).

The air still smells like fresh paint and vanilla from the blondies cooling in the kitchen. The combination shouldn't work as well as it does.

The wall beside me catches my attention. Photos from the renovation, tucked between snapshots of birthdays, family dinners, and honest victories: Elliott's crooked grin, his favorite Spider-Man comic held up beside his face—Green Goblin on the cover—Jonathan squinting into the sun next to him, both of them probably nine and seven and completely unaware anyone was watching. Jonathan's Mom holding up the blondie tray after she won a blue ribbon at the county fair, a yellowed recipe card smudged with fingerprints beneath the glass. Dad and Bobby dancing at their wedding, Mom laughing at something Larry said. Nova and me doing cartwheels across the yard when we received our acceptance letters to the same college.

And Dawson, smiling at the camera, grinning over a book.

I stare at the picture for a while—the ornery glint in the green eyes we share, his mess of curls wild and unbothered like they always were.

Even at nine, he had that look—like he already knew something you didn't and couldn't wait to tell you all about it.

My eyes drift down from the photo to the shelf below it. The journal Dawson started and I finished stands open, pages rippled from handling and healing. Next to it, *Anne of Green Gables*. And something that I know I didn't put there. A new novel I've never seen before, with no author on the cover. I pull it off the shelf and read the title.

That Time Mazey Lane Stopped Pretending and Started Living.

My eyes flood instantly, which is a problem because I spent an embarrassing amount of time enhancing my freckles. I flip through the pages anyway. Each chapter holds my story over the past eight months. The arc of it. The growth I apparently achieved while mostly feeling like I was holding on by my fingernails.

"You want some more coffee, Sawyer?" My mom says from the kitchen. I put the book back on the shelf and walk towards the laughter and coffee-mug clinks.

"I'm just so proud of Mazey."

I pause mid-step in the hallway at Bobby's voice, one hand on the wall.

A beat. Then Sawyer's voice. "Yes, please."

Slowly, I peek around the corner so I can see my people, my family.

Sawyer is dressed as Aunt May, cardigan buttoned to the top with baby powder throughout her hair to make it appear as if it's graying. "I don't think she realizes the ripple she's started. This place is more than cozy corners and clever signage. It's a haven. It's what so many of us didn't know we needed."

The hush that follows feels like a held breath.

Then Jonathan's voice, softer than I've ever heard it: "I'm just glad she took the chance. On this place… and on me."

"We all had bets on when you two would finally figure it out," Elliott says from beneath a Green Goblin mask—a choice he made with the specific energy of someone who has been waiting his entire life for a socially acceptable reason to wear a full supervillain costume.

Bobby, in-between giggles, says, "By the way, Larry won. He got twenty dollars from me."

The room dissolves into laughter.

My first instinct is to sprint in and say *I didn't do it! This wasn't me! It was all Dawson. I swear!* The second instinct is to wonder why my first instinct is always to throw myself out the window before accepting a compliment.

A tear slips down my cheek instead.

It's true—it wasn't just my idea. It was Dawson who planted the seed one afternoon on the beach after I told him why I'd been crying. A group of teenage assholes had mocked me for reading during study hall instead of passing notes or whispering about who was dating who that week.

"Wouldn't it be cool if there was a place where no one judged anyone for being a book nerd? Like it was celebrated? We could call it Reading Lane... Get it?"

And now, here we are. Well, here I am.

I wipe my eyes, mindful of the makeup situation, and walk into the room.

"Oh babe, what's wrong?" Nova adjusts the flower crown. She's dressed as Gillian Owens from Practical Magic—loose, freshly dyed bright red waves tumble over a rust-colored slip dress, a thin chain catching the light at her collarbone. She looks effortless in the way that takes hours. It's the perfect costume for her, really. My best friend matches Gillian's confidence so well that I almost think Gillian wraps her arms around me. "Whatever it is, we'll figure it out."

"Everything is wonderful." I sniffle. "I'm just so thankful to have you"—sniff—"and everyone"—sniff—"in my life." I gesture vaguely at the cottage that absolutely should not be called a cottage. "And this cottage."

"Seriously, who decided to call it that?" Sawyer says from the breakfast nook, adjusting her cardigan. "It's massive."

"I finally feel like I'm the person who should be living this life."

These words are not small. They're the kind of words that, a year ago, would have lodged in my throat like something I wasn't allowed to say yet. Like I'd slipped through a side door meant for someone more certain, more *right.* I smiled on cue and hit my marks and nodded through applause that never felt like it belonged to me. The spotlight never felt warm. Just borrowed.

Now, I dare someone to tell me I'm not supposed to be here. I'd raise an eyebrow and ask who exactly they think this life belongs to, if not me. And then, just to be petty, I'd tell them how whatever book they're currently reading ends. Spoilers for all.

"So, these are happy tears?" Jonathan says, exhaling with what sounds like genuine relief.

"Very happy tears." I shake out my hands, putting my business owner face on. "People should be getting here, so if you need to get changed, now's the time. "

Jonathan glances down at himself, then back at me with a slow smile. "I should probably go get dressed." He leans down, his mouth close to my ear. "Want to help?"

$$+ \cdot +$$

The courtyard hums with life. Laughter spills between tables. Folding chairs scrape against the brick patio as people squeeze in shoulder to shoulder.

A woman dressed as Elizabeth Bennet is deep in conversation with someone in full Dracula regalia. A group of kids are dancing with someone I'm fairly certain is Dad (the bookmark to Bobby's book).

Across the courtyard, Larry moves through the crowd in his BFG costume—enormous and gentle—bending down to hear every person who stops him. Mom, dressed as the big, friendly giant's companion, Sophie, is tucked beside him, talking to a couple of the authors that Sawyer invited. They look, objectively, like the best thing I've ever seen.

I move through it all with my arms full of thank-you bags tucked against one side, braids swinging. A girl is dressed as Anne Shirley at her own grand opening—which, now that I think about it, feels exactly right. Anne always did throw herself into things headfirst and sort out the embarrassment later.

I can feel eyes on me. For once, I don't feel the gut punch of forgetting to do something or the nagging feeling of dread in the workplace.

Instead, I feel light and full. Excited for the rest of my day, and all the days that follow.

By the refreshment table, two women clutch their limited-edition tote bags like golden tickets, whispering about the reading room with the candle that smells exactly like vanilla and old paperbacks.

"If you book a stay, you get thirty percent off your next candle order," I say, handing them a business card for the maker I met at the pop-up market.

They make the sounds people make when they are genuinely delighted, and I direct them toward Nova, who is already stationed near the information table because she has been waiting her whole life for a job like this.

Nearby, a handful of wide-eyed readers hang on every word from an author signing books beneath the pergola, fans lined up, dressed as characters from their books.

I spot Margot hovering near the back. Instead of the familiar clench of self-consciousness, I grin. She offers a smile and congratulations. After I declined her original offer, she offered the Pixel Perfection software at a discounted rate in exchange for honest feedback. Reading Lane said yes before I finished reading the email.

Evie, in a very elaborate Spiderman suit, sits with a group of kids her age, all of them bent over a table rhinestoning bookmarks and laughing like they've been friends for years.

Then I find him.

Jonathan. I knew he was coming as Gilbert Blythe. He described the costume in exactly the way a man describes something he is so nervous that he'll get wrong, but badly wants to be right—vest, rolled shirtsleeves with suspenders, and his hair tousled into *what product? I woke up this way* perfection.

Knowing didn't help.

He's standing with a group of his team, drink in hand, scanning the crowd—and the second his eyes land on me, they stay. A slow smile spreads across his face. The kind that starts at the corner and takes its time.

I murmur something to the woman beside me and start weaving

through the crowd. He says something to the group beside him and moves at the same time, both of us cutting through the noise toward each other. We meet somewhere in the middle of the fairy lights and the noise and the everything.

"Hello, Clover." His eyes trace the braids, the ribbon, the flower crown on my head. "You look—"

"Don't."

"I wasn't going to say anything embarrassing."

"You absolutely were."

His smile widens. "Hello, Anne."

Jonathan's gaze settles on me, and he bites his lower lip. I have thoughts about that, which I will not be putting into words right now. "You tonight, Mazey." He shakes his head slightly. "You're glowing."

A laugh slips out. "Thank you. It's a beauty secret. Very exclusive."

"Oh yeah? What's it called?"

"Sweat," I say. "I've been running my ass off for three hours."

His smile tilts, knowing. "You're loving every second though, aren't you?"

It's not a question.

"So freaking much." I slip my arms around his neck, pulling him closer. "This is just the start, you know. Silas and I have been talking about the cabins, the financial impact, the cosplay book clubs and craft nights—and you heard Elliott's whole vision for the kids' camp. It's going to be something."

"You'll do amazing," he says, squeezing my hand three times.

I look at him. "Have you heard from Brody? About the offer?"

"Did you see the cookies Larry made? They're little books with the Reading Lane logo."

"Yes, they're adorable." I pull my hand back. "What happened with the studio?"

"It's your day, Clover," he says. "I don't want to take anything away from it."

I put my hands on my hips. "Does that mean it's bad news?"

"It's not good news." His chest expands on an inhale.

Not good news. My mind starts running the math—other locations, more work, higher costs. Silas might be able to help put together a financial plan—

"It's great news," he says. "I got it."

I smack his chest. "You are so annoying."

He catches my hand, laughing. "Have time for a dance?"

"You'd better believe I do."

Right there, in the middle of the fairy lights and the laughter and the clinking glasses, Jonathan and I dance. And then everyone joins— Elizabeth Bennet and Dracula, Spiderman and the Green Goblin, the BFG and Sophie, a Reader tilting slightly under the weight of her tote bag—all of them spilling into the courtyard in a scene that would absolutely work as the final act of an '80s rom-com, complete with terrible moves and a dance battle that Evie—still in her Spiderman suit—rightfully wins.

The courtyard spins around us. My people in their costumes, doing terrible dance moves in the glow of everything we built. A party thrown to celebrate the beginning of the next chapters of my life at Reading Lane.

Acknowledgments

There are so many people I want to thank. People that have listened to me ramble on and on about the story line, how much I want to be an author, how I don't think I can be an author, questioning if Mazey should have shoulder length hair or bra strap length hair… the list goes on and on.

My husband. This man has played interference so I can write when I'm behind on my imaginary timeline. Wore witty t-shirts to conventions to promote my work and even sat in the lobby of a hotel, encouraging me to hand out Valentine's to potential readers. He may have also helped work out some specific scenes *wink emoji*.

My kiddos, that helped me come up with names for the town, the lake, and almost every side character—Thank you. Without you, Honeyville would be named something really silly because I'm terrible at naming things.

Carley Fortune gave me her One Golden Summer shoes right after I finished the first draft of this book. She gave me a giant hug and told me that I can do it. Every time I feel like I can't, which is more than I care to admit, I look at the beautiful footwear and push forward. Thank you for believing in me, Carley.

My brother, Drew, read an early copy of this book… so early that there was no magic and it was dual POV. He would call me and tell me what he thought—the good and the bad. He did this while going through a time in his life that his attention didn't need to be on me or my writing. He's just that incredible and I am so thankful. Elliott may have bits of my brother woven into him.

All of my writing friends—Austin, Augustine, A.D., Erica—thank you for reading random excerpts, pushing me forward, and battling impostor syndrome with me. I could not have felt confident enough to put this into the world without your support.

Thank you to my editors, Amy, Kelly, and Sarah. I've learned so much from your feedback. I have valued everything you've told me and Happily Ever Chapter would be a hot mess without each of your inputs.

Avery Flynn. Thank you so much for writing Muffin Top, getting me back into reading, and taking time to read Happily Ever Chapter. I'm so incredibly grateful for your kindness.

The biggest thank you goes to every person who has told me I can do it, has said they are proud of me, has talked about books with me, and has made me feel like part of something bigger. I am so thankful for the bookish community, specifically the romance one.

About The Author

Samantha Wren believes in two things above all else: that love is the most powerful kind of magic, and that Pokémon is a perfectly acceptable hobby for a grown adult. Her magical realism romances blend the everyday with the extraordinary, because she's convinced the two were never really that far apart. When she's not writing, Samantha is drawing, reading, or wrangling three kids—all under the watchful eye of her two dogs: one who cheers her on and one who gives her a very disapproving look when she skips a writing session. She shares her chaotic, joy-filled life with a very patient husband.

Find her at @samantha.wren.writes—she'd love to hear from you.